# Men of Khyber

## *A Historical Fiction*

### Before You Take Me Away Series

Happy Reading!!
03-22-22

## Om Soni

This book is dedicated to my late father, Sh. Ram Avtar Soni, who taught me the art of imagination and the value of perseverance. This book would not have been possible without stories he told me from his childhood in Peshawar.

# Contents

# Prologue

My name is Yama. I am the god of the dead. It is said that I am the first man who experienced death. I am also known as *Kala*, meaning "time," because time brings people one step closer to death. In most Eastern religions, I have been given the responsibility of helping the dead pass to the next life. While many people expect some sort of judgement after they die, I don't judge all the dead. I only judge the ones who can't make a choice for their next life for themselves. Passing judgments on others is a painful part of my job. I rather like to be the one to cheerfully remind people of their departed ancestors.

Death can bring out different emotions in people. Some peacefully pass away to the next life without needing any intervention. Others choose to linger after death, refusing to move on. Many lack the conviction and strength to make a choice. They desire to surrender their right to make their own decisions in death and leave their fate to my judgment.

And I do judge them for their deeds. There is a lot of work involved. Wars, unrest, diseases, and disasters have kept me very busy. Luckily, I have assistants called *Yumdoots*. And let us not forget Chitragupta, my record keeper, as well as my pet dogs and birds. Together, we perform our solemn duty to help the dying transition to the next life.

Most people don't like to talk about death. They worry about leaving the known and going into the unknown. The fear of being judged for their deeds worries them. Humans, I have noticed, can be very clingy, especially to their bodies and their identity. They are too attached to material things and people they have known and loved. They don't want to leave their past situations. Because of that, they let their bodies linger in pain; some linger even after they die. But there is no escape from death, and there never will be. Death will remain the ultimate truth.

Death and destruction have haunted humans since the beginning of time. It has especially haunted people of particular areas on Earth. One such area lies between Afghanistan and Pakistan. In recent times, this place has been called Pashtunistan, or the land of Pashtuns, after the name of the tribes that live there. But the story that I have for you is from before Pakistan was created; before it became a separate country by partitioning from India in 1947. During this story's time, the areas of Pashtunistan lies between Afghanistan and India.

From the times of Alexander the Great to Ashoka the Great, until the Soviet occupation and Taliban control, the mountains and valleys of Pashtunistan have seen significant death and destruction. Now infamous for the Taliban and Islamic terrorists, that area was not always like that. People of the land respected freedom of thought and different ways of worship; they favored discourse and discussion over beheadings and bombs. They listened to new ideas and philosophies even when they disagreed, and embraced ideas of their own free will.

Before recent times, this land flourished with culture and trade. Those were great times for this land; different cultures lived and thrived together. There once was a pure alliance between Hindu-Sikh and Pashtun clans who fought together to protect freedom of thought and defeat bigotry and hate. The fighters of these clans were spread over the lands and mountains of Pashtunistan. The story of this clan is special to me because there was a boy in that clan that negotiated his time of death with me. He was not afraid of death. He just wanted to get a few things done before I took him away. But before I tell you more about the story of the clan and this boy, you should know a bit about the city where they lived.

This clan was centered in the beautiful and lively city of Pashtunistan. They called it Peshawar, meaning a "frontier city." For almost two millennia, Peshawar was the frontier town for ancient kingdoms of India, including the Mauryan Empire and the Gupta Empire. It was a trading hub—a place for traders to rest and enjoy their time before moving on to their destination. Since the times of Ashoka the Great, warriors roamed these lands and mountains, guarding the Hindu Kush Range and Khyber Pass, protecting their country from foreign invaders. Later, Kushans spread the influence of Buddhism in the area and built beautiful monasteries. But their lands were overrun by White Huns from Central Asia, who destroyed the thriving city and most of the Buddhist monasteries in the region. Soon came the onslaught of Islamic invaders, who destroyed remaining monasteries and temples, converting their people to Islam by force and killing those who resisted.

The warrior clans fought hard to protect their country and culture. Even though they lost, they didn't give up. Eventually, the Marathas and Sikhs among them turned the tides against the invaders and raised their flags on Peshawar. As rulers and reigns changed, some of their warriors stayed behind and adopted Peshawar as their home. Some even settled in the mountains and lived peacefully with Pashtuns. But the peace of Pashtun lands was destroyed by Islamists who came from distant lands.

When Sikhs took over the city in 1831, they pursued the Islamists in the mountains. And there, the

Islamists hid, influencing the Pashtun tribes against infidels, encouraging hate and violence against other religions, and destroying the peaceful co-existence Pashtuns had with other cultures. Then, a man named Syed Ahmad came from the East and introduced *jihad* to the people of Pashtunistan. Although Sikhs defeated Syed Ahmad and his men, they could not defeat his ideology. The violent *jihad* he preached continues to destroy the lives of Pashtuns and others to this day. Even for me, it is painful to see so many young men destroying theirs and others lives for nothing. In death, I only see bitterness and guilt on their face.

When the Sikhs lost Peshawar to the British, many of their warrior clans settled in Peshawar and the mountains of Swat. One such clan was led by Kalyan Dil. After losing the battle with the British, Kalyan left with his people for the Upper Swat mountains to seek help and refuge with his friends among the Kalasha people. On his way towards the town of Chitral, his caravan ran into hostile Afridi tribes. Kalyan and his militia fought hard. His wife, Raye Devi, fought bravely and killed many Afridi fighters but was killed in the battle. Kalyan lost both his sons and was left for dead. As Dils lay there dying on the cold, snowy mountains, I saw peace and satisfaction on their face of a battle fought hard and a life lived with dignity and pride. There was no fear of death tormenting their souls. As if they always knew not only about the certainty of death but also the uncertainty of its time.

As much as Kalyan wanted me to take him away with his wife and sons, it was not his time. He was saved by the Kalasha people. There, Kalyan married a Kalasha woman and rebuilt his clan, eventually settling in the town of Tarnab. The Dil clan thrived in Pashtun lands for three generations until the British decided to divide India in June of 1947. The partition of India created the Muslim-only country of Pakistan, while India remained a country for every religion. Peshawar and all properties of the Dil family were now on the Pakistani side of the border.

Provoked by mullahs and politicians, Muslims in Khyber went on to eliminate the "infidels" from their lands. But Dils would not leave their homes for India. After they died, defending their pride, they lingered in Peshawar, refusing to pass to the next life. I still see them today in Qissa Khwani Bazaar and in their mansion, Dil Mahal. They tell me they will linger till the reign of terror and bigotry ends on their lands. They will only pass to the next life when tolerance and freedom of thought return. Their presence reminds me of the glory of the frontier city and the clans who defended the people and cultures of ancient India.

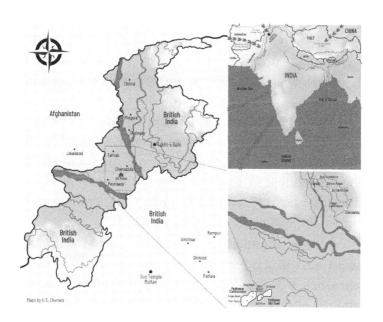

# Chapter 1
# [1936] Kedar, the Crazy Gambler

It was a cool day in November of 1936 in Peshawar. In a *haveli* courtyard in Qissa Khwani Bazaar, a young man ran around the well playing with five children. He hoisted a little boy on his shoulders and made the sounds of a steam engine to entertain him. The four other kids were running behind him to form a train. The man had removed his chappals on the side so that he didn't slip on the wet marble floor. The little boy smiled and laughed while enjoying the ride in the steam engine around the well.

The entrance to the haveli opened onto the street next to the bazaar. The gate was made of solid nine-inch wood and braced with metal plates. An engraving outside on the cement said *Dil Mahal* in Pashto. The literal meaning of the engraving was 'heart palace,' although Dil was the family name of the clan. Dils established themselves in Qissa Khwani Bazaar after the British occupation of Peshawar. Under *Dil Mahal* prominently engraved was the name *Lala* Jawar Dil, the family patriarch, under whom the influence of the Dil clan had peaked before he retired to the Upper Swat mountains. 'Lala' was a salutation used for wealthy merchants and a general title of respect for rich landlords.

Joga, the estate manager-cum-watchman, sat comfortably outside the entrance on a chair, cracking open and eating peanuts with one hand, having lost the other arm in the battle as a young man. Next to Joga, the family's driver-cum-security guard, Lal Singh, a thin framed but tall turbaned Sikh, sat reading a newspaper and sipping tea.

In the right corner of the yard, Rustam Baloch, the cook and helper, was laying the wheat for drying after washing it. Rustam, a thin man with a light beard, was always in a hurry. Zahir Fakir, the old man with a long goatee, was on the roof of Dil Mahal sewing a quilt. He intermittently beat the quilt with a stick to settle the cotton he had stuffed inside, causing the dust to blow into the yard.

"Will you stop beating quilts at this time?" Rustam yelled. But knowing Zahir, who was hard of hearing, wouldn't hear, Rustam ran upstairs to talk to him.

The front yard of the haveli was lit by beautiful sunshine that extended into a part of the veranda that led into a large drawing-room. A meeting was going on in a small room attached to the drawing-room. This room was used for private and important conversations on clan matters. The room had three chairs and a table that faced the wall with a large map drawn on it. The map prominently marked Dil Mahal at the center and all other properties owned by the clan around it. Among others marked was Preet House, the family mansion in Peshawar Cantonment three miles west of Dil Mahal and the town of Charsadda, where Jawar's sister Amrit and her husband lived with their family. Just further north of Charsadda was marked the family's farmhouse on the road to the town of Tarnab. The map also included other places important to the clan. During clan meetings, it was frequently used to discuss family affairs, tribal conflicts and carefully chart routes to hostile tribal areas.

There were two bedrooms on the ground floor primarily used for guests. On the right side of the veranda was a kitchen with a clay oven built just outside the entrance. A large room used for dining opened into the veranda from one end and into the kitchen on the other. A lady sat on the chair talking to two housemaids chopping vegetables near the kitchen. A clay oven had just been fired up to make fresh bread.

"Put Hari down, Kedar. You are spoiling him," said the woman in the maroon *salwar kameez* as she opened a bunch of carrots and started cleaning them in the water bucket.

"No, no, he is having fun, sister," the man replied, catching his breath.

Kedar was Hari's uncle, the brother of Lakshmi, the little boy's mother. He had been living at Dil Mahal since after her marriage to Jai Dil, the youngest son of Jawar Dil. Kedar named the little boy Hari, as the boy was born on the night of the birth anniversary of Lord Krishna, one of the incarnations of God in Hinduism. Kedar declared that the boy must be named after one of the Hindu God names. Lakshmi and Jai had gladly accepted the proposed name. The boy took his features from Jai, his hazel eyes from Jai's mother, but his demeanor was as calm and gentle as his mother's.

About three years back, on the day of Lakshmi's wedding, Kedar had come to Dil Mahal with the wedding procession and decided to stay there. His father had initially allowed him to stay for a few days, but Kedar refused to go back. It was not considered respectable to live at a married sister's house, and his father disapproved of it. Kedar's elder brother picked him up a few times from Dil Mahal, but he would run away from his family home, the Maggu House, to join his sister. Eventually, Lakshmi convinced her father that it was best Kedar stayed with her. Lakshmi's husband, Jai Dil, did not mind Kedar living with them. But Jai's elder brother, Mehar, could not stand Kedar's prolonged stay. He often asked Kedar to leave the room during family meetings. Usually, Kedar stayed away from the haveli when Mehar was around.

Kedar was younger than Lakshmi by four years. He had spent his entire childhood playing with her. He had learning difficulties and was held back at school a few times. After five years at school, he could barely read or write anything. Eventually, he refused to go to school, complaining that everyone at school teased him. Things were hardly any better for Kedar at home. His father showed his disappointment every time he saw him. His elder brother called him dumb. Although everyone had given up on his education, Lakshmi had slowly home-schooled him to read, write a little Urdu and Pashto, and do some basic math.

Before Lakshmi's marriage, Kedar spent his time helping her manage their haveli. There, he loved decorating the place with pottery and brass. Lakshmi kept him engaged and excited by supporting his interests. Their mother had died when Kedar was only three years old. Unlike everyone else, Lakshmi loved her little brother and had raised him like a mother would. She protected Kedar from everyone, even her own father and brother, who refused to tolerate his tantrums. After Lakshmi's marriage was fixed, the thought of her leaving him behind at Maggu House gave Kedar panic attacks. "I can't live in this house without you. They hate me here."

"No, they don't hate you. They are a little less patient and a little less accepting, but they are your family."

"I will go with you," he insisted.

"Maybe." Lakshmi would smile and calm him down.

At his father's house, Kedar had occasional bouts of anger that would make him aggressive. His father and brother often ordered servants to lock him in his room during these times. On days when his brother picked on him, and his father ignored him, he would get very frustrated and charged at everyone around him, except Lakshmi. But since his stay at Dil Mahal, he never got into one of those fits. Although he still picked fights in the bazaar with traders and had to be rescued by Joga. Unlike Maggu House, where there were rules around everything, including when and where you could eat, at Dil Mahal, there was plenty to eat all the time, and life was fun with a continuous stream of visitors who were warm and friendly. Lakshmi cared for him, and Jai was nice to him. And the best part of all, he could play with little Hari all day long.

Jai had explained some basic rules for Kedar to stay in Dil Mahal. "If you need something, only ask Lakshmi or me. Greet everyone inside the haveli, and don't enter any room except yours unless invited."

Kedar understood those rules and never broke them. There was another set of rules in Dil Mahal that were not usually told but were expected to be followed all the time. They included things like decency or *tahzeeb*; things like dressing correctly, not coming in drunk, being kind and generous, and so on. There was a rule to respectfully call everyone by their given name or relation. The only exception was for mothers, who could call their child by any name. Then there were the rules of Pashtunwali, Sikhism, and Hinduism that were practiced in a strange mix unique to the Dil clan. Dils were known for their hospitality, courage, and fiercely defending their honor, land, and clan. In line with the core value of Hinduism, they were also very tolerant of other cultures and religions and believed that the right to practice religion and pray to God in whatever manner is an inherent principle of freedom. But Kedar did not necessarily need to know those rules. He was not considered part of the Dil clan in that sense.

It had been three years since Kedar had arrived at Dil Mahal, but he had never ventured outside Qissa Khwani Bazaar. One day, Jai asked him to accompany him on a hunting trip. While there, Jai taught him how to handle the rifle. Jai bought him a holster with two daggers and a pistol on the way back.

"Well! Now you look like a Dil clansman," said Jai, who loved dressing up young clansmen as fighters. He called this brief ceremony *sajana*, or 'decorating' a clansman. And most of the time, it happened without much planning and was a private ceremony between Jai and his new 'soldier.' Sometime back, he decorated his nephew Lakhbir, who was just about the same age as Kedar. Jai had learned that from his uncle Jurnail, the greatest fighter the clan had ever had before he retired to live as a sevadaar, or servant, at a gurdwara. Jurnail had fought so many battles and seen so much blood spill that he really didn't wish to have his own family. Instead, he chose to serve the community and *connect with God* by volunteering at a Sikh temple.

On their return, when Lakshmi saw Kedar with a handgun, she immediately took it away, saying, "He does not need a gun." She jabbed Kedar, "Go first and find a job and earn your handgun."

"Soon, he will earn it. Right, Kedar?" Jai said and smiled.

"Please don't take him on one of your battles," she whispered to Jai as she passed him into the kitchen. Jai followed her.

"He won't fight my battles, and maybe you shouldn't fight his. A man should be prepared to face all kinds of situations, good and bad. We live in Khyber. Don't make him weak," Jai said.

"What are you thinking? He will pick a fight and shoot someone in the streets." Lakshmi shook her head, "He does not have the maturity to wield a weapon."

"He seems fine to me. Your family needs help. Kedar has lived here for, what, more than three years? No issues. Right?" Jai grabbed a handful of raisins and started shooting them into his mouth as he walked out of the kitchen.

Oblivious to tribal conflicts and to the Dil family's interests and life in and outside Peshawar, Kedar spent his days enjoying the small pleasures of life. He could barely read and had little interest in the news. At night, he would sneak out to smoke and play cards with a group of young, aspiring businessmen in Qissa Khwani. Like Kedar, his friends, Mangat Bakshi and the twins, Ved and Tej Sahani, were in their late teens. They had not built any social standing yet and craved the respect established merchants, and influential clansmen enjoyed. While Bakshi liked Kedar and considered him a friend, the Sahani twins associated with Kedar because of his affluent family and connections with the Dil clan.

\*\*\*

As little Hari grew older, Jai started taking him out on his day. Hari's homeschooling also started. A

Hindu priest started teaching him Sanskrit and Punjabi in the morning. A mawlawi came in every afternoon to teach him Urdu and Farsi. Hari's evenings were usually spent with Jai taking him along on his business and social interactions. Kedar now spent most of his day outside Dil Mahal exploring and experimenting on life with other young men of his age. He had picked up social drinking and started gambling the little money that his father would send for him, only returning to Dil Mahal late at night. This made Lakshmi worried about the future of her brother.

One night, Kedar returned home drunk from an evening with the Sahani brothers, who were mischievous and had spiked his drinks. In Dil Mahal, this was considered disrespectful. Lakshmi and Jai made sure no one else found out about this transgression. Lakshmi begged Jai to help Kedar settle down. The next day, as Jai left to go to his farms in Tarnab, he asked Kedar to join him. They mounted the horses and rode towards the countryside. A small militia of riders followed them. Having been severely reprimanded by Lakshmi, Kedar told Jai, "I apologize for last night. It was very inappropriate of me."

"Well, we all make mistakes. The question is, what do we learn from them?" After a pause, Jai asked as he slowed his horse, "What is your plan for life, Kedar?"

Kedar's face lit up. "I want to open a handicrafts emporium, where I can sell the best handicrafts in copper, brass, clay, and stone."

"What is stopping you?" Jai asked.

"You know I don't have any money. My father doesn't trust me with money." Kedar's father, Partap Maggu, thought little of him and didn't trust him with any responsibility. For his part, Kedar had given him enough reasons to lose his trust.

"How much money do you need?" Jai stopped the horse.

"I don't know, I really don't know." Kedar was unprepared to answer this question.

Jai smiled. "You need to first find out. You have to know your business a little before you start it."

"I can't take it from you. Father will be mad. He gets very upset with me on this issue."

Jai again stopped his horse. "He won't know. Lakshmi wants you to settle. Any help I can provide will be my pleasure. And when you become successful and rich, you can pay me back."

Kedar smiled. "Well, I will tell you soon. Thank you. I will be successful at this. I know this business. Lakshmi and I used to buy lots of pottery together." Jai smiled as they went on chatting about the different types of pottery and brass on their way to Tarnab.

Soon, they reached the farmhouse at Tarnab. Jai's militiamen camped outside the farmhouse as servants helped Kedar off the horse.

"Is this our place? I mean, your place?" Kedar asked.

Jai laughed. "Yes. It is our place. Do you want to see the farms? I can show you around."

Helpers brought a pot of water, soap, and a towel.

"Let us first wash our hands and eat something."

"This place looks like a fort." Kedar dried his hands with a towel.

"Well, it is a fort as well. Let's go inside the drawing-room."

Jai walked into a large room whose thick wooden doors were held open by the servants.

"This is a nice room. Just like the drawing-room in Dil Mahal." Kedar looked around the room with engraved wooden pillars, painted ceilings, and beautiful rugs and pillows. "Whose portraits are on the wall?" he asked, looking at four portraits, one on each wall.

"That is my grandfather, Lala Kalyan Dil. That is my uncle, Jurnail, also known as 'Mountain Hawk.' And that, you should know, is my father, Lala Jawar Dil. That there is *Diwan* Krori Mal, our ancestor. I don't know much about him except that he lived in Jalalabad and was a rich and influential man." It was quiet as Kedar keenly observed everything in the room.

Jai walked closely to the portraits and stared at the faces of his elders. Why am I so alone? I miss *you all, father, Uncle Jurnail… and all those who are gone…. I wish I was as brave.* Jai's thoughts clouded his face with sadness. Then he turned around and, in a firm voice, said, "Let us eat," startling Kedar standing just behind him.

They sat down to eat the lunch laid out on two low tables before them.

"Did you send food for the men outside?" Jai asked the farmhouse cook before he started eating.

"Yes, *sahib.*"

"Let us pray, Kedar."

Jai prayed, and Kedar just observed and tried to copy him.

"Why do we need that militia?" Kedar asked as they started eating.

"It can get dangerous around here."

"Do you have a lot of enemies around here?"

"We have enemies, and we have friends, and that is how things work 'round here."

After finishing their meal, Jai asked his farm manager to show Kedar the farms. He went himself around his estate with his militia. After that, Jai spent some time with his farmworkers, asking about their well-being and listening to their needs. Then they headed back to Peshawar.

"Your farmworkers, they are all Muslims?" Kedar asked.

"Almost all."

"Do they like you?"

"They will die for me if need be," Jai said as he looked at Kedar's face.

"Dils are Afghans?" Kedar asked, confused.

"Not sure." Jai paused to think. "We are *Khatri*, just like your family. But unlike your family, there is a lot of Pashtunwali in our blood."

"So, you are Khatri-Pashtuns?" Kedar asked, perplexed.

Jai burst into laughter. "Khatri-Pashtuns? I like that. Yes. You are absolutely right." Jai laughed again.

"We are the people of this land. We have been on both sides of Khyber over the generations. We may have once settled in Punjab. But who knows? We have been roaming these lands for generations."

"Did your people move around a lot?" Kedar asked.

"Uncle Jurnail used to say that our clan covered these lands by protecting *dharma* and fighting oppression for centuries." Jai's face became grim. "If you were my brother, I would teach you how to fight." He smiled.

"I don't like fighting," Kedar said in a low voice.

"If you believe in something, you should be willing to fight for it, and if you are blessed, you won't be alone in that fight."

Soon after the death of his wife, Jai's father, Jawar, decided to hand over the clan to him and left for a *dera*, a spiritual retreat in Jalalabad, to be a monk. Along with him, Jawar also took his goodwill, relationships, and experience of thriving as a Hindu-Sikh clan in Khyber. Once Jawar was gone, Jai felt unprepared, with no one around he could trust or ask for guidance. His elder brother, Mehar, didn't have much interest in clan affairs. As such, Mehar had no interest in anything.

Sensing Jai's mood, Kedar decided to change the topic. "Thank you for taking me out on this trip. This is the first time someone ever took me outside Peshawar."

"You should come with me more often," Jai said and smiled.

As the sun began to set, Jai's farmhouse manager came in to inform that the militia was ready to head back. When they reached the outskirts of Peshawar, it was already dark. Near the Bara River, they came across a group of armed men. Jai signed his militia to stop.

"You have been out too late, Lala. Getting too comfortable is how you die in these lands," a medium-built man on the horse with his face half-covered shouted from a distance.

"Mind your business, Ali."

"Just brotherly advice," Ali said as he looked around at men with him. "Not everyone is as friendly as I am."

The men sneered at Jai.

"Let us go," Ali signed the men as Jai watched them leave.

"Who are these people?" Kedar asked, trying to hide his fear by smiling.

"That man Ali, he is our enemy within the clan," Jai paused and grimaced, "he has my father's protection. The man who was standing right behind him, he is Haji Khan. He is our enemy. But because he is not protected by our own people, he is afraid of talking to us like Ali."

"I am confused. Why is your father protecting Ali?"

"Let us leave that story for another day," Jai replied as he signed his men to move.

"The moral of the story is, an enemy that is treated with leniency and tolerance for too long becomes bold and can be very dangerous," Jai rubbed his lips together and then spat as if trying to get rid of the taste of bitterness. There was silence.

Kedar nervously tried to read Jai's face but stayed quiet for the rest of the way. The group reached the Qissa Khwani Bazaar. The few men waiting outside Dil Mahal stood upon seeing Jai. Servants took Jai and Kedar's horses to water, and the militiamen dispersed after a few instructions from Joga.

"Tomorrow, tell me how much money you need for your business. Don't worry; this will stay between you, me, and your sister."

"Yes. Thank you. No one ever helped me like this before. I am so grateful."

Jai patted his back. "You will do well in life. I know that."

On his return from the trip, Kedar was exuberant. He stopped to say thanks to Lakshmi. She looked into his eyes. "Remember, it is a loan. Irrespective of what you were told by Jai, you have to pay it back soon." She grabbed his arm to get his full attention. "I know you won't let me down."

Kedar nodded. He understood that she had put her reputation at stake for him.

That night, Kedar celebrated with his friends, who were eager to be partners in his business. They made business plans and drank till late at night at Mangat's father's grocery shop. They proposed a lot of numbers for the investment required for business, and they discussed a lot of partnership options. They decided that twenty-thousand would be a good starting capital. As per the plan, the Sahani brothers would pitch in five thousand together, and Bakshi agreed to invest the same amount for a one-fourth stake. Kedar would hold half of the shares in the business, with a ten-thousand-rupee investment. For the Sahani brothers and Bakshi, opening any business with the Maggu and Dil family was a dream come true. Their families were excited to support them with financing.

The next day, Jai asked the family accountant to give the money to Kedar. As Kedar walked out with the money, he ran into Lakshmi, who had come out of the kitchen to confront him. She looked into his eyes, and he looked down, shook his head, and left. He knew what she meant to say. She knew he got the message.

In the evening, all partners of this new enterprise met at a *kahwah* tea shop. There, they formalized their partnership by exchanging turbans, a custom in the Punjabi community, to formalize commitment and friendship. Although Jai did not like Kedar dealing with the Sahani brothers, he thought it more appropriate to not interfere. The Sahani family was not considered respectable because of their involvement in criminal activities. Although breaking the laws of the British Raj, the rule of the British Crown in India, with a larger purpose of doing general good, was considered honorable, the Sahanis broke the law just to benefit themselves at the cost to their community.

Jai knew Mangat Bakshi and his father well. Although the Bakshis' were not rich, they were honorable people. Mangat was a young man of integrity. Mangat's father, Mohar, had raised him alone after his wife died during Mangat's birth. Kedar's partnership with Mangat gave Jai some assurance. He asked Mangat to keep an eye on things for him. As much as Jai disliked the Sahani brothers, he understood that the partnership allowed Kedar to hide the source of money from his family. Kedar had told his father he was helping his friends in their business. BSM Handicrafts opened its doors within a month after Jai gave the money to Kedar. They named the store by taking the first character from the last name of each of the four partners.

"That is too fast, Kedar," Lakshmi cautioned, concerned at the pace of his new business.

"You know there is not much to do, sister. We rented a shop, and we are going to procure pots, pitchers, rugs, and things to display there with a price tag."

Lakshmi worried about her role in this new enterprise. She held the biggest stake. Not only had she put her reputation before her in-laws on the line, but also her trust in Kedar and the reputation of her father. She had never seen Kedar act responsibly but believed he should be given an opportunity. She worried that Kedar would fail because of his immaturity. But she also believed that if there was one reason for Kedar to give his best, it was for her and Jai.

Kedar's hard work and dedication to his business made Jai happy. Lakshmi constantly worried that her father would find out Jai had financed his business and that he would not forgive her for facilitating it. She wanted Kedar to pay back the money as soon as possible. But Jai had told her clearly, "Businesses don't get established so fast," and that she should refrain from talking about it anymore.

In his heart, Jai was ready to lose the money. His hope of any chance of its success lay in Bakshi's ability to keep Kedar safe from Kedar's own poor decisions.

For BSM Handicrafts' opening day, they agreed it would be good for business if Jai inaugurated it. Jai was hesitant. He did not want his name publicly associated with the enterprise but agreed because of Kedar. After the inauguration, Kedar showed Jai the merchandise and proudly told him how he had procured each piece painstakingly from different towns and cities in Swat.

"These are beautiful pieces." Jai picked up a red pot with white polka dots and green stripes. "Where did you get these from? You have a good collection of pottery."

"I order these from the same places as others, but I provide my own specifications."

"Nice. That makes your collection unique."

"Yes. That is why I charge many times more than others," Kedar said as he smiled.

Jai congratulated Kedar on the successful opening and cautioned him to be careful with his partners. "I know the Sahani brothers are kind of mischievous, but they will not mess with us."

Kedar identified himself with the Dil family more than with his own. In the coming weeks, he traveled around Peshawar, Charsadda, and tribal areas looking for craftsmen that made unique pottery. He prepared his own designs on paper and showed them, then he got them painted by other artisans. That ensured his designs were not sold by craftsmen to other traders. Bakshi helped manage the finances of their business. The Sahani brothers became the salesmen.

They visited the houses of wealthy merchants and sold them the pottery at high prices.

Soon, the shop became popular among elites and the rich of Peshawar for its unique collection and no-haggle prices. Within six months, the business started making good money. They divided the revenue into four parts: two parts to Kedar and one each to Bakshi and the Sahani brothers. When Kedar made his first payment of five hundred rupees back to Jai and Lakshmi, tears of happiness and pride ran from Lakshmi's eyes. Jai gave Kedar a big hug and told him how proud of him he was.

With the success of the business, Kedar had become more confident about his life and decided to move out of Dil Mahal. He believed he should pay for his expenses since he was making money. He would have preferred a place by himself but knew both Jai and his father would not like that. Jai had suggested that either Kedar stay at Dil Mahal or return to Maggu House. Kedar didn't want to stay in Dil Mahal anymore. In addition, at Dil Mahal, he felt the burden of the loan every time he saw Lakshmi and decided he would move back to Maggu House next month after the Diwali festival.

The approaching Diwali filled Hindu and Sikh homes with excitement. Everyone in Dil Mahal kept busy cleaning and decorating. Servants had been cleaning every corner of the haveli for days. Maids were working hard on preparing for the Diwali feast.

All this happened under Lakshmi's supervision. Being the only lady in the Dil family was not easy for her. She had to take care of all household matters and attend to a continuous stream of visitors. Diwali always brought unending energy to Lakshmi. She was excited in anticipation of the visit to her father's house. This one day in the year that she got to see her father, brother, and his wife all together. She bought gifts for everyone: a European leather handbag for her elder brother, Anand; a sari for his wife, Meera; a beautiful sherwani stitched from a family tailor for Kedar; a Swiss watch for her father that Jai had bought from a returning British army officer.

This was a special Diwali for Kedar. This time, he had money he had earned himself. He was proud to buy gifts with his own money; a silver Lord Krishna idol for Lakshmi, decorated gold tobacco pipes for his father and brother, and he bought a specially engraved handgun for Jai from a tribal leader in Swat. On the Diwali morning, he dressed up in a new sherwani that Lakshmi had gifted him. With newfound confidence, he looked handsome.

Lakshmi was so proud of him. She had tears in her eyes as she handed him the gun from Jai and said, "You have grown up to be a responsible and very handsome man." She took some money from her bag and circled it around Kedar's head to stave off the evil spirits and gave it to her maids before he left to greet everyone at Maggu House.

As per tradition, early in the morning of Diwali, all members of the Dil family went for prayers at Goraknath Temple. After the visit to the temple, Jai and Lakshmi visited the Maggu House to greet the family. Partap Maggu was disappointed that Kedar was not with them. Jai did not want to engage in conversation about Kedar. After spending a few minutes at Maggu House, he returned to his office in Qissa Khwani to meet clansmen from nearby areas who had shown up for festival greetings.

Kedar had already visited the Maggu House in the morning and found himself alone. His father, Partap Maggu, had gone to the temple. His brother was still in his bedroom. After waiting for some time, Kedar met all the servants at the haveli, and gave them cash gifts, and returned to Dil Mahal. He had exciting plans for the day. This was a special Diwali for Kedar for one particular reason. He had received an invitation to Diwan Prem Chand Uppal's Diwali party; Diwan-ji, as people called him with respect, was known for his extravagant parties. He was a rich and well-respected man in Peshawar. Many years back, Kedar's father, Partap, and Diwan-ji were partners but slowly parted ways over lifestyle differences. Partap Maggu was serious about how a Hindu should live his life, and Diwan-ji's parties with gambling, alcohol, and opium didn't sit well with his ideology.

Since the Maggu family had never attended Diwan's Diwali party, he had stopped inviting them. The Sahani brothers, who had been helping with the arrangements of Diwan-ji's parties for many years, had assured him that the Maggu family would show up this year and convinced him to write a personal invitation.

Diwan-ji had two haveli's in Peshawar, one known as Rang Mahal, which in Hindi meant something like 'palace of enchanting entertainment,' and the other, Diwan House, where he lived with his wife and three sons. Every year on Diwali night, Diwan-ji hosted a big feast in the Rang Mahal. Every man of high society and good standing in Peshawar was invited.

Diwan-ji served delicious delicacies by cooks and *Halwais* specially hired for the day. There were Hindu, Sikh, and Pashtun guests. But no British men were invited. As Diwan-ji used to say, "British needed to be handled separately." For one reason, no one trusted the British; and two, as colonials, they were thoroughly despised, even by the rich who were otherwise eager to curry favors with them.

Diwan-ji's Diwali party was famous for fun, entertainment, and food. He served alcohol for those who drank and planned all-night gambling for those who preferred it over going home to their families. Diwan-ji's high-profile guests didn't need any money with them to gamble. He provided sureties based on the status and standing of his guests. Only the very rich and respectable gambled big and lost big and still maintained their big smile. As the news of winners and losers would spread the next day, the big loser with the big smile earned the most respect. Diwan-ji put every effort into making it a memorable night so the party would remain the topic of conversation until the next Diwali.

Kedar did not like being in the middle of lots of people. He felt vulnerable as if they were all watching his every move and making judgments; the bad ones that made him quit school; the ones that made him leave his father's house. The only reason he wanted to go to the party was to prove himself as a man of standing in the city. He wanted to be recognized as a successful businessman in the town. Besides, the Sahani brothers had told him this would be a good opportunity to get more business.

Kedar spent a lot of time getting dressed up for the event. With the new sherwani gifted by Lakshmi and a gold chain gifted by Jai at the birth of Hari, he looked more royal than any Maggu had ever looked. His gold-embroidered *jutti* shoes had been given to him by none other than Jawar Dil on the birth of Hari. He had picked the attar-of-roses fragrance especially for this day. With a beautiful red rose donning his sherwani, Kedar strolled up and down outside BSM Handicrafts as he waited for Bakshi to pick him up. W*hat would happen if father found out I had gone to Diwan's party?* His stomach rumbled, *but I have to take the chance.* Partap Maggu considered gambling and drinking a vice and decried Diwan for hosting this event on the religious and pious day of Diwali. There was no way Kedar would have been allowed by his family to attend Diwan's party.

Bakshi and Kedar were received by the Sahani brothers outside of Diwan's haveli, who quickly took them to introduce Diwan-ji.

"Diwan-ji, this is Kedar Nath Maggu, Lala Partap Maggu's youngest son."

"Now, this is a surprise! This is a very special Diwali!" Diwan was intrigued to see Kedar at the party. "Diwali *Mubarak*," he said with a smile.

Kedar presented the gifts he had brought for Diwan-ji: a pashmina throw and a copper vase.

"What a day! I can't believe it. Welcome. Welcome," Diwan-ji hugged Kedar. "Hey, you, come here. Hold these and keep them safe. These are special gifts," Diwan said as he handed over the gifts to the attendant. Then turning to his manager, "Mister Maggu should be seated next to me at my table."

The manager added a chair to an already over-crowded table, and Kedar joined the important guests on Diwan-ji's table.

"Does your father know you are here, son? He never comes here; your brother never comes to my parties. They really don't think we deserve the pleasure of their company."

"No, no, it is just that my father believes gambling and drinking are two evils that one should stay away from."

"I never ask anyone to gamble or drink, do I?" Diwan looked around for approval from the guests sitting around his table.

They all shook their heads.

"It is for you to enjoy if you wish," Diwan said. Everyone on the table nodded in agreement.

Diwan, a heavy, middle-aged man, wore a silver sherwani and *pakol* that hid his mostly bald head with long thin grey hair left dropping down his back. He believed the Maggus had belittled him by not accepting his invitations. He was holding a grudge. Dils always sent a few men to attend his parties, but they had firm instructions to not stay after the dinner. Diwan was okay with it. No one was required to stay longer than they wished.

Kedar knew Diwan was unhappy with his family. "Well, I am here to clear things up. I hope my presence will make up for that," Kedar said as he cleared his throat with apparent nervousness.

"We are glad you could join us. But does your father know you are here?" asked Diwan-ji, making Kedar even more uncomfortable.

"Diwan-ji, let us get a picture taken," interrupted Ved Sahani, the elder of the Sahani twins.

Kedar was hardly twenty; his small thin frame made him look even younger. Diwan, being a man of principles, wanted to make sure that Kedar had not disobeyed his father by showing up on his own. In reality, the Sahani brothers had never sent the Maggu House any invitation. They wanted to impress Diwan with their influence, and at the same time, push Kedar into a vulnerable situation. So, they had maliciously worked on the plan to just hand over the invitation to Kedar and convince him to attend for the sake of their business. Bakshi had agreed as well, as long as Kedar only stayed a few minutes.

There were lots of guests. The Dils were represented by Mehar, who expressed his surprise to see Kedar there. Bakshi noticed tension on Kedar's face. As Diwan's attention strayed to greet other guests,

Bakshi took Kedar out to the back porch of the haveli, where a few men were smoking and drinking.

"Won't he be offended if I don't sit with him?" Kedar asked.

"Maybe, but he will be more offended if he knows you came here without your father's approval."

Kedar felt uneasy. His anxiety shot up. He wanted to leave, but the Sahani brothers told him to stay at least till dinner. "Here, take this. Relax," the younger Sahani, Tej, said and gave Kedar some opium.

"What is this?" Kedar asked.

"Just a pill to relax you. Take it for today," Tej said.

Kedar swallowed the small pill and soon felt a little better. He sat on a chair on the porch, thinking, *This is a way better place; a large porch with the few men here too intoxicated to judge anyone.*

Ved handed Kedar a drink, and they all toasted "Happy Diwali" and bottomed up.

The twelve or so men, including three partners, on the porch on the back of the haveli were intoxicated enough by now to feel comfortable with each others' presence. Soon, everyone was a friend, and they talked about each other, business, Peshawar, India's freedom movement, local politics, and tribal wars and disputes. On the right end of the porch, a back door led to a big room, where five tables with light velvet covers were set up in the four corners and middle. On each table, neatly laid, were a deck of cards, a bottle of alcohol, a jug of water, cigarettes, an ashtray, and four upside-down glasses.

Soon, dinner was served in the lobby. Diwan-ji rounded up everyone around the haveli to ensure they ate. "No guest should go hungry," he told his manager. Diwan would be offended if he came to know that any of his guests had left without eating. Groups of hungry, drunk men piled up their favorite dishes on their plates and left to find their tables. Some just looked around for someone important to sit with or an acquaintance they had not seen for a long time.

Kedar stayed behind on the back porch to avoid Diwan-ji and Mehar. He had asked Bakshi to make his plate. "We should get out of here soon."

Bakshi handed Kedar his plate and left to get food for himself. A server filled Kedar's drink.

As Kedar took the first spoonful from his plate, someone placed their hand on his shoulder. "Eating lonely on Diwali is not acceptable," said a voice behind him. As Kedar turned and saw Diwan-ji behind him, he almost dropped his plate. Kedar struggled to say, "No, no, I'm just here… for the card game to…."

Diwan smiled at him. "Oh, I didn't know that a Maggu can have fine tastes like gambling," he said and pulled on Kedar's arm, laughing.

"Let us first eat. Then you join me on the gambling table," Diwan said.

"Do you gamble, Diwan-ji?" Kedar asked as they walked towards the lobby, trying to confirm what Bakshi had already told him.

Kedar followed Diwan-ji, who walked quite fast for his heavy frame and age.

"I can't today," said Diwan-ji. "The host has to be fair. But I will watch. …What an exciting Diwali. Someone in the Maggu family finally showed their presence here. I am honored. Convey your father my thanks." He put his arm around Kedar and introduced him to some of his key friends. Then he asked an attendant to get drinks for a toast with Kedar.

Kedar felt nervous and, at the same time, felt great to be part of the elites of society. He felt his time had finally come. Diwan made him feel comfortable; he'd invited Kedar to join his forthcoming hunting trip, and Kedar had gladly accepted. Then they talked about Kedar's business. Diwan asked him to decorate his haveli and told him that he could spend two thousand rupees. That thrilled Kedar. This, by far, was the biggest order for his business.

Soon, the dinner ended. Diwan stood up for his Diwali speech. "To all my friends who have gathered here, thank you for making this day so special with your presence. I wish all of you and your families a happy Diwali." The gathering erupted with greetings. "As is tradition, everyone is invited to watch the fireworks after puja. Then we will start the card games. You can play with whatever pleases you, stake whatever you want, or just watch the game."

Then he turned to Kedar and said, "Today, we have a special friend here from the Maggu family. We are so blessed to have the Maggu family participate. Gentlemen, meet my guest, Kedar Maggu."

As Diwan-ji introduced him, Kedar nervously smiled, bowing his head with folded hands to clapping guests.

Diwan continued, "It is most important that you all have fun. Eat, drink, and have fun as long as you wish. Happy Diwali, and may next year be prosperous and auspicious!" With that, Diwan walked towards the room set up for card games with his arm over Kedar's shoulder, followed by other close friends. Bakshi and the Sahani brothers followed them. Outside, servants lit the fireworks. The rockets, fountains, and custom-made firework arrangements fixed on bamboo structures with jute ropes enthralled the guests. Among the ultra-rich of Peshawar, Kedar occupied the central table. Bakshi and the Sahani brothers sat at another table. The stakes were put at five hundred rupees, and the cards were distributed. Kedar thought it risky but decided he could afford to lose five hundred to gain some influential friends, a nominal fee for making big connections in high society.

Diwan-ji was known to be good at reading a poker face and telling the hand. But today, he was not playing. "Okay, gentlemen, I wish you good luck. Stay as long as you wish. I will be keeping a tab on you. Remember, it is all for fun." This was Diwan's way of telling them, *you are welcome here, enjoy, and don't gamble too much.* But he wanted the night to be memorable, and what better way to do that than gamble big. Diwan-ji left the room for the lobby, where he raised a toast with everyone and then left for his residence, Diwan Bhavan, two streets away, to celebrate Diwali with his family.

As he sat in his car, Diwan felt content that as a host, he'd done a good job. He felt happy that someone from the Maggu family had joined. *But did he get his father's permission?* The question stayed in his mind. Diwan had a reputation for being responsible for the community, and he had the community's best interest in mind. He asked his driver to wait and rolled down the window and called to his manager, "Let me know if the kid loses over ten thousand rupees."

At the Diwali party, in the room with velvet tablecloths, Kedar had lost his first stake. It did not take much time. Before he could think, the cards were distributed. He had placed his next bet of five hundred rupees, and his mind told him that two-thousand-rupee business that Diwan-ji had given him should generate enough profit to cover it. Anyway, if he left that early, Diwan-ji would think little of him. Unaware that Diwan had already left, he kept looking at the entrance to the room in the hope Diwan-ji would show up and talk to him.

As alcohol went around, the night matured, and the gambling continued at Rang Mahal. At Maggu House, the Maggu family had gathered for Diwali dinner. Kedar's absence was noted, but no one missed him. Partap Maggu found another reason to prove how irresponsible Kedar was.

That night, Diwan did not receive any calls from his manager because Kedar only lost seven thousand before Bakshi, fearing Jai's anger, took Kedar out of the gambling room as the stakes were raised. At first, Kedar refused to come out. But then Bakshi lied and told him Jai was outside. On hearing about Jai, Kedar dropped the cards and asked to be excused to use the restroom.

Bakshi followed him. "What are you doing?" Bakshi asked him, staring into his eyes angrily.

"What? What am I doing?" Kedar looked dazed as if someone had woken him from a dream.

"You are either drunk or crazy. You have already lost seven thousand rupees!" Bakshi shook him by the shoulders. "What? Yes. Is Jai Sahib outside?" Kedar suddenly looked scared. He was sweating on his forehead.

"No. I lied. but we need to leave."

"I can't. I lost so much money. I need to win."

As he turned to go back, Bakshi ran in front of him to block him. "You will lose more. They are long-time gamblers with lots of money. You don't have anything. You just lost Jai's money. Let's go back, Kedar, for God's sake."

Kedar whispered to himself, "Yes. I lost Jai's money. How will I pay it back?" He looked at himself in the mirror. His sherwani reminded him of Lakshmi. "You are right. I have nothing. This chain was gifted by Jai, the clothes by Lakshmi, the money I lost did not even belong to me... What should I do, Bakshi?" As the reality of the situation hit Kedar, he felt cold and sick.

Bakshi pulled his arm, "Let us first get out of here." Ved Sahani also joined them in the conversation.

Kedar looked at both and said, "But can I leave here without paying?"

Bakshi assured him, "Yes, of course. You go back in the room and announce that you need to join your family for dinner and that money will be paid to Diwan-ji tomorrow."

Kedar looked at Sahani. "Can I, Ved? Can I go?"

Ved Sahani, who was enjoying the situation, said, "You only have one option. Ask your father for money. He is the richest man in the town. If he pays, you will have a name tomorrow. No one has lost even half as much as you have."

"He will never give me a penny for gambling."

"Your brother lives such a lavish life. He has cars, businesses. Why can't your father give you some money?"

"Yes, okay. I will go home... Yes, let us tell them," Kedar said, sweating and trembling. The fear that he had done something awful gripped his mind.

He feared that Lakshmi would know and that Jai would find out, and he would lose the only people in the world who really cared for him.

He followed Bakshi back to the hall. Bakshi stopped outside the room and said, "Wipe the sweat off your face and keep a smile on. Just say as we discussed."

"What? What should I say?" Kedar asked as fear gripped his mind. The opium and alcohol had further diminished his ability to think coherently.

"Say that you have to leave, and money will reach Diwan-ji."

"But how? How will I pay them, Bakshi?"

"Just say it, Kedar." Bakshi pressed his hand as he entered the room with a smile, his arms around Kedar, and announced, "Everyone, our friend, Kedar, has to leave for home now to join the dinner with his family. Before he leaves, he would like to say a few words."

"As Bakshi said, I have to go. Money will be paid to Diwan-ji. Thank you." Before he could hear Diwali wishes from others, Kedar rushed out of the room. There was a storm in one part of his brain, complete numbness in the other.

Bakshi followed Kedar. "Wait. I will drop you off."

"No, I will walk," he said, irritated and restless. "Please leave me alone."

Kedar walked down the lobby to the entrance, ignoring guests who greeted and waved. He came out on the street, his feet moving fast in one direction and then another, his brain in many. He stopped at the corner and leaned against the wall to breathe. He started crying, "What do I do? They ruined my life. Lakshmi must never know. Jai should never know…." He felt sick as he crouched in the middle of the street and cried. He wiped the cold sweat on his forehead. Then he quickly got up and walked towards Maggu House again. "They must give me money. I need it. It is the money of my ancestors. They can't just keep it for themselves. They must share." He walked faster still. Maggu House was only three blocks away.

He stopped as he wanted to throw up. But on seeing two men approach, he got up and started walking towards Maggu House. His steps staggered. He could see Maggu House and hear the family dogs barking. He stopped outside the gate and stared at the doorman, who immediately recognized him and opened the door after salutations.

"Where is Lala-ji?"

"Inside, sahib," said the doorman, a little surprised at the tone.

Kedar walked inside. He could hear the laughter, the family enjoying the Diwali dinner. He went into the dining room.

"Here comes our dear brother," said his elder brother, Anand.

"Where have you been? Have you no shame?" said Partap Maggu.

Kedar's ears were frozen. It was like he did not hear anything. "Can I talk to you, Papa?" he said with a shaky voice.

"You could at least greet your family for formality's sake, but no — a little manners are too much to expect from you."

"Can I talk to you alone? It is important." He trembled.

"What is it now?"

"Please."

"What did you do?" Maggu got up from the chair. He looked puzzled; never before had Kedar told him so firmly and clearly what he wanted. "What is going on?" Partap stepped outside the dining room.

"I need money."

"What do you need money for?"

"I made a mistake." Kedar's voice trembled. "I lost seven thousand rupees in gambling. It won't happen again, but I need money to pay Diwan-ji."

"Are you mad? You went to Diwan's party?" Maggu's face turned red, his voice suddenly raised. He yelled, "I will never give you a paisa. I knew you were useless. I never knew this useless. You went to Diwan's party — who gave you the permission?" Partap Maggu yelled louder.

"Listen. Say whatever you want. I will return every paisa. Please. I made a mistake." He held onto his father's arm as Partap Maggu tried to walk back to the dining room.

"This is my only chance. I made a mistake," he screamed. "All will be ruined."

Maggu pushed Kedar's hand away from him and ordered the doorman, "Tell him to leave. If he does not leave right away, throw him out."

As Partap Maggu returned to the dining room, the doorman and servants surrounded Kedar, hesitating to intervene.

Kedar looked at the servants standing around him. His eyes were dead with hopelessness and despair. His face became as pale as a corpse as he whispered, "Throw me away?" Then he yelled, "What is new? That is what you have done with me since my childhood. You have thrown me away. You were never a father to me."

Maggu had already gone inside the dining room, where he could be heard cursing about Kedar.

Kedar opened the dining-room door as servants waited respectfully to follow Partap Maggu's orders. He stood in the middle of the door. By now, everyone in the dining room knew what had transpired. His brother had joined their father in yelling at him. They were telling Kedar that he had no right to come here asking for money, but Kedar had stopped listening. With his head shaking with anger, he slowly stepped inside and locked the dining-room door behind him as the servants hesitated to get involved in the family matter. Kedar shivered and cried as he pulled out his handgun and aimed it at Partap Maggu. "I don't need this life. You are nothing but a hangman's noose around my neck, a suffocating burden my entire life. I will die, and so will you. All of you will die."

Everyone was stunned as Kedar shot his father.

There was silence for a second. Outside, servants tried to break open the solid wooden door. Sounds of screaming and gunshots joined the sounds of servants shouting and pulling on the door and Diwali fireworks outside. One by one, eight shots rang out, and then it all became quiet. Kedar had shot every bullet in his handgun. There were no more bullets left for him. He dropped his gun. Outside, there were still shouts by servants trying to break the door open. Kedar opened the door and sat there in the dining room on a chair, the one where his brother had been sitting before. Anand was lying in front of Kedar on the floor along with his wife, Meera.

Some servants ran for cars and others for doctors or the phones. The news of carnage spread like fire in the town. Kedar was taken to the police station. He stayed quiet and barely moved. He was breathing, but there was no expression of life on his face. Jai came to see him in the police station and asked him, "Why?" There was no answer. Jai and Mehar spent the night at the hospital, mortuaries, and in cremation arrangements.

\*\*\*

When Lakshmi learned about it, she went into shock. The housemaids tried to keep her conscious. For days, Lakshmi talked incoherently. "I should have known before handing over the gun to him. I should have known better," she cried and repeated over and over.

"Why did he do this?" she asked Jai. "He was doing so well. I raised him like his mother. He was part of my heart, and he killed my father. He killed my brother." She cried inconsolably.

Jai tried to console her: "All Kedar wanted was love, a little respect, some support. And more than anyone else, he wanted it from his father. He didn't get that. And he just lost it. I cannot explain what happened. We are all lost here."

"I am so broken inside. I will never be the same again. My father, brother… gone. Kedar in jail for life…" she said every time she saw Jai.

Jai discussed Kedar's case with the family attorney, Chaman, and asked him to represent Kedar. He thought that might help Lakshmi feel better. "I have not abandoned Kedar. I will try to help him. Please don't lose hope for him."

"Rustam, call Chaman here," Jai said. He wanted to discuss it with Chaman in front of Lakshmi to reassure her that everything was being done to help Kedar. Chaman lived with his wife and two children not far from Dil Mahal and often visited Dil Mahal about the court cases he handled for the clan.

As days went by, Lakshmi became quieter and quieter. She stayed in bed for most of the day. At Dil Mahal, maids handled all the work. Jai's aunt, Sukhi, who was visiting to care for Lakshmi, had also returned to her farmhouse. With Lakshmi in severe depression, Hari was being neglected.

"Hari and I need you. The family needs you," Jai begged Lakshmi.

"I am broken. I will never be the same again. You and Hari don't deserve this," Lakshmi cried.

A few months passed like this, and Lakshmi did not recover. Jai tried everything. Then he asked his aunt, Sukhi, and his grand-aunt, Amrit, to come to stay at Dil Mahal for some time. Both matriarchs tried to help Lakshmi to move on with life, reminding her of her duty towards the clan.

"If you are not strong, this clan has no future. Hari needs his mother. Jai needs his wife," Sukhi said.

"Clans are built by women. They nurture them. The children are reflections of their parents. More so of their mother. You should consider what effect your life has on Hari. What happened was so terrible that I can only imagine your pain. But it has been three months now. It is time to move on and rebuild your life," Amrit said.

"I am aware of that. I wish I could just go away. Life is very hard for me to live."

"Send Hari for some time to Tarnab," Sukhi said. "It is not good for a boy to be exposed to such an environment and thoughts. There, he can play with Satwant's daughter, Raji, and his son, Jigar. They are the same age." Then looking at Jai, she said, "That way, you and Lakshmi can also spend some time together. Maybe take her out on some excursions. Lakshmi, what do you say?"

Lakshmi had nothing to say on this. That night, she stayed awake, lost in her thoughts.

Jai, unable to bear the pain of watching her suffer, came out of the bedroom. He prepared the hookah and sat in the dark on the veranda, smoking till late at night. The next day, when Jai and Mahar left early in the morning for the court hearing for Kedar, the maids had not arrived yet. Lakshmi was awake and still in bed. She didn't get up. She had no energy or motivation to do anything.

At court, the charges against Kedar were read, and the Dil's family attorney, Chaman Talwar, filed the papers to represent Kedar. In the afternoon, when Jai and Mehar returned to Dil Mahal, the maids were concerned about the absence of Lakshmi.

"How is Lakshmi?" Jai asked the older maid, Amira.

"Lala-ji. We didn't see her. We thought she went with you."

"Was she not at home when you arrived?" Jai asked.

"No. We have not seen her since morning."

Jai, Mehar, and the servants searched for her everywhere, but she was nowhere to be found. Little Hari kept walking back to the front yard. Then Mehar heard him say, "Ma," as he pointed to the well.

They found her drowned in the well.

Jai was heartbroken. He sat in Dil Mahal's guest room for three days without sleep. There, he mourned with his clansmen, who had come in numbers from surrounding areas. For days, he didn't let Hari away from his sight. As his clansmen camped there to grieve with him, he pretended to stay strong as their leader. Inside, he was shattered. His heart ached for little Hari. "He just turned four. She didn't even think of him."

Mehar knew his brother's pain but felt helpless. Unable to contact their father, Jawar, the family's trusted estate manager, Joga, came with a suggestion to send Jai on a pilgrimage to immerse Lakshmi's ashes in the Ganges River.

The following week, Jai left by train with Hari and Daler for Haridwar in the hope this would give him time and space to grieve. Jai spent two months traveling to pilgrimage sites at Amritsar, Haridwar, and Kashi with Hari and Daler. When they returned, Jai was a different man. He had lost a big part of himself with Lakshmi's death and looking at him, it was not hard to tell.

\*\*\*

Kedar knew his sister had killed herself. He had left her little choice. The burden of what had happened was too much to bear for him. He would sit in his jail cell and murmur all day long. Some people who knew him thought he was remembering Lakshmi,

Jai, and Hari. But others thought he was praying for forgiveness to Lord Krishna and Goddess Lakshmi. Soon after Lakshmi's death, Kedar was convicted of his crimes and sentenced to life in prison. In jail, Kedar barely ate or talked with anyone. He mostly spent time in the corner of his jail cell.

After a year in jail, Kedar was declared mentally unfit and transferred to a madhouse. Jai tried to get him out, asking his attorneys to present the case as temporary insanity. Eventually, he succeeded, and in May of 1939, the court sentenced Kedar to five years in prison for murders under temporary insanity. Kedar was sent back to jail, where he spent his time in self-imposed solitary confinement. In three years, he had turned into a walking skeleton with long hair and a long beard, a man with a scary appearance. But as the jailer had said in the court, "He gives no one any trouble." With Jai's efforts and the jailer's recommendations, Kedar was released after serving three years.

On the day of Kedar's release in June of 1942, Bakshi came to receive him. Kedar looked old and sick. Bakshi's eyes teared up as he looked at Kedar. *What a pitiful sight,* he thought.

On seeing Bakshi, Kedar hugged him and cried loudly, begging him for forgiveness.

"Jai is the one you should be asking for forgiveness," Bakshi said.

On hearing this, Kedar ran back towards the jail, saying, "Please don't take me to Jai." He repeated it until Bakshi told him, "Fine. I won't take you to Jai. We are going to our store." Jai had himself suggested Bakshi lodge Kedar in his shop.

Bakshi led Kedar to the tanga carriage that had been waiting. As they traveled towards the shop, Kedar told Bakshi he wished to leave town.

"I understand. I will help you. Let us first settle a few important things. Our business has been profitable. You and I own it since the Sahani brothers have sold their stake and left a few days after that forsaken Diwali party. I have kept your share of the profits. In total, it is a decent amount from the last three years."

"Are you out of your mind? I don't deserve any of it. I owe Jai money."

"I offered to pay him back. He refused. He told me to keep the money. In addition, you also have all the money your family left."

Kedar was the only heir to the large Maggu fortune put in trust for him by the court.

"You have inherited lots of money. You may want to take care of it."

"Money," Kedar said as he started laughing loudly. He laughed a few times, and then he said, "What good is it?" and started crying.

The following day, Jai arrived at their store to meet Kedar. Kedar cried upon seeing Jai but stopped when Jai yelled at him to stop crying. "I am doing this in the hope your sister will feel happy in heaven. You don't owe me anything. No money and no apology. I agree with your plan to leave the city. Settle somewhere in the East. You have a lot of money for you to rebuild your life."

When Kedar asked to see Hari, Jai responded, "You can see him outside the haveli, but it is better that Hari does not know about you or any of the unfortunate events."

Before Kedar left, Jai handed him urns containing the cremated remains of the Maggu family. On seeing the urns, Kedar ran outside the storeroom crying like a madman.

That night, Kedar spent most of his time walking around the streets of Peshawar. In the morning, when he returned, he asked Bakshi to help him dispose of the inheritance. He went to see Diwan to ask if he'd gotten paid his seven thousand. Diwan refused to meet him. His manager told Kedar the winners had refused the money. Walking out of Diwan's haveli, Kedar said, "When I needed money, no one would give it to me. Now that I have it, I don't want it."

"It is tainted money. Who will want this money? Even you don't want it," Bakshi replied.

On Jai and Bakshi's suggestion, Kedar donated all his inherited money to temples and gurdwaras. He kept a small part of his share of profits from the business. He gave away his share of BSM Emporium to Bakshi after Jai had forgiven the loan.

The next day, Bakshi made preparations for Kedar to leave Peshawar. Everything was settled for him to leave. Kedar refused to leave without seeing Hari. The following morning, Bakshi dropped him off on the street outside Dil Mahal. There, Kedar waited for Hari to come outside the haveli. When Hari emerged from the gates playing with his cousin, Raji, Kedar approached him as a beggar asking for food. To his immense happiness, Hari went inside and brought back some bread and *sabzi*. Kedar took the food from Hari and walked away, crying loudly. People in the Qissa Khwani Bazaar stared at the crying madman with long hair and a beard.

A kahwah shop owner told his curious customers, "He is Kedar, the crazy gambler. Just got out of jail."

That was the last time Peshawar saw Kedar. His name was never mentioned in the Dil family.

Bakshi, on his end, lived under tremendous guilt for being party to all this. The questions like *Why did I let him gamble?* And *why did I drive him to the party?* And *why did I let him go to Maggu House?*

tormented him. When Bakshi's father died in 1944, he sold his house and emporium and left Peshawar. Before leaving, he met Jai to try to return Kedar's share in the business. Jai refused the money, saying, "You are young, Bakshi. Take this money and settle someplace safe in the East. One day, God willing, we will meet."

Bakshi bowed with folded hands.

"You know where you are going?" Jai asked.

"I will look for Kedar for some time. Kedar told me that he will live in Haridwar and pray as a penance."

"If you are going to Haridwar, do you mind taking some ashes to our family purohit?"

"Anything for you."

That day, with his little belongings and the few urns given by Jai, young Bakshi left Peshawar forever, hoping to see Kedar. Little did he know he would never be back to see the city again.

# Chapter 2
# [1940] Orphans of Bara Bandai

It was the third Friday of January 1940. Jai had been handwriting invitations for Mehar's wedding. Earlier in September, Mehar was committed to Kirat, daughter of Jung Singh of Mingora. The wedding procession, the *baraat*, would go through many Pashtun tribal areas hostile to Dils to reach Mingora. In Dil Mahal family elders, and friends had gathered to plan the wedding. Jai and Mehar's father, Jawar Dil, had arrived from a dera in Jalalabad, Afghanistan, where he had retired as a spiritual recluse after the death of his wife, Preet. It was there, at the dera, Jawar's old friend, Jung, had proposed the marriage of his daughter to Mehar.

"Jawar, if you bless my daughter and accept her into your clan, it will be a huge relief for me. It is dangerous for a Sikh man to live in Khyber and an especially terrible place for a young Sikh woman. I would like Kirat to get married and settle in your clan."

Jawar was very pleased with Jung's proposal; with his eyes wet with emotions, he held Jung's hands and said, "Jung, you are a close friend. It is my duty to help you by accepting Kirat into my family. It will also be my honor. Besides, after the tragic death of Lakshmi, I worry little Hari is not being cared for properly. And you know Jai refuses even to entertain the idea of him getting remarried."

"His heart is broken after the horrible events," Jung said as he put his hand on Jawar's shoulder.

"I don't think Jai will ever marry again. My eldest son Bhole…he never belonged in the family. Maybe it was a mistake to send him to London for studies." Jawar looked away and then said, "Mehar, his first wife, died too soon."

Jung pressed his hand on Jawar's shoulder to comfort him.

After a brief pause, Jawar looked with a smile at Jung and said, "I would like to have more grandkids. Dil Mahal and my family will be blessed to have a girl as smart and beautiful as Kirat to put the house in order."

"Well, come with your family to Mingora. We will marry Mehar and Kirat and bind our friendship in their relationship." Jung vigorously shook Jawar's hand as they laughed in happiness.

Even though Jawar had committed to the marriage of Mehar and Kirat, in his heart, he was deeply concerned about taking the wedding procession to

Jung's place at Mingora. Jawar had raised his concerns: "Jung, you have put me in a predicament. You know how much I love Kirat. She is like my own daughter, but to bring the baraat to Mingora could be troublesome." Jawar worried about Masood Khan, the influential tribal leader of the Nikpikhel tribe, who was also one of the orphans of the village of Bara Bandai near Mingora.

"I won't say a word, and you won't say a word to anyone. We will keep the wedding a secret till the wedding day, and then you can leave the same day with the wedding procession." Jung assured him of secrecy. "And then your friend, Dostan, he will help you, won't he?"

*** 

In Dil Mahal, below his full watercolor portrait on the wall, descendants of Kalyan Dil had gathered to plan the family wedding. In addition to Jawar Dil and his two sons, his cousin Balwant was there with his two brothers and their sons. *Baba* Balwant, as he was known in the clan, was head of the Trehan family. He always traveled with his favorite grandson, Lakhbir, who helped the aging Balwant during his excursions. Jawar's close friend, Dostan, a Yusufzai leader in Tarnab, was sitting close to Jawar. The family's most trusted man, Joga, was standing against the wall waiting near the door, welcoming all the clansmen who had come from different areas of Khyber. As clansmen arrived, they congratulated Jawar and Mehar on the wedding and displayed great excitement. Many younger clansmen wondered the reason behind so much military planning.

As in every clan meeting, Jawar started with the story of the clan's history. He always made sure that everyone involved had a good understanding of the facts and reasons behind the matter at hand. "So, some of you may not be familiar with the history of our hostilities with some of the Upper Swati tribes," Jawar said, then he paused and looked around the room. "Where is Hari? Bring him here. He must listen to some family history." Jawar smiled, and his long grey mustache broadened his smile. As young Hari walked in, Jawar invited him to sit with him.

"This story is important to the clan. It is important to our future. Every clansman should hear it. You must understand the hostility we faced, the sacrifices the clansmen have made, and the hard decisions we must make to survive in Khyber." Jawar paused and rotated his sword-cane. "This particular issue stems from the assassination of my father on our farmhouse. At the beginning of 1900, Baba Kalyan came down from Chitral and settled in Tarnab. Some tribes didn't like the idea of a Hindu-Sikh clan settling in the valley." Jawar paused and looked around the room. "Where is Joga? There you are." Jawar smiled with affection at Joga and said, "And this is also the story of how Joga lost his arm. Joga, why not you to tell the story. You know it better than anyone."

Joga paused and then started telling the story that he had so fondly told so many times. "I think it was September of 1908... Provoked by mullahs, tribes of Bara Bandai attacked the Dil farmhouse in Tarnab. Baba Kalyan and some clansmen, who were out working on the farm, were ambushed by fifty or so Nikpikhel tribesmen. The ensuing battle left fourteen tribesmen and five of our clansmen dead. Baba Kalyan himself was badly injured in the battle. I quickly arrived with all the militia I could muster, and Dostan, our friend" — Joga pointed to Dostan as he bowed down to him — "had gathered more than a hundred of his fighters. Shortly after we brought him inside, Baba Kalyan died from his wounds." Joga looked around the room and noticed everyone was intently listening. "There was a lot of anger in the clansmen. After all, Baba Kalyan was our leader in the true sense. A father figure who protected us. Seething over his father's killing, Baba Jurnail ordered clan fighters to pursue the tribesmen into the Bara Bandai village. Only after we had killed each one of them did we return to Tarnab to cremate *Baba-ji"* Joga paused as he looked at Jawar to continue.

"That is how Joga lost his left arm in that battle at Bara Bandai," Jawar said as he looked at Joga and smiled. "After the attack, we moved our residence out of Tarnab to Qissa Khwani Bazaar, in what is now our office. It would be almost thirty years until we would be back in the same area of Swat. Although, this time, not for war but a wedding."

"We have seen extreme hostility in Khyber. We have also seen extreme loyalty. My friend here, Dostan, has always stood by us. He has given as much of his blood and sweat for us as any Dil clansman. He has lost many of his tribesmen in our battles. There is no blood relationship here. Only of heart and mind. Just as our bond with Joga and his family has been, so is our bond with Dostan," he said, then looked at Jai and added, "But loyalty can't be assumed. We can only count loyalties that are gifted to us. While I can count on Dostan anytime, I can't assume his son, Ullas, will be loyal to us. But I know Ullas is a loyal son. So, because Dostan is with us, Ullas will support us too." Jawar paused to clear his throat and take a sip of water. "There was one more man who had shown that much loyalty and sacrificed his life for us. Azmat. He was a Muslim. Just like Dostan. No blood or religious relation either. I am telling you because it is important to know how we thrived in Khyber. It would have been difficult without the support of these fine men.

"But as I said, never assume loyalty. Azmat's son Ali. He is not a friend. So, we have to be careful what goes outside this room. Don't trust anyone in this case. Don't tell any details about the wedding to anyone outside the family."

"You know who raised Ali," Dostan interrupted Jawar. "Mullah Arfan, a Popalzai Pashtun and a Wahabi Muslim," Dostan said, implying that Arfan was radical mullah.

Jawar ignored Dostan's comment, as he avoided discussing religious ideologies in clan meetings. "Unfortunately, women can't join the wedding procession. It is not safe. And if you are slow and heavy, you can't join either." The room erupted in laughter as a few big clansmen shook their heads in disappointment. "Sorry, but you can enjoy all the food at Dil Mahal." Jawar smiled. "And those of you who will join must prepare for anything. Now you have more background, I will ask all except Joga, Dostan, and Jai to enjoy the evening with Mehar, as we have to discuss some important matters."

As clansmen were leaving the room, Jawar turned to Hari and asked, "Hari, what did you learn today?"

"Papa had told me Baba Kalyan and Bara Bandai story earlier."

"Oh, yeah? Your Papa is doing something right, for sure. What had you not learned?"

"I never heard about Wahabi and Popalzai."

"You have more questions to ask your Papa next time. Now, you go with Baba Balwant and Uncle Mehar, as I have to discuss some business matters here."

"Jai, let us look at the map of the area," Jawar said and walked into the meeting room to the wall with the map. "Above the city of Mingora across the Swat River is the village of Bara Bandai. Below the river, in the Lower Swat, we have great relations with the Yusufzai tribes. My worry is the tribes of Bara Bandai. They would not miss the opportunity to attack us."

"What about Haji Khan? His village is after Barikot on the way to Mingora," Jai said.

"Haji Khan is in the lower valley. He won't take the risk of direct conflict with us."

At Dil Mahal, lights and lamps were on until late at night. They were debating the safe passage for the wedding procession. A route was charted from Tarnab to Mingora. Places to camp were finalized, and they decided where to change horses. After midnight, they finalized their plan to safely take the wedding procession to Mingora.

"I will re-state what we agreed here," Jawar said as he stood near the wall with the map. "Jai, you will lead the baraat with forty fighters that are loyal to the family, the men from the Trehan family, and our militia. You will reach Tarnab farmhouse before noon, where you will be joined by Ullas with fifty or so of his tribal fighters. Ullas can negotiate with tribal leaders to secure safe passage and recruit more fighters if needed. I think we have a plan. Keep it to yourself. No one outside this room should know anything. Let us make sure we stick to the plan."

After everyone else left, Jawar and Dostan sat together to catch up on old times.

"Why are you so worried?" Dostan asked.

"Because we are not going there for war. It is a wedding, and I know if Masood Khan finds out, he will not miss the opportunity. I have no experience in defending wedding processions."

"I must say, wedding processions are highly vulnerable and very difficult to protect. But now that we have a plan, I hope you stop worrying and enjoy the festivities," Dostan said.

"The memories of Jurnail's attack on Bara Bandai have haunted me my entire life. That was my first battle," Jawar said as his face became grim. "In that battle, Jurnail was not the brother I had known all my life. The caring and kind Jurnail became a warrior with a vengeance. After the village fell to him, on his orders, no man of fighting age was spared. They either fled or were killed. There were only women and orphans left in the village."

"Because of Jurnail's actions, your clan enjoyed safety in Peshawar. If he had shown weakness, they would have come hunting for you all the way here in Peshawar," Dostan said. "Now, what you really should worry about is Ali."

"I find it ironic that Azmat died fighting these radical mullahs in Bara Bandai, and his son is a Wahabi radical."

"Azmat really gave his life to protect the Sufi culture of Pashtuns. Mullah Arfan was furious with Azmat for his loyalty to you. He has been filling Ali with hate since his childhood against your clan. I know this. You have been away in Jalalabad. I am here. I know what is happening, how Arfan and Ali are building alliances to destroy your clan," Dostan said as Rustam brought a hookah and placed it in front of him.

Jawar tried to speak but, struggling to express his thoughts, he looked around the room. Then in a low and firm voice, he said, "As Azmat lay dying in the mountains after the battle, he asked me to promise that Ali would be taken care of by the clan. I promised him I would personally make sure his son was safe and well cared for."

"Ali is connected with all these radical tribal leaders. Did you help him connect to them before you left for Jalalabad?" Dostan asked Jawar.

"Ali asked me to introduce him to my tribal connections to help him set up his dried-fruit business. I connected Ali with many Lower Swat tribal leaders that are friendly to us. You know them. I only introduced him to good men like you."

"His grandfather is a cleric here in the mosque in Qissa Khwani. He knows all the elements, good and bad, to connect with Ali. Ali came to you just to know who your friends are," Dostan said as he stared into Jawar's face.

"We will have to deal with it. Are you afraid of him?" Jawar asked with irritation.

"I am afraid for your clan. Ali and Arfan are weaving this net around your clan. All you need to do is let Jai take care of it."

"I never stopped him."

"Jai will never go against your word. He will not act against Ali unless you tell him."

"I can't order his killing if that is what you are asking."

"There will be a heavy price to pay," Dostan said as he shook his head in disappointment.

"Did you talk to Mullah Arfan? Ask him what his problem is with us?" Jawar asked as he slowly rubbed his thumb against his fingers.

"I have asked him. He is a mullah. He almost enrolled me against you."

"Yeah? What did you say to him?" Jawar smiled.

"I said to him, if he is asking me to choose between him and you, then I believe you are a better person. He didn't look happy."

Dostan and Jawar laughed.

"You live in a castle in Qissa Khwani as an infidel, by his terms, and Mullah Arfan's key purpose of life here is to remove infidels. Besides, he lost his son-in-law, Azmat, to you — both ideologically and literally. How much it must have hurt him that he could not convince his own son-in-law to join his ideology. He must be really upset." Dostan took a few quick puffs from the hookah. "Since you left Peshawar to this retreat, Ali has started to conspire to outsmart your sons. He knew Jai and Mehar neither had the tribal-social skills and acumen to match their father, nor a thorough and practical understanding of Pashtunwali."

"My sons are smarter than me. You know what my sons are missing? A friend like you."

"They are not getting any friends like me. No one wants to go to hell. Ask Mullah Arfan."

They laughed.

"Arfan is a cross gone wrong between Wahabi and Deobandi Islam," Jawar said. "Mullahs like him are very dangerous."

"They will destroy Pashtunistan and its culture," Dostan said as he took a few puffs from his hookah. There was a moment of quiet. "When are you going to give up this bitterness with Bhole? He is your son," he asked Jawar, though he knew the question was too personal.

"What do you mean?" Jawar asked as he raised his eyebrows.

"Did you invite him to the wedding?" Dostan put the hookah aside.

"What would he do at the wedding?"

"Look, I find your behavior towards him a little too harsh. Fine, he married an Irish woman."

"Without telling me," Jawar said as he showed disappointment with his hands stretched out.

"Okay, that was bad. But it has been, what? Seven years?"

"Don't pretend that you don't know why I am upset with him."

"Well, everyone is serving the British now," Dostan said as he pulled the hookah back and took a puff.

"He is serving the British army. If he cared a bit about my happiness, or family honor, country, and all the sacrifices people have made to push the British out, he would not have joined or at least should have quit."

"Thousands of your Sikh brothers have been serving the British Army, dying in battles for them far away from home. What if your son joined? He is an officer."

"My family does not serve the British," Jawar said loudly, turning away his face.

"I didn't mean to make you upset. I feel if he is around, he may be of help to Jai."

"He is of no help. He will never help, and his help will never actually help. I know him very well. It is better he is away."

"All I am saying is that you left for Jalalabad. Jai needs some help here." Dostan said as he pulled the pillows and sat against the wall.

"Jai and Mehar must learn to manage this clan on their own," Jawar said as he lay down on the bed across Dostan. Then he covered his eyes with his right arm. "Jai was very brave and wise. Lakshmi's death has left him a broken man. He is still struggling to re-cover from that tragedy."

Dostan and Jawar talked late into the night un-til they were too tired to respond.

***

Since the day Ali heard of Mehar's wedding, he had been working hard on finding the detailed wedding plan so he could pass it to Masood in Bara Bandai. He had found out from a horse handler who worked at Dil Mahal that the wedding procession would start from the Dils' Tarnab farmhouse. But what Masood wanted to know was the destination of the baraat.

"All you need to do is find out when and where. I will take care of the rest. Your name won't even come in the middle," Masood had assured Ali.

"I will try. But Jawar, the old man, is back in the haveli, and he will keep it a secret."

Despite his rigorous efforts, Ali failed to get any information on the destination of the wedding procession. Frustrated, Ali walked into the Dils' office to disrupt the meeting on the pretext of congratulating Jawar. He showed great happiness and interest in the wedding and continued with his probing conversation with Jawar. Jawar did not reveal any specifics about the wedding location and instead invited Ali to join the wedding procession.

"I would love to join, but unfortunately, I cannot be away from my business that long," Ali explained.

"That makes two of us. I will not be joining the wedding procession either," Jawar replied. "Just getting too old."

Ali was relieved. *That is great. Dealing with his stubborn sons is way easier in his absence. Of course, the best revenge would be to see him suffer,* Ali thought as he walked out. The words of his grandfather Arfan echoed in his head: "They used your father to kill the clerics and sheiks in Bara Bandai and then left your injured father there to die."

"Jai has barred him from our office," Joga said as Ali left the office.

"Why? What happened?" Jawar asked Jai.

"He repeatedly walked in uninvited on important *jirga* meetings. He also crashed a meeting to settle Masood's conflict with the British over passage rights," Jai said.

"Let us not create more enemies. We don't need enemies in Peshawar. Since when has this been going on?" Jawar asked.

"About a year back, a British army officer in charge of the garrison near Malakand had sent Haji

Khan of the village of Kabal and some tribal leaders from the town of Malakand to Jai for mediation. We were in jirga to resolve disputes when Ali walked in uninvited. I asked him to leave. As he walked out, so did Haji Khan, claiming that I had insulted his friend. Their walkout derailed the entire negotiations. It was a setup," Jai explained.

"His actions are causing significant damage to our credibility and influence. It is like he is planning something behind our backs," Mehar added.

"Why do you think he is conspiring?" Jawar asked.

"After that meeting, he officially became Haji's agent in Peshawar. He has been representing him in tribal disputes. Haji and Mullah Arfan are also very close," Jai explained.

"Handle him tactfully. You should always know what he is up to," Jawar said.

"You know Haji Khan. He preys on weak Hindu and Sikh families in Khyber. He has close ties to Arfan," Jai replied.

"Haji Khan's grandfather fought along with Syed Ahmad Barelvi in the Balakot. He is a real hardliner. Wants to destroy Sufism," Dostan said.

"You should have known about Haji's connections with Ali and Arfan," Jawar said to Jai. He was already worried about the wedding, and this situation with Ali in Peshawar irritated him. "There are always rivals in our businesses. They may conspire, hate, backstab, or attack. They will do anything that works for them. Your job is to neutralize them. And you can achieve that by defeating them and destroying them, or by being their friend and ally. But they should not be a looming and persistent threat," Jawar advised Jai.

"You had Baba Jurnail to help you. I am alone here," Jai said with frustration. "I work under tremendous constraints here."

"I also have Dostan. Make friends. At least spend as much time making friends as you invest in making enemies," Jawar said. He was not amused at Jai's response.

Dostan was uneasy. He felt Jai was right about working under constraints. But didn't want to interfere between father and son.

"If you know the solution to the problem. Then solve the problem. Don't worry about anything else," Dostan said to Jai.

Jawar frowned with disapproval as Dostan shrugged it off.

*** 

In Peshawar, news of Mehar's wedding was the talk of the town. The ceremonies had started many days in advance. Many tribal and political leaders, civil and army officers were invited for dinner at Dil Mahal. A big reception was planned for the baraat's return.

At the Dils' farmhouse in Tarnab, hundreds of farmworkers, clansmen, and locals from friendly tribes had gathered to enjoy the festivities. Free food was offered to the poor, large donations were given to Hindu, Sikh temples, and Sufi shrines. There were henna and dance ceremonies for women. Jawar's sister, Sukhi, had also arrived from north of Tarnab with her husband and their two sons. Special horses were selected for the journey and decorated the night before.

In the morning, the baraat left Dil Mahal to fanfare. The family priest and a few servants and horse handlers also accompanied the baraat. Jai led the procession with his militia. There were only two women in the caravan; one Jawar's sister, Sukhi, and the other a domestic helper named Amira. They were sitting in a *palki*, a boxed carriage attached to horizontal poles and hand-carried by men. Jai's mounted fighters covered the palki on both sides. Ullas, a tall young man with a long beard, was on his horse a few yards away on the middle-right side of the procession. He usually kept to himself, only talked when necessary, and kept his sentences short and to the point.

A few hours later, Jawar and Dostan, with some close friends and their militia, followed the baraat in a separate convoy that included local tribal leaders close to Jawar. The convoy stopped at friendly villages on the way, as Jawar wanted to thank them for their support. Jawar and Dostan then camped with two dozen or so of their fighters on the riverbank after crossing the village of Aboha. From there, he wrote notes to Jurnail detailing the events of the last few days and the uncomfortable feeling about being in the valley: *Last night, I woke up from a nightmare that felt real. Ghosts of the past surrounded me as I slept. When I woke up, I had my dagger in my hand. I had pulled it out in my sleep.*

They camped near the area where the Swat River ran low. Jawar believed if anyone attacked the baraat, they would cross the river from here. It was easy to cross the river from there to escape to the Bara Bandai and other Upper Swat villages.

"I am so worried, Dostan, that something will go wrong," Jawar said. Unable to sleep, he sat down close to Dostan, who was smoking a small hookah. "I think part of being old is that you just get so good at worrying."

Dostan looked at Jawar and said, "There is no way to keep this a secret. Half of Swat already knows about this wedding. As far as the location is concerned, they just have to follow the baraat." Dostan leaned back on the rock and took another puff from his hookah.

Jawar was not at all surprised by Dostan's words. He was sure that Masood's men were following the baraat. "Dostan, thanks for being here. Your support means heavens to me."

"I gave you my word."

When they were young boys, Dostan had promised Jawar to always be there when he needed him.

"Now, let us hope our old bones have enough strength to fight," Jawar said and smiled.

"Let us hope we won't have to. But if we do, it will be an honor to fight alongside you again." Jawar patted Dostan's shoulder to acknowledge his loyalty.

Dostan, Jawar, and Jurnail were childhood friends. They were born in Tarnab and grew up together. They studied Urdu, Farsi, Punjabi, Sanskrit, and Hindi together. They went on long hunting trips together and visited Sufi shrines, and engaged the fakirs and Sufi saints in discussions on the nature of God. Nothing ever came between their friendship and loyalty to each other. While Dostan was dedicated to friendship with Jawar and Jurnail, his son Ullas only fought alongside Dils because Dostan ordered him to.

His fighters knew that Ullas had no personal connection to Dils.

The following day, the wedding procession safely reached Batkhela. They camped there to spend the night. Tribespeople greeted Jai and Ullas and prepared good food as they celebrated with dancing and a bonfire. On the way, the procession camped in many tribal areas, enjoying the hospitality of tribal leaders friendly to the clan. After two days and changing horses four times, the baraat reached Mingora. The marriage was solemnized as per Sikh rights. After one night's stay, the baraat left for Peshawar with the bride.

As Jawar and Dostan had feared, Haji's men were tracking the movement of the baraat. Although Haji stayed away from directly getting involved, his fighters had already gathered near Aboha to help Masood. Many even passed close to where Jawar and Dostan were camping, alerting them to an impending attack. As the baraat headed back with the bride, Masood and fifty or so of his fighters intercepted the procession near Barikot. Masood had underestimated the preparedness and number of Dil fighters in the baraat. In the fierce fighting that followed, the women in the palki became sitting targets. As Masood's men retreated, they attacked the palki.

As the guns roared, Jawar and Dostan quickly caught up with Masood. They surrounded Masood's fighters from the side of Aboha and blocked their escape. As the battle raged, despite all their efforts, Jai and Ullas could not save Mehar's bride. She, being the main target, was shot and killed by Masood's men. In a hand-to-hand fight near the palki, Jai was stabbed with a bayonet in his thigh and fell to the ground. A bullet hit Mehar's left shoulder, leaving him bleeding. Balwant's son, Hazoor Singh, fought bravely but died in the battle. Masood lost his two brothers and most of his fighters, but he himself escaped after crossing the Swat River, leaving his dead and injured men behind. Daler quickly ran to the palki as Mehar carried his bride out and laid her on the ground. There, with her head on Mehar's lap, she took her last breath.

With his anger boiling, Ullas asked his militia to shoot the captured fighters. Although the attack was not unexpected, Jai had not mentally prepared himself for it. He was in shock. It was his first battle of this size. He felt like a general who had a bigger and better army but still lost the battle. He felt shame and guilt at not being able to protect his brother's bride.

Jawar, however, was not surprised. He quickly took charge and started working to manage the danger of a second attack.

"*Inna lillahi wa inna ilayhi raji'un*," Dostan prayed over the dead in his militia. He turned to his son and said, "Ullas, bury your dead. We are too far from home to carry them."

"Daler, you heard Dostan. Please prepare for the dead's cremation. Leave Hazoor; I will take him myself." Jawar insisted that Maher's bride be cremated on the bank of the Swat river that ran close by.

"Hurry up, people," Jawar yelled.

Thus, Kirat was cremated on the banks of the Swat River in her bridal dress by Mehar. Many tribal leaders looked on as the Dil's bride was consigned to fire. In brutal tribal culture, many saw this event like the falling clout of Dils in Lower Swat.

"Priest, will you dress Hazoor's wounds? I would like to take him to his family. He will ride with me. I will face his father, Balwant, and his son, Lakhbir, myself," Jawar said and sighed in grief as a priest prepared Hazoor's body for travel on horseback with Jawar.

Jai was furious and wanted revenge. Hurting and bleeding, he wanted to go after Masood. *How dare he!* His anger over what had happened made him shake. He took it as a personal failure.

Jawar stopped the restless and angry Jai. "As long as you are alive, there is always a second chance," Jawar told Jai as the priest dressed his wounds.

"The wound is deep. He cannot ride," the priest whispered to Daler, who was helping with dressing Jai's wounds. After that, the priest checked Mehar's wounds and decided to remove the bullet.

"Leave it in there," Mehar insisted.

"It is right near the shoulder joint. It is best if I take it out. It will hurt but heal way quicker than leaving it in there," the priest said.

After wounds of Mehar and the other men hurt in the fight were dressed, they all joined for the cremation and burial of the soldiers. Eleven men in Ullas' militia lost their lives and were buried on the foothills. Heavy stones were moved to cover their graves.

After the cremations of the bride and eight Dil fighters, Jawar told Jai, "We need to clear the area soon. Masood's men may reassemble. Go to Dil Mahal and get better." On hearing Jawar, Daler pulled the palki near Jai and helped him inside. Jawar went around visiting each of his fighters and personally asking their well-being, then he stopped his horse near Ullas. "Ullas, will you be kind enough to station some of your men here so the cremation goes through completely? The priest and Mehar will stay behind."

Ullas ordered a few of his militiamen to stay behind.

"Please come to Peshawar. We need you there," Jai begged his father as he lay in pain in the palki.

"I have no desire to go back to Peshawar. It is your time to handle this situation." Then he whispered to himself, "I should have stayed in Jalalabad."

As Jawar turned his horse, he looked at Mehar, who was sitting against a rock, with pain and misery written large on his face. Jawar hated his son's situation. His eyes shot up with anger, and he yelled sternly, "Mehar, go with the priest to the farmhouse after the cremations are complete. Fulfill your obligations of last rights and ceremonies of your wife and our men. Stay there for some time till things settle down." Then he turned to Ullas and said, "Please escort Mehar and the others to Tarnab when they are ready."

"Ullas, make sure everyone safely reaches Tarnab," Dostan ordered his son, who then immediately directed his militia.

Jawar mounted his horse and moved it close to the palki. "Sons," he said, "this clan is in your hands, and I fully trust you will recover. My blessings will always be with you. Remember what your grandfather taught us. Attack like a hawk. A hawk's eyes, timing, and speed leave little chance for its prey. A hawk is observant and patient."

With that, Jawar and Dostan left with their men.

Jawar knew this attack was just the beginning, and things would only get worse for the clan. He realized that his sons were not mature enough for the task at hand. Many thoughts ran through his mind as he rode towards the town of Charsadda with Hazoor's body. There he wanted to hand over his body to his father, Balwant. He also wanted to meet his elder brother, Jurnail, in Charsadda and seek his counsel. *I cannot go to Jalalabad without addressing this situation. Jai has become so weak. A man cannot become weak for a woman. It does not matter who she may be. He has to take care of his responsibilities. Oh, God! How will I face Jung?* He was deeply disturbed by the death of Kirat, and there was no one who could have provided more solace and guidance than his brother, Jurnail, who had always looked after him.

# Chapter 3
# [1940] Curse of Messa

In Peshawar, news of the attack on Mehar's baraat reached Qissa Khwani Bazaar. Riders of Ullas Khan delivered the news with little compassion. At Dil Mahal, celebrations quickly turned into mourning. A crowd of well-wishers gathered outside the haveli to convey their condolences. Among them was Ali, who wanted to see and enjoy the Dils' misery. But there was no one at Dil Mahal except little Hari, who was briefly informed by Joga of the family situation.

Unable to meet or even see anyone from the Dil family, visitors to Dil Mahal were concerned about the well-being and safety of the Dils. Joga had arranged a cordon around the mansion and had refused to speak to anyone. In the absence of information, many rumors about the Dil family were spreading around Peshawar.

\*\*\*

After cremating the Dil clansmen who died in the battle, Ullas and his men left Mehar and the priest outside the Dils' farmhouse in Tarnab. At the farmhouse, servants waiting for celebrations and gifts were shocked to see Mehar bloodied and hurt as he rode in on his horse with the priest. Mehar and the priest were both stone-faced as they trotted through the entrance of the farmhouse. Farmworkers and orderlies helped Mehar down from the horse. With bloodstains covering much of his wedding attire, Mehar walked to the drawing-room as everyone watched in dismay. Mehar put the urn containing the ashes of his bride on the table and sat there on the chair.

"Please get some buckets of warm water," the priest said as he tried to catch his breath. Then he added, "Please layout some cots."

Priest and Mehar sat down on the cots as servants helped them wash their hands and feet. Then the priest asked for many other things from the housemaids and farmworkers for the ceremonies of the last rights of deceased clansmen.

After bathing and dressing, Mehar retired to the guest room. There, he grieved in bed as he remembered the dying face of his bride, her blood-covered hands, and the gushing gunshot wound on her neck. The events of the last few days raced through his mind. He remembered the tribesman that had dug his bayonet into Jai's thigh. He remembered Jai shooting him in the face. Then, two riders had fired at Kirat's palki before he and Daler could take them down; one had shot at him. He remembered how she had looked at him as she was dying, that he had picked her up, and she was as light as a flower and as beautiful as a dove. She looked so pretty in her red dress when he'd laid her on top of the funeral pyre. When the priest had asked him to light it, he had hesitated for a moment. He felt she would wake up from sleep. Then the lit wood just dropped from his hand at the place the priest had asked him. With that, his bride was consigned to fire before he could share a word with her. He felt powerless and ashamed of himself. *There was nothing we could have done to save her. Nothing I could have done to protect her. Those vows that I took to protect and cherish her were all false.*

The worry about Jai's condition, the clan's future, and the tragic death of his second wife kept him awake till late at night.

In the morning, relatives of the clan's militiamen who died in the battle joined the priest for ceremonies for their last rites. Mehar was troubled as the names and ages of these men were announced by a priest. In all, twenty-one people in Dil's and Dostan's militia lost their lives.

Mehar had never been in a battle before. He was devastated by the loss of life. *Too many young clansmen died too soon. All for my wedding.*

The priest tried to explain to him, "They died because it was their time. The reasons are created to help things happen that have to happen. Now the ceremonies are over, you should go back to Peshawar and help Jai."

Mehar did just that. He left in the evening on a horse for Peshawar. He wanted to be with his brother in this difficult time.

*** 

It was with great care and difficulty that Daler had brought Jai to Dil Mahal from the battlefield. He wanted to get him needed medical attention. British doctors were called in to attend to him. As Jai lay suffering in bed injured, sick, helpless, and alone, the clan was looking to him for answers. Every time he faced a family member or friend, Jai wished he had died in that battle. He had taken the events of the last few days as his personal failure. His anger over the incident was so much that it had made him sick. He had developed a high fever and had difficulty breathing. If he could, he would have gone back and attacked Masood in Bara Bandai. But all he could do was lie in bed and lament and suffer. *Death is easier than indignation.* In this defeat and loneliness, Daler was the only one around that Jai could trust.

In Peshawar, continued streams of family and friends visited Dil Mahal every day. As the days passed, Jai's health got worse. Girdhari, the family *vaidya,* the traditional ayurvedic physician, said that it was the anger that was killing him inside. Daler was very concerned about Jai's condition. He pleaded with Jai to not stress about taking revenge at this time, "I swear on my life that we will take revenge."

Jai told Daler the true cause of his worry and urgency of action. "Daler, I am deeply worried that the clan may not survive under the circumstances. I am bedridden when I should be out there destroying our enemies." Then, with pain on his face, he said, "I will get better when Masood is dead. You keep an eye on any opportunity."

"I would work day and night to find out if that opportunity existed," Daler assured Jai.

In his effort to give Jai some hope, Daler put several of his informants on Masood, Haji, and Ali. He wanted to know anything that would provide an opportunity to take revenge.

Masood and Ali knew Jai was seeking vengeance with every breath. They had already started making plans to set him up. The opportunity came sooner than they had anticipated.

\*\*\*

Messa Khan was the leader of a small tribe in the town of Sardheri. He was a Sufi poet, fakir, and *dervish* who was well respected by the Yusufzai tribes of Charsadda. He was a good friend of Dostan. He had one son named Abdul, who he loved dearly. Before Messa became a dervish, he gave control of his tribe to his son and moved to a shrine near the town of Haripur. Although Abdul was a young man, he was wise and kind and exceeded his father's expectations. His wedding was fixed with the daughter of another Muslim scholar. Messa loved his son and was looking forward to a great future for him after his wedding.

Masood, like Haji, did not like Sufis for their tolerance towards other religions. When Masood and Ali learned about the wedding of Messa's son, they planned to set up Jai. Through Ali's contacts, one of Daler's informants was tipped off that Masood was planning the wedding of his younger brother. It was said that the wedding would be in two months and the baraat would go to Sardheri. It was also hinted that the marriage was kept a secret to thwart any attack from Dils.

Masood and Ali knew that Messa Khan was highly respected by the Yusufzai tribes and Dostan himself. Any harm to him or his family by Dils would create an unbridgeable rift between the Dils and Yusufzai tribes. The plan was to trick Jai into attacking Messa Khan and the wedding procession. Ali was sure the Dils could not survive in Khyber once the Yusufzai tribes of lower Swat turned against them, and he had laid a perfect trap for Jai. To eliminate the possibility of Ullas providing any help to Jai, Ali had already facilitated reconciliation between Ullas and Masood, and they agreed to forgive and forget the battle at Barikot.

After receiving the information from Daler, Jai already felt better. His wounded thigh had not fully healed, but that did not deter him from assembling his militia. Jai started working with Daler and Mehar to take revenge on Masood. Although he had to be helped onto the horse, he had resumed routine rounds of his estate in Tarnab.

This time, Jai had no support except his own clansmen. Jawar and Dostan were not there, and getting help from Ullas alone was unlikely. Jai just had not built that strong of a relationship with Ullas. Besides, Dostan and Ullas would not have participated in the attack on a wedding procession. This time, however, Jai was supported by the Trehan clan, led by Baba Balwant and his two brothers. Together the brothers had nine sons and fourteen grandsons. Trehans lived outside Charsadda together in the Trehan farmhouse. They had brought about thirty fighters. Jawar's sister, Sukhi, was represented by her two elder sons, Satwant and Zorawar. The brothers resembled each other as if twins, except that Zorawar was three years younger and a little taller than Satwant.

Concerned, Joga said, "This looks like a Sikh army. We need some tribal warlords with us."

"But there is no time to organize that kind of militia," Daler said.

Ali had learned that Messa had planned for the baraat to spend the night in the town of Dargai. He'd carefully kept it a secret. Two days before the wedding, he tipped off Daler. This was a shrewd plan by Ali. He wanted to give Jai less time to plan and force him to move in haste.

Ali had been keeping an eye on the movement of Jai's men and told Masood to position his fighters on the east side of Dargai. When Ali saw Messa Khan leading the wedding procession towards Dargai, he knew his plan was working perfectly. *If everything goes according to plan, and not only today, we will kill Jai and Mehar, Dils will be one of the most hated clans in the Khyber,* thought Ali as he nervously observed the situation from a distance.

As Messa Khan and his family left Dargai with the baraat, Masood followed the procession at a distance with a large number of his fighters. As the procession reached Dargai, Jai's militia attacked Messa Khan's baraat, thinking it was Masood's brother's wedding procession. Before they realized their mistake, Abdul was already dead. Jai had himself shot the bridegroom. When Jai saw Messa Khan, he realized his mistake. Jai fell on Messa's feet and asked for his forgiveness.

Messa was heartbroken, and in his anger, cursed Jai, "May Allah's curse destroy your clan, and just like my family is destroyed here today, may you one day see your family dying in front of your eyes."

Shortly after, Masood reached there with his fighters as planned and attacked Jai's astounded militia. In the ensuing fight, lots of Jai's men were killed, including his three nephews. Masood also took two of Jai's cousins hostage.

Jai escaped with Mehar and Daler through the mountains of Dargai. His thigh wound had started bleeding again. The pain was unbearable, but even more unbearable was the blunder he had committed by killing Abdul. Having understood that Daler had fallen for Ali's plot, Jai was dying to meet Messa Khan and explain the entire conspiracy. But Masood and Ali had already made their plans. Messa Khan and everyone else in the baraat was killed by Masood and his men. Ali and Masood made sure no witnesses were left. Jai realized his mistake, but it was too late. The deafening words from his father's past advice exploded in his head: *Always include tribal leaders in your actions,* Jawar had told him. *If they don't support you, you should seriously rethink pursuing your plan.*

Masood took Abdul's bride with him and performed *nikah*, the Muslim marriage ceremony, with her the same day to 'restore her honor.' Ali and Masood ensured that news of a Hindu clan attacking and killing a Muslim fakir reached every corner of Khyber. News spread in Khyber that Dils had attacked the wedding procession of Messa Khan to avenge the attack on their wedding procession. It was also told that had Masood not reached there with his men to protect a fellow Muslim brother, a Muslim bride would have been taken by the Dils.

Although Ali and Masood failed to kill Jai, they had done even better. They had killed his spirit, undermined the Dil clan, cut its social standing, captured two of his cousins, and ruined the Dil family reputation in Khyber. As Jawar used to say, *reputation is all you have when you have nothing.* The defeat devastated the clan. When Jai and Mehar arrived at

Dil Mahal, Jai had fainted on the horse. He was immediately helped to the cot.

In Dil Mahal, Jai was lying surrounded by a *vaidya* and a British doctor. The clansmen gathered outside were worried if he would survive this time. Some had given up hope, and for them, it was just a matter of days.

\*\*\*

Jawar, Dostan, and Jurnail were still in Charsadda when they heard the news about Jai and Mess Khan. There, they were approached by a mercenary named Khuda Baksh. He had watched in disgust as Masood ordered the killing of Messa Khan and lived with remorse for his part in it.

"His witness could win back Yusufzai leaders," Dostan told Jawar. Then together, they worked out a plan.

"This will be our last battle, Dostan. We are so fortunate to have you as our friend. Times have changed. We would like you to keep all the land of the Dil clan in Tarnab. There will be no more involvement of the Dil clan in tribal affairs."

"As long as I am alive, that land will always belong to the Dil clan."

"Your son has always followed your orders and put his own and his men's lives in danger for us.

Give this land to him and his militiamen as a token of our gratitude."

As part of the plan, Dostan left for Tarnab to assemble his militia. Jawar had left with Khuda Baksh for Mingora, and along the way, sought help from his old friends and tribal leaders. And Jurnail decided to go to Qissa Khwani and sort out clan affairs.

In Tarnab, Dostan told the Yusufzai leaders that Dils could never kill Messa, "They are righteous people; they live their life within certain believes and principles. They call it *Sanatan dharma*, living a life of honesty, refraining from unjustly injuring living beings, purity, goodwill, mercy, patience, forbearance, self-restraint, generosity, kindness; these principles are central to their life. I know Masood killed Messa, and I will prove it to you all. Till then, please support the Dils and me as you always have. Give us one more chance."

While tribesmen had little interest in supporting Dils, they had a great deal of respect for Dostan. They were ready to fight and die for him anytime.

***

At Dil Mahal, Balwant, the family patriarch and eldest cousin of Jawar and Jurnail, had arrived to take charge of the situation. He asked that a telegram be sent to Bhole Nath requesting his presence at Dil

Mahal. "With Jai being sick, there is no one with more military experience than Bhole. In the absence of Jawar and Jurnail, he is the only one I can think of, and he may be able to get the British involved to secure the release of our boys."

Mehar objected to engaging Bhole in tribal affairs, "He will completely get it wrong."

"Tell me a better option. You have always shied away from leading the family," Balwant said.

The same day, a telegram was sent to Bhole: *Jai very sick. Come immediately.* Bhole and his wife, Mary, arrived at Dil Mahal the next day after receiving the telegram. A family meeting of elders was held under the leadership of Balwant, where he asked Bhole to leave his military job and move to Peshawar to act as head of the family.

"I would be happy to support the family in this difficult time. But I have a few conditions."

"We would like to hear those," Balwant said.

"One, that Mary stays with me at Dil Mahal, and the family will accept her."

"The family didn't have any problem with Mary. We always wanted you to serve the family and not the British," Balwant replied.

"Second, we need to stop hostilities with tribesmen."

"We are doing hostilities? Are you crazy?" Mehar said as he got up to walk out of the meeting.

"Mehar, he does not know. Let us explain it to him." Balwant tried to calm Mehar down. Then, turning to Bhole, he said, "They have an agenda to destroy us. They attacked the wedding procession and killed Mehar's wife and my son. But if you help kill Masood, we will scale down our militia."

"I am willing to talk to Masood to make peace. But there will be no more battles. Our job is not to enforce laws here. That is the job of the British government."

"You are so clueless. The British government is here to extract money, not to create law and order for people. They take our help to resolve tribal issues. Do you understand that?" With that, Mehar walked out of the room.

"Let us take a break and regroup in the evening," Balwant announced.

Later that day, the family elders met again for jirga. Bhole promised to secure two hostages held by Masood if he got a free hand in negotiating on behalf of the clan. The elders agreed on the condition that any deal with Masood be approved by them first.

"Another important matter is that we need you to take care of Hari. His safety is at risk here," Balwant said and looked at Bhole for a response.

"Mary and I would love to take care of him," Bhole happily agreed. He even offered to adopt Hari as his son.

"Thank you. Jai will derive great comfort from this news," Balwant said.

All other details regarding the clan jirga were kept secret from Jai. The family was worried about his health and didn't want to stress him out. They also understood that Jai would never give his approval to the terms Bhole was proposing.

# Chapter 4
# [1940] Old Mountain Hawk

The following Friday, after destroying Jai's militia in Dargai, Masood and his men entered Qissa Khwani Bazaar openly. Ali had invited Masood and Haji to join the Friday prayers at the Qasim Ali Khan Mosque led by his grandfather, Mullah Arfan. Ali had planned far ahead, and he intended to color the conflict with the Dils as a religious battle with infidels. Mullah Arfan always did a great job inciting the crowd.

In the past, Masood had visited the bazaar discretely and made sure he never crossed paths with anyone in the Dil clan. But today was the day of retribution for Jurnail's actions in Bara Bandai. He took an open victory procession, and his men fired in the air as a crowd of late-nighters gathered. But Masood was oblivious to the presence of Jurnail, who had followed him with a few other riders into the bazaar. Jurnail had been in distress since he'd learned from Jawar the events of the last two months. He had recruited some fighters from Charsadda and picked up some mercenaries on the way and stationed them outside Peshawar on the road to Tarnab.

In Qissa Khwani, the large presence of Masood's fighters had attracted the attention of the British army. Before the situation escalated, Ali brokered an arrangement for Masood and up to ten of his fighters to stay in Qissa Khwani. The rest of his men had to go outside the city boundary.

As Jai lay dying in Dil Mahal, Bhole met Ali to broker the peace with Masood. Ali explained the terms for the release of the Dil clansmen in Masood's custody.

In a nearby kahwah shop, Bhole met Masood and agreed to the terms, pending the elders' approval. "Masood, I come here in friendship and very favorable terms for the release of our men," Bhole said. Bhole not only agreed to everything Masood had asked for but gave even more.

"As you demanded, all the land of Tarnab would be surrendered to you. In return, you will release two sons of Sucha held by you."

"All farmhands in Tarnab should also be transferred to me," Masood said.

Bhole thought it natural for farmhands to go with the farm. They agreed there would be no attacks from any side unless negotiations failed.

"I need Preet House," Masood demanded.

"That will be almost impossible," Bhole said.

"Khan is willing to pay," Ali said.

After some negotiation, Bhole agreed to sur-render Preet House in Peshawar Cantonment for twelve thousand rupees. Masood made it clear the deal had to be approved by midnight the next day while he waited in an inn in Qissa Khwani Bazaar.

By transferring the farmhands, Bhole handed a big gift to Masood. It made him happy. Farmhands, who were almost all local Pashtuns, had always sup-ported the Dil family until recently. Masood had used the death of Messa Khan to breed hate in their hearts for Dils. Bhole understood that it would be hard to change course and make these men loyal to the family again. He took the easy path.

After Bhole left, Ali and Masood celebrated their success.

"Khan, now they have no Pashtun support, no farm, and no farmhands. Soon we will have their haveli in Cantonment. Now, all we need to do is drive them out of Dil Mahal," Ali said as he smiled.

"*Insha Allah,* it will happen soon," Masood replied.

"Remember, I want Dil Mahal," Ali said.

"Of course."

*** 

In Qissa Khwani Bazaar, inside the Dil office, the jirga was called to discuss the proposed deal with

Masood. All elders from Tarnab, Charsadda, and surrounding areas were summoned by Bhole. There were elders from the Trehan and Bedi family who had never participated in clan decisions before. They had never needed to. They would agree with anything that Jawar or Jai proposed. They had no knowledge of complex tribal disputes, long-term and short-term consequences of decisions, or the political dexterity to understand the impact.

As Bhole sat with elders to discuss the deal, Masood decided to take a tour of Dil Mahal. High on opium, he and his henchmen walked outside Dil Mahal in the street. In the dark, their half-open eyes stared at the beautiful mansion. They could see the two gunmen guarding the huge wooden entrance. Masood smiled as he read *Dil Mahal* on top of the gate. Standing on the turrets, Jai's militiamen could see Masood's fighters in the street. But Masood was not alone near Dil Mahal. Jurnail and his fighters followed him as they watched from a distance.

Inside Dil Mahal, Jai Dil lay sick, barely breathing. Two men continued to massage his feet. A little boy slowly massaged Jai's head. Two old men, a priest, and a vaidya sat nearby.

Outside, Masood and his men fired into the air.

"Who is outside?" whispered Jai as he heard the gunshots.

"No one in particular, *Chacha*," Lakhbir, who was guarding Jai, replied.

Lakhbir, considered an exceptional fighter, was specially assigned by Baba Balwant to protect Jai.

"Where is my boy?" Jai asked in a low voice.

"I am right here, Papa," Hari said.

"Listen, Hari. In a few days, you will move to your uncle's place. He will take care of you better than I have been," Jai whispered.

"I want to stay here with you. Nothing will happen to you." The boy held Jai's hand. Then he walked over to the wall to look down on the street through the loophole.

In the street, Masood stood staring at the gate of Dil Mahal with two of his key henchmen, Ismail Khan and Ajmal Khan, as Joga watched them closely.

"He is inside," Ismail said with a smile.

"I heard he is dying slowly," said Ajmal Khan with a smile.

"We can make it fast," countered Ismail.

"Let him suffer. Let's go. We wait for Ali," said Masood as they walked away.

\*\*\*

Unaware of Bhole's arrangement with Masood, Jai lay sick in bed, fearing the curse of Messa would not only kill him but also everyone else in the clan. It had been a week since the battle at Dargai. Daler and his father Joga, along with other men loyal to the family, continued to guard Jai and Dil Mahal. The clan's future was a concern on everyone's mind. Being the sole heir, protecting Hari became one of the key priorities for the clan. He was not allowed to leave Dil Mahal. The boy had learned earlier that when he was asked not to leave the haveli, it meant that enemies of the clan were nearby and had the upper hand. He secretly wished he was old enough to fight the hostile tribesmen. But most of the time, he prayed for his father's recovery. At night, Hari stayed awake late, walking along the walls of the haveli's balcony, looking at the dark streets of the bazaar. Sometimes, he would go outside the room and sit under the stairs to shed a few tears for his father's condition. And many times, every night, he would return to Jai's bedside to check on him.

Daler stood the watch on the balcony, keeping an eye on everyone in the streets. In the quiet of the night, the sound of a trotting horse on the brick streets captured the attention of Daler and his men. As the rider neared the entrance, Daler and a few other men came downstairs from the roof, where they had been keeping watch around the clock. The rider wore a blanket that covered everything but his eyes. As he removed the blanket, Daler's face lit up. He immediately identified the old man as Jurnail, the elder brother of Jawar. "*Sat Sri Akaal*, Baba-ji," Daler said and touched his feet, then helped the old man get down.

"May you live to see many generations, Daler. Where is Jai?"

"Lala-ji is upstairs," Daler said and led the old man into the haveli. "Baba-ji, Lala-ji is not well." Daler's voice cracked. Jurnail walked past the men guarding the haveli as if inspecting them. Daler walked behind to catch up with the old man.

"I know. I know. Can someone get my horse to water?" the old man asked the men guarding the entrance and went upstairs as Daler followed him. "I need to see Bhole before he meets Masood. Don't tell him that I sent you. Also, call Mehar. Tell him I am waiting. Go now. They are at the office, almost ready to leave."

"Sure, Baba-ji," Daler said and ran out of Dil Mahal.

Upon reaching the roof, Jurnail declared, "Keep the watch," so as not to disturb the attention of men who were unfamiliar with him. Hari came out after he heard the commotion outside. "Is this my boy Hari?" The old man got hold of the boy and hugged him strongly. "Do you know who I am? Do you? I am the brother of your grandfather."

Hari bowed to touch his feet.

"Where is your father? Let us see him."

Hari led the old man to Jai's bed.

The vaidya came out and bowed down to Jurnail.

"Ah, Girdhari, you can't fix my boy? They say you are a great doctor. I only believe if I see." Then he sat on the edge of the bed. "Jai, open your eyes. This is your uncle, Jurnail."

Jai, who was half asleep, tried to get up. "No, no. Stay. Stay." The old man uncovered his sheet to inspect his wounds and covered him back.

"I am here to remind you that evil may win in the short term, but dharma, the righteousness, always prevails. Just let go of your fears. I was praying this morning, and my mind lightened up. It was like the Almighty said things will be fine."

Jai looked at Jurnail. "Is Papa here?"

Jurnail got up from the bed and replied, "If he was here, he would be right here in front of you. Don't you worry anymore. I am here. And I am not going anywhere now."

Jai looked at Jurnail and mumbled, "It is Hari I worry most about. He lost his mother, and now I am lying here counting my time."

Jurnail covered Jai's back with another sheet and tucked it under his arms. "Don't worry. Hari will be fine, and nothing will happen to you either. We're not dead yet. We will not drop dead just because some people want us dead. If that was the case, we would have been dead centuries ago." Then he added after a pause, "I have aged. But I can still settle scores. You rest, and tomorrow will bring a new day, a brighter one."

When Jurnail arrived at Dil Mahal, the family elders had already gathered at the Dils' office for a jirga. After discussions, they approved every part of the deal, except releasing Preet House in Peshawar Cantonment.

Mehar was very unhappy with the decision. "Bhole, I can't tell which side you are on?" Mehar said as he walked out of the jirga.

Sarup, son of Amrit and cousin to Jawar, told Bhole, "I know you are in a hurry. You want to wrap things up. Remember, what is built in centuries can be destroyed in days."

"Jai made some mistakes. We have to pay for them," Bhole argued.

"He built a lot. It is sad what happened. But work on it. Be a leader and build this family. We did not call you to dispose of it. We called you to lead it."

Sucha, the youngest son of Amrit and father of both men in Masood's custody, voted for the deal. While Sarup and their eldest brother Balwant did not vote. Two more elders, who were too old to understand the whole thing, gave their approval as well. Bhole walked out of the Dils' office to meet Masood and Ali. He was surrounded by fighters the clan had provided for his security.

As clansmen watched them leave, Sarup became angry and said, "There is no Dil pride in him. No love for the clan. He has no understanding of the purpose that Baba Kalyan had once communicated."

"Dil pride is dying with Jai or crying inside the office," Balwant said as he saw Mehar sitting below Kalyan Dil's portrait, crying with hands over his face. Mehar sobbed uncontrollably as he looked at *Our Position*, a family proclamation framed in gold. *Our Position* was a letter written to a British army officer by Kalyan Dil in 1897, in response to the question on whose side the Dils were in British battles with Pashtuns near Malakand. The letter stated:

*We are here to protect freedom, the right of people to live their life the way they choose without disrupting or destroying others. We are here protecting the culture of this land that has accepted everyone for thousands of years. We can kill and die for those simple ideas. Happily, we live by Pashtunwali.*

That letter was hand-delivered by Jurnail to General Biggs. Angry after reading it, Biggs threw the letter on the floor. Jurnail picked it up and brought it back with him. After Kalyan's death, Jurnail framed the letter and hung it in the Tarnab farmhouse. When Jawar moved to Dil Mahal, he hung it in the office under the Kalyan portrait for everyone to see. He called that letter, *Our Position.*

Despite writing that letter, Kalyan had helped the British avoid many conflicts with Pashtuns by mediating. Kalyan knew very well how to deal with the British and tribesmen without giving or taking too much.

Bhole, Satwant, Zorawar, and other clan members gathered outside the office, waiting for Ali to receive them. Bhole's wife, Mary, arrived at Dil Mahal in a separate car with Lal Singh and was lodged in the guest room by Daler. She worried about her husband and wanted to stay in Qissa Khwani during negotiations with Masood.

As Ali walked into the office, Mehar felt disgusted by his presence and walked out. "See, that is the attitude that got them here," Ali said to Bhole. "Let's go."

As they prepared to leave for the meeting with Masood, Daler came running to Bhole. "Some elders have arrived at Dil Mahal and need to see you immediately," he whispered in Bhole's ear.

"Who exactly?" Bhole asked.

"I am not allowed to say that. We need to go now. The rest should all wait here for you. It should only take a few minutes."

As Bhole left for Dil Mahal, he waived to Ali and said, "I'll be back in a few."

"Come to the inn. I'll wait for you there," Ali replied.

After arriving at Dil Mahal with Bhole, Daler ran back upstairs and signaled to Jurnail, who abruptly left the room. "Is there a place I can talk to him?" Jurnail asked.

"In the drawing-room downstairs," Daler suggested.

Jurnail and Daler went down to the drawing-room. "Daler, once I am done talking to Bhole, I need you to go with him and inform me of everything that happens at the inn with Masood. I want to know as much about Masood's next steps as possible. Take Rustam with you. I have him waiting on the side street."

Rustam was a loyal Pashtun who had served the family since childhood.

"Listen, boy, keep an eye on Ali. I want to know who he meets and where he goes," Jurnail told Daler, who nodded firmly.

Jurnail walked briskly into the drawing-room.

"Baba-ji, if you allow me to ask…." Daler usually kept his opinions and questions to himself unless they were related to the situation at hand.

"Daler, you are family. Ask without hesitation."

"It is common knowledge that Ali is behind all this. Why do we always let him go?"

"His father was loyal to the family. He gave his life for us. If Jawar had not given his word to Ali's father to protect him, he would've been dead long ago. But no one else gave their word to his father. So, all you imbeciles could have taken care of him. Now he is grinding lentils on our chests."

Bhole was shown to the drawing-room by Daler.

"Greetings, Bhole."

Bhole looked bewildered to see Jurnail. "My respects. This is a big surprise."

"Oh, this has been a season of surprises for all of us," Jurnail said. "Whoever thought Bhole Nath would run the clan or rather run down the clan?" Jurnail sat down on a chair below his father, Kalyan's, portrait.

"I was asked by family, Baba-ji."

Jurnail pointed to everyone else to leave the room.

"May I know some details of the deal with Masood you have brought forth?"

"We have very few options. I am trying to buy peace and secure hostages." Bhole stood at the entrance to the drawing-room, waiting to be invited in.

"Please explain the terms." Jurnail moved to the chair facing the entrance as Bhole handed over the paper to Jurnail's hand, who quickly went through the terms. "All farms of Tarnab will go to Masood. How come?"

Jurnail got up and walked over to Bhole. "Isn't that tribal land? We can give it all to Masood, but without the approval of the Yusufzai leaders of the Tarnab, Masood can't take control of it. There will be a war between tribes."

Bhole was surprised. "I didn't know that land belonged to the tribes."

Jurnail laughed as he looked at Bhole's face and said, "It was our land. Two decades back, Jawar and I decided to give the land to Dostan. A small gift for all the support he had given us and all the men he had lost in our battles. This arrangement worked well for the family for many reasons. You know the rules of *firangis* don't work here."

Although *firangi* was a term used disrespectfully for white people, Bhole understood that in this case, Jurnail was referring to him.

"I did my best," Bhole said.

"You do your best for yourself — common white-man thinking. Also, you are offering to sell Preet House to him for twelve-thousand rupees. I won't bother you with the minor detail that your father built that beautiful haveli for your mother. It has the name of your mother on it." Jurnail's voice had anger and pain. "Have you ever thought how a tribal man, or even leader, will manage that much money? Do you know who is funding him?

"Well, I should not be too hard on you. Let's make a necessary correction. Tell him that the Tarnab-farms deal will need approval from local tribal leaders. He will understand. He knows well how tribal laws work. Also, take Daler with you."

"If I may, Baba-ji, Daler should be here for Jai's protection."

"I will cover for Daler here. Your protection is equally important. After all, you haven't been used to our ways here."

"I will be fine," Bhole insisted while bowing his head in respect.

"Also, take Rustam." Before Bhole could say anything, Jurnail preempted him. "I insist."

Bhole bowed down, folded his hands for a silent namaste, and left along with Daler, Rustam, and a dozen fighters that had come with Jurnail. Bhole knew that, unlike his father, Jawar, his uncle, Jurnail, was not a deal maker. On his way to the inn, he asked Daler the reason for Baba's visit. "*Bhai* sahib, as much as I know, he came to check on Lala-ji."

At the inn, Masood was sitting on the floor against the cushions, smoking a hookah with his henchmen by his side. Ali was already there to receive Bhole. Ali looked at Daler and Rustam, who greeted him with, "Salaam."

"Those two stay outside," Ali told Bhole.

"They will stay with me," Bhole replied. Daler and Rustam followed him.

Ali whispered in Bhole's ear, "They should wait outside."

Bhole raised his hands, insisting it was okay for them to come.

"As-Salaam-Alaikum, Lala ki jaan. Do we have good news or bad news from you?" Masood had gotten up from his comfortable posture.

"Elders have approved all that is in their hands. Everything you have asked for. But the farms in Tarnab need to be approved by local tribal leaders. The elders asked that the boys be released tonight, unharmed."

"What about the *sadar* haveli?" Masood asked, referring to the Preet House.

"That option is approved as well, for twelve-thousand rupees, but you cannot have possession before a year." Bhole looked at Masood to read his face.

"I believe the rate is negotiable, and one year is too long."

Bhole walked a few steps closer to Masood and said discreetly, "You understand that the family has to find another place. Let us know when you are ready to make the payments, and we will try to vacate it early."

"I would like to make the payments tomorrow," Masood said.

"*Janab*, let us work on it together," Ali intervened.

"Well, good deal. I like you." Masood put his hand on Bhole's shoulder. "You don't have arrogance like the rest of your family. Although, one thing bothers me. I heard that you work for the British."

Masood moved closer to Bhole and whispered in his ear, "I believe you will be very successful if you embrace Islam. You and your white wife, Islam will accept her. I can even give you part of the Tarnab farms."

Bhole looked around the room. "I appreciate your generosity. When can I see the boys?"

"The boys will be released tonight. They will be dropped off outside Dil Mahal." Masood had a smirk on his face, and he raised his eyebrows and said in a taunting tone, "We like that place as well. Is your brother dead yet?"

Bhole extended his hand for a respectful and appropriate departure to signal a deal. "Thank you. I hope this will end all hostilities going forward."

Bhole and the entourage left the inn for Dil Mahal, where Jurnail was waiting for them.

# Chapter 5
# [1941] The Last Battle

At Dil Mahal, Bhole arrived to report to Jurnail on negotiations. On hearing his voice, Mary, who had been waiting in fear and anticipation, came running to the door and then stopped after she saw Jurnail. As Bhole told Jurnail that all had gone well during negotiations, Jurnail, who could see Mary behind the drawing-room door, waited for her to come inside, but she stayed behind the door. "She could use your blessing, Baba-ji," Bhole said to Jurnail. Then he added in a low voice that felt more like a complaint, "You know when our Pashtun friends visit us, we have separate utensils for them. Although we believe in so many things that they don't, and the same is true for them of us, we respect each other's feelings and cultures. She's never received the same accommodation."

"She is your wife. We will respect her," Jurnail said and looked at the door, waiting for her to enter the room.

"Will you meet her? No one has met her since she has come here," Bhole asked in a low voice.

"Of course, I will."

Bhole stepped near the door. "Mary, darling, will you come here? Meet my uncle, Jurnail."

Mary stepped in, touched Jurnail's feet, and said, "Namaste."

"God bless you, girl," Jurnail said and looked at her with a smile. "She looks more like a Kalasha girl. Not very different than Maher's first wife. It is a pity that our women have died so young." Changing tone, Jurnail turned to Bhole, who looked happy, and said, "Did you quit your military job?"

"No, I am on vacation," Bhole announced.

"It is not a part-time job to manage the clan. It is a very important job," Jurnail looked in Bhole's eyes.

"I am posted in Rawalpindi Cantt, not too far from here," Bhole said.

"It is a shame you won't commit to such an honorable job and choose to serve the British instead. This family business is brutal. You are too sophisticated and too much of a sellout for this. British payroll suits you better." Jurnail paused and looked at Bhole as he took a few steps towards him, "I heard you will take care of Hari."

"We would love to take care of him," Bhole said, looking at Mary, who smiled and nodded.

Jurnail walked back to the drawing-room wall, and looking at his father's portrait, he said, "Hari is the only hope for this family. You take the boy and go to Rawalpindi. Keep him safe. Train him to be a strong man, a great leader, a wise one."

Jurnail walked back to Bhole, then he called Daler, who was waiting outside the room. "Daler, can you ask Mehar to take Bhole, Mary, and Hari to Preet House tonight. From there, tomorrow morning, they should leave for Rawalpindi."

As Mary bowed to leave the room, Jurnail said. "Daughter, we never banished you. We banished your husband. There are so many reasons for that. But it was a decision I had made in everyone's interest. I am very happy to see you."

She stopped, turned around, and said, "He loves this family so much, and still he is disrespected, and his loyalty questioned."

"What is she saying?" Failing to understand her accent, Jurnail asked Bhole, who stood near the door waiting to be dismissed.

"She is complaining?"

Jurnail stepped closer to Mary and said, "I want to hear her complaint."

"She believes you are not fair with us," Bhole replied.

Jurnail's face turned grim as the smile on his face disappeared. "What do you two think we are doing here, among hostile people? We could go some-where east and live a peaceful life, but why leave this land, the land of our ancestors? Why just surrender to ideas that are full of hate and destruction? The ideas that want to destroy our peace, freedom, and way of life."

Then he turned back, looking at Kalyan's por-trait, and said, "I know the meaning of the battles my father had fought. They were battles against oppres-sion and injustice, and we choose to continue to fight those battles and have paid a heavy price.

"Your husband chooses to side with the British. He chooses to side with oppressors. I will fight till my death to protect our people, our culture, and our values. This is what it is all about. It is not about your husband or you."

Then Jurnail turned to Bhole and said, "It is time to leave the town. Tell her I am happy to see her. I hope she understands. Besides, women in our clan had such misfortune. It is better she stays away from us."

"Daler, bring my little prince to me. I want a word with him alone," Jurnail said.

Daler went to Jai's room and brought Hari with him.

"Son, sit here close to me," Jurnail said.

Hari came and sat on the chair that Jurnail had turned towards the west wall, facing Kalyan's portrait. "You know this man?"

Hari nodded.

"Can we please have time alone? Daler, please pull the curtains and go pack Hari's bag while the two of us talk."

"Hari, my son, people, friends, enemies, family, even parents can change. They may not be the same person you know them to be or want them to be. Eventually, one day, they all leave this world. Attach yourself to ideas, great ideas, and you will continue to find purpose in life even when you are alone."

Hari nodded again.

"Are you ready to go?"

Hari looked at Jurnail, then whispered, "I want to stay with Papa. If I leave, he will die." Tears rolled down his cheeks.

"My father's first wife — I called her Rayema. She was a brave lady. I never got tired of hearing stories of her bravery from elders and even my mother. Her stories are imprinted on my heart. I feel as if she had raised me. Because she was an idea in my mind, the idea of bravery in the most difficult circumstances, she will always be alive in my mind. People only matter because of their ideas. Hold the idea of your father in your head. He will always be with you. The sacrifices he made for a life of dignity for everyone. His love for his clan. His willingness to make the difficult decisions that needed to be made. There are a lot of things you can keep in your heart to remember him and keep him alive for a long, long time."

Jurnail wiped the tears from the boy's face, adding, "I promise you that your papa will be in a better place. I will take care of him."

"When will I come back here to see him?"

"Soon. Now give me a hug. There is your bag," Jurnail said, pointing to Daler, who stood in the door waiting for Hari.

"Go see your father, and then join your uncle Bhole. You will be a great man one day." Jurnail hugged him tightly and let him go.

Hari went upstairs with Daler, his cheeks wet and eyes still full of tears. He touched his father's feet and left the room with a small bag that had been packed in haste for him. After Mehar had left to drop off Bhole, Mary, and Hari at Preet House, Jurnail came outside the haveli to talk to Daler and Rustam, who were waiting for him.

"Was Ali there?" Jurnail asked.

"Yes, Baba-ji."

"Then, I guess nothing exciting happened," Jurnail said as he adjusted the gun on his shoulder.

"Did you tell Hamdard to keep an eye out? You know Hamdard supplies kahwah and snacks at the same inn where Masood is staying?"

"Yes, I did. I specifically asked him to take a note of everyone who comes and leaves the inn and to send a message as soon as Masood leaves."

"Good. Are you ready?" Jurnail moved the dagger tied around his waist in and out.

"Any time, for you, Baba-ji. Order me, and so I will act. At this age, you should not go to battle."

"Why? I may not be able to summon strength in my old bones, but I can always summon courage. This battle is the last battle of the clan. I can't pass up this last opportunity to fight against oppression and injustice." Jurnail smiled for a moment, and then his expression became grim. "How many men can we get?"

"There are twelve men guarding the haveli, and then there is Rustam, Lal, and I, and ten mercenaries we hired for Bhole's protection, and then the ten-to-twelve men that came with you."

"Leave four men to take care of Jai here. Tell the rest of our men they can see their families tonight and should be ready with their horses tomorrow, early before daybreak. We'll meet at Bara River Ghat. Don't tell anyone anything. No mention of my name."

"Baba Jurnail, what is the plan?" Daler asked as Jurnail mounted the horse.

"Plan?" Jurnail looked in the distance. "You know I am old. My hands are not that steady, but I will always fight for a good cause. If we find steady men, the fighters like we used to have — loyal, diehard faithful men — then we can win with only a few."

"What should I tell the men if they ask?" Daler beseeched Jurnail with folded hands.

"Don't say anything. Times have changed. People can't be trusted. And without steady men, plans are doubtful. That is why you have to believe in Him." He pointed to the sky. "If all was certain, a man wouldn't need Him."

"We can count on these men to fight for a cause, but we will need more men to defeat Masood."

"Numbers don't have anything to do with a desire to fight for a cause. I have asked Jawar and Dostan to arrange another hundred fighters and head to Mingora. We need real, loyal men. There is no pride in fighting with mercenaries. See you all at Bara River Ghat in the morning." With that, Jurnail left into the dark backstreets of Qissa Khwani Bazaar.

***

Jawar had reached Mingora with a militia of over a hundred fighters. There, he joined Jung and his men to attack Bara Bandai. Soon, more than fifty mounted men, under the command of Ullas Khan, also joined Jawar.

"Where is your father?" Jawar asked Ullas.

"He has not been doing well."

"I wish him a full recovery. This is the first battle I will fight without him."

"He really wanted to come but has been running a high fever."

"I would like to see him first thing after we have won this battle."

"What is the plan?" Ullas asked.

"We attack after sunset."

Together, Jawar, Jung, and Ullas, with their two hundred or so mounted fighters, attacked the village of Bara Bandai after sunset. Surprisingly, they met little resistance, as most of the men had gone with Masood to Peshawar. But Jawar captured Masood's cousins from the village and brought them along as they marched back towards Tarnab.

Unaware of the situation in his village, Masood, along with his men, trotted on his way to inspect his newly prized farms in Tarnab. Jurnail and Daler were on his trail with about thirty fighters. When he reached Tarnab, he got information about the attack on his village. Upon hearing the news, Masood rushed towards his village, gathering more fighters along the way. Jawar and Ullas were hoping to engage Masood in Tarnab, but to their surprise, both sides ran into each other near the village of Ghalegay. In the open grounds, there was no place to hide. In the ensuing close combat, Masood had the advantage of numbers, whereas Jawar's fighters and Ullas' militia were highly organized.

As the battle raged, hot on Masood's trail, Jurnail reached there with his three dozen or so mounted fighters. His eyes were searching for Masood. When he saw him a few hundred yards away, he charged at him. As he reached close to him, Jurnail gave out a big scream that for a moment had drawn the attention of every fighter on the ground. Then he lunged at Masood, and with one swing of his sword, he beheaded him.

Jurnail's attack took Masood's fighters by complete surprise. Masood's fighters were in disarray. Many deserted the grounds and were chased and killed by Ullas' men; those who surrendered were captured and taken to Tarnab. In Tarnab, a jirga was called by the tribal leaders. A large number of clansmen and tribespeople gathered at Dostan's haveli, many of whom had only heard stories about the bravery of Jurnail and had come to see him. Ali was captured from his home and brought to Tarnab by Ullas' men. In the jirga, Masood's cousins were sentenced to death for the killing of Mesa Khan. Despite Jawar's requests for clemency, many of Masood's fighters were executed. Jawar insisted on saving Ali's life.

"I gave the word to his father to protect him. Please allow me to honor my word." Then he addressed Ali. "When you were a little boy, you called me Chacha. I was your uncle. Jai is like a younger brother to you. Why do this?"

Ali never expressed remorse or asked for forgiveness.

"You will have to leave Peshawar, Ali. It will be in everyone's best interest," Jawar said.

Ali accepted the jirga's decision but took the humiliation of being captured and produced in a jirga to heart.

"You are a fool, Jawar. If not for your family and clan's sake, this man should die because that would be justice. He's had enough chances," Dostan told Jawar. But Jawar insisted, and Ali was released.

Jurnail was livid, "Your children will pay the price for your foolishness."

"Well, this one will be last. I will not return from the dera again, and because I promised Azmat, I will honor it. None of you are bound by that promise. So, in my absence, do whatever you want."

"I am tired as well. I want to go to Charsadda and spend my last few years there, but I think I am needed in Peshawar. Those sons of yours need supervision," Jurnail whispered to Jawar. Then he looked around with pain in his eyes and said, "This farm is gone. The place we were born, grew up, and played."

Jawar patted Jurnail's shoulder with teary eyes.

"You even married Preet here. This is where the boys spent a lot of their childhood," Jurnail continued as if trying to change Jawar's mind.

"Someone always takes your place in this world. Now, this land belongs to Dostan and Ullas. Good people. Not to Masood," Jawar said as he looked around.

"I should leave now," Jawar said loudly to grab everyone's attention as Daler ran to prepare the horses.

Dostan became sad to see his childhood friend leave. "Please stay with your clan in Dil Mahal. They need your help," he implored Jawar.

"Dostan, I am leaving and not coming back again to Dil Mahal. I hope you can come to see me."

"I am old and tired. I won't be able to visit Jalalabad to see you. For the little time I have left, we should be able to spend it together here. Why do you want to leave?"

Jawar held Dostan's hand and said, "I have to go, Dostan. That does not mean I can't come back to see you. Who knows what life has in store? Did I ever think I would be fighting these battles at this age?"

"I am not keeping well. Stay for a few days more," Dostan said. Then he turned to Jurnail, "Why don't you stop him?"

"I think he knows what he wants. I don't mean to make it more difficult for him," Jurnail said.

As Jawar mounted his horse, Dostan stopped him from leaving by holding his arm. "Don't you want to visit Dil Mahal one last time?"

"I will never leave if I go back there. I must go now and spend the last years of my life in prayer. Jung is also coming with me." With that, Jawar gave hugs to Dostan and Jurnail.

Jung and Jawar left on their horses with a few men. As they reached the bank of Bara River, Jawar stopped and turned around to look at Tarnab. A flash of memory of his days with Preet and his children ran through his mind. Then he and Jung left.

After Jawar left, Jurnail asked Dostan if they could ride the horses around the farm. They shared the memories of their childhood and laughed. "Jawar looked like he was in pain about letting go of this farmhouse. As far as I am concerned, this is your family's farmhouse," Dostan said, turning serious.

"Jawar is the one who proposed that we transfer it to you. Times have changed. We had a gift of a loyal friend in you. A gift of these loyal tribesmen. The waves of hate are sweeping. Religion is about hate now. We can't live here anymore," Jurnail said with a grim look on his face.

"I wish it wasn't true. But I find it harder and harder to get support for the Dil clan. Ullas can give away his life on my orders, but I can only be sure of that while I am alive," Dostan said as his eyes were filled with sadness.

Then they trotted a few minutes without saying anything until Jurnail stopped near the barn, "I should leave now."

"Why? Stay tonight."

"I should leave. I would like to check on Jai."

"There are few things that you should not leave here. They are very dear to you."

"Ah, those things of great Kalyan." Jurnail smiled.

"And those things of great Jurnail and great Jawar," Dostan said, smiling.

Jurnail said, "Send it over to Jai. He would be pleased. He needs something to lift his spirits." After a quick hug, Jurnail turned his horse towards Peshawar.

"I hope to see you soon at Dil Mahal."

Dostan raised his hand as Jurnail, Daler, Satwant, and Lakhbir rode off towards Peshawar with their clansmen.

# Chapter 6
# [1942] Shirtless Prince

In Peshawar, the news of Masood's defeat had reached Qissa Khwani Bazaar. In Dil Mahal, Mehar gave the news himself to Jai. "We have great news from Tarnab. Baba-ji and Papa engaged Masood and his men, killing him in the battle."

The news had an uncanny effect on Jai. He started feeling better the same day. Although Mehar shared in Jai's happiness, he felt like less of a man compared to his old uncle and father. From the balcony of the haveli, he saw Jurnail, Daler, and others arrive outside Dil Mahal.

"Uncle Jurnail has already arrived."

"Where is Papa?" Jai asked.

"You should learn to let go," Jurnail said as he entered Jai's room. "Your papa became a monk many years back. Now I don't think we should expect him back. But I am going to be staying here from now on."

"That is wonderful," Mehar said as he rushed to touch Jurnail's feet.

"Oh! Thank heavens!" Jurnail's decision to return to Dil Mahal made Jai very happy. "I thought our elders had deserted us."

"Elders were hoping they had already raised their kids. Apparently not," Jurnail said and laughed.

On Friday, special permission was arranged from the mayor to organize an armed procession in Qissa Khwani Bazaar. Ullas, Dostan, and more than a hundred of their militiamen entered the bazaar in the afternoon and gathered outside Dil Mahal. There, they were welcomed by Jurnail, Maher, Joga, and Daler.

"You came," Jurnail laughed and hugged Dostan, who was still unwell.

"I could not resist. This, I didn't want to miss."

"We are so happy to have you and Ullas here."

Sounds of celebratory gunfire, dance, and drums echoed in the air. *There are celebrations, smiles, and hugs again. The dark clouds on the clan have cleared, for now,* Jai thought as he watched from the rooftop with the help of attendants. Outside Dil Mahal, tribespeople did the *Khattak* dance till late at night. The celebratory gunfire continued to amuse Jai, who kept thinking about Jawar and Hari. After midnight, the tribespeople dispersed into the inns and kahwah shops of the old city. This show of strength displayed relationships, alliances, and the power of tribal leaders.

\*\*\*

A few days later, Dostan sent the Dil family portraits and other items of importance to Dil Mahal. Despite being unwell, Dostan himself packed each item. Hari was visiting Dil Mahal from Rawalpindi. Both Jurnail and Hari started opening the items in excitement.

"Those, my boy, are Kalyan's swords and shield. These should be hung on the wall."

"Did Baba Kalyan have a gun?" Hari asked.

"He had a long gun. I don't think we will see it here today."

In one of the packages, wrapped in silk cloth, Jurnail found a painting and a handwritten note from Dostan: *I hope this painting will make you as happy today as it used to in our younger days.*

"Oh, I totally forgot about this. This painting…." Jurnail could not complete the sentence as his breathing became heavy. He was so excited after looking at the painting that Rustam called Mehar to help calm him down. It took him some time to calm him down, as a scared and worried Hari watched. Rustam and Mehar waited to call the doctor.

"No… No. I am fine now. Look what I found. This is Raye-ma, my father's first wife, painted by my mother. This should go on the wall at our office. Right by *Our Position*." He looked at the painting, again and again, stopping to catch his breath.

"Did you know that my father had a wife and two sons before he married my mother?"

"No. Where are they now?" Hari asked.

"They died on Lowri Pass."

"What is Lowri Pass, and how did they die?"

"Your great grandfather was going with his caravan to Chitral, and he was attacked by Afridi tribesmen. Your great grandmother fought so bravely that she killed four tribesmen before she was killed."

"What happened to the boys?"

"Unfortunately, the boys died fighting as well... My father was badly injured and was saved by Kalasha people."

"Who are Kalasha people?"

And so, Jurnail and Hari went on and on in a question-and-answer session.

Hari had become rather fond of Jurnail and always looked forward to seeing him. He loved to hear stories about their clan from him.

"Now, let's open the other packages."

Among the things Dostan had sent were swords and guns of Kalyan, portraits, and a box full of gold coins and jewelry with a note: *I found it behind your father's portrait.* "See his honesty. God bless him. Hope he recovers fast."

After a few days, Dostan developed a high fever. He died within a week. Jawar was informed, and he sent his condolences in a letter detailing the great times they had spent together since childhood. The letter was read by Jurnail to Dostan's clan.

***

In Rawalpindi, as directed by Jurnail, Bhole and Mary put Hari in a Hindu religious boarding school. Dils had a long tradition of going to Gurukul Rawal for their primary education. One of the reasons that they liked the Gurukul Rawal was that it didn't practice the caste system, neither did it use family background for accepting students. It only relied on children's consciousness and interest to accept them and differentiate them into different levels of education.

On the day of his admission, Jurnail, Jai, Bhole, and Mary arrived at Gurukul to drop Hari. There they listened to the *Acharya,* the Hindu teacher, as he introduced students and their guardians to the functioning of the school.

"In Gurukul, all students are equal. We believe everyone is equal. Respect everyone. That is one key rule here. Hinduism believes that God lives inside every person, that the Atman is part of Brahman. We, however, also believe everyone is born with a different level of consciousness."

Then with a pause, Acharya added, "We don't differentiate on your birth caste. The two most revered people, Valmiki and Vyasa, the greatest sages in Hinduism, belonged to a so-called lower caste. One wrote Ramayana, and the other wrote Mahabharata. We will be studying both epics here. We will also study English and Science. You will learn multiple languages here that will prepare you for seeking knowledge and debating on issues."

After Acharya was done explaining schedules and daily routines, he asked the children, "Is any of you being forced to come here by your parents?"

There was silence.

After a pause, Acharya asked, "Does anyone here disagree with our teaching methods or have any questions?"

There was silence.

"Alright. Parents and guardians can meet their children on Mondays. The next break is for Diwali. You can take your child home for seven days during Diwali. Unless you have any questions, all parents and guardians can leave now."

Mary raised her hand as she looked at Bhole and said, "I have a few questions."

"Come inside," Acharya asked the Dils to join him in his cottage.

"You said all people are equal, but there is so much inequality. So many people suffer so much in poverty while others live sumptuously. There is casteism in India and racism all around the world. I don't understand how world can see all humans as equal," Mary asked.

"When you look at people from the lens of the material world or Maya, they look very different. Maya hides the ultimate reality. People look rich or poor. They look black or white. All that is destroyed, but Atman remains. In Hinduism, your Atman is part of Brahman. We are all equal in that sense. The problem with Maya is it is an illusion. It makes you believe rich people are happy. That their life journey ends better. In fact, most poor people are happy as long as they don't compare themselves to rich people. You don't know how happy a hermit can be. It does not matter what your situation is. With higher consciousness, you are always happy."

"But people think differently. They are so different in many ways."

"Yes. There are differences in consciousness in each person right from birth. Your karma in your previous life affects how much consciousness you carry to this life. That is why two twins are not equal in consciousness and nor are siblings born of the same parents. But nothing stops you from raising your consciousness irrespective of what you were born with.

So irrespective of different family background, children here at Gurukul do generally well."

"I get that. Thanks for answering my questions. Hari had unusually difficult circumstances. His mother died, and sometimes, he gets sad. He may need some attention from that sense," Mary said.

"He will be fine here," Acharya said. "Can I ask you a question?"

"Please," Mary said.

"How are you related to Hari?"

"I am his aunt and foster mother. He has been living with me and my husband," Mary said as she stepped close to Bhole.

"What is your experience about Hinduism?"

Mary thought a little, then replied, "Good. I am very impressed that I am not asked to convert. That as I learn more, I am drifting towards these philosophies, and still, I feel I have not converted to a new religion."

"Glad to know that. I was asking if you have knowledge of Hinduism."

"I am learning. There is so much philosophy, though, it takes time to process. But as I said, I am reading more and more. I am drifting towards it."

"This drifting is what Hinduism is, the desire to seek knowledge, exploration of oneself, Atman and

Brahman. Once you start doing that, you are a Hindu, and you still can be a Christian. Hinduism does not exclude anyone."

Acharya then paused and looked around at everyone, then said, "Hinduism allows freedom of spiritual thought. For more than ten thousand years, people have written their experiences within the framework of Hinduism. It has created many religions, sects, and philosophies. Once you read a few, you will see they are all the same with little differences here and there. Be careful what you read, though. There is also a business of Hinduism. Some pandits have created a lot of ritualistic literature. It is useless."

"How could you tell one from another?" Mary asked.

"You read a little, and you can tell. It is for the consumption of low consciousness people. These pandits created all kinds of nonsense to exploit them. Many of these greedy priests have done worse things to Hinduism."

Although Mary understood Hindi, Bhole was still trying to explain Acharya's answers to her. Jurnail said to him, "You have just become a translator. Ten years of marriage, what have you taught her about Hinduism? She is still asking basic questions."

Then shaking his head, Jurnail said, "Whom am I kidding? What do you know about Hinduism?"

Mary thanked the Acharya as they walked out of the cottage. Then they met Hari before they left the Gurukul. As they walked out, Mary asked Jurnail, "Baba-Ji, why didn't you ask me to convert to Hinduism."

Jurnail stopped and smiled, "There are only two ways to convert someone's religion. Either by sword or by a bribe. None of these are acceptable in Hinduism. People can adopt whatever they choose consciously. Once people understand our spiritual values, we let them walk into Hinduism by their choice. And you already have. And you can stay a Christian. As Acharya said, Hinduism does not exclude anyone.... except hate and bigotry. We don't tolerate that."

As Bhole explained Jurnail's answer, she nodded and smiled. Then she asked, "But isn't Baba-ji a Sikh? And Sikhism has a difference in philosophies from Hinduism?"

When Bhole explained the question to Jurnail, he got upset. His face became red, "What is not there in Sikhism? Is Brahman not there, or is it consciousness not there?"

As Bhole tried to explain to Mary, Jurnail interrupted him, "Don't be a translator for firangis. I am asking you what the difference is? I am not a *lakeer da fakeer*."

"I got what he said except the *lakeer da fakeer* part," Mary said.

"I think he meant I don't just parrot lines from religious books," Bhole responded.

"What I read, I understand it. What I understand, I decide with my own judgment what to take and what not to take. If all I want to do was to parrot a religious book, then I could have joined Mullah Arfan's madrasa."

"Baba-Ji, I get it. We don't mean to offend you," Bhole said. "She had a genuine question."

"You offend me by your ignorance. You offend me because I answer Mary's question because you have no knowledge. She is more Hindu than you."

"Why are you upset with me. There are lots of clansmen who don't know the basics of Hinduism," Bhole said. "It was not my choice. You and Papa sent me to London. I didn't see my family for eight years."

"So, now you want me to count you in the rest of the low-lives?. Unlike them, your family dedicated their life to country and dharma and granted you all the privileges and opportunities to learn," Jurnail said. Then he tried to calm down and said, "Look. I don't really care what your religious beliefs and choices are. I am saying that you should have the knowledge."

"Mary is doing my part," Bhole smiled as he looked at Mary. "We will go to Cantonment now if we have your permission," Bhole asked.

Jurnail raised his hand, "God bless you both."

As they left, Jurnail said, "The whites had the material world, now they are trying to explore the spiritualism world. Our people are going in the opposite direction."

"You are too harsh on him," Jai said as they traveled back to Peshawar. There was quiet for some time. Then they changed the topic and started talking about Hari. Both felt they had made the right decision by sending him to Gurukul.

"I am happy that Hari is gaining the knowledge needed to lead our clan," Jurnail said.

"He looked comfortable there," Jai said.

\*\*\*

Bhole Nath and Mary visited Hari at the school every weekend. Jai and Jurnail also visited him every month. A year passed like this. At Gurukul, Hari was learning History, Philosophy, Sanskrit, Hindi, English, Persian, and Urdu. Hari learned about Hindu, Buddhist, Sikh, and Muslim religions. His prowess in horse riding and rifle shooting was better than most clansmen.

But Jurnail had noticed unusual softness in Hari's demeanor. When Jurnail took him on his hunting trips, he found Hari to be unnecessarily kind. Jurnail would get upset when Hari wouldn't take a shot at the animals in the forest.

"We came here for hunting. Why didn't you shoot the deer? You had a clear shot."

"I don't feel like hunting," Hari said.

Jurnail saw in his eye's hesitation and doubt. On return from a hunting trip, Jurnail would lash out at Jai. "The boy does not have the spark of a fighter. How did you raise him, Jai? He is too soft. He won't be able to kill a man in battle."

"He gets the kindness from his mother," Jai replied.

"Kindness has nothing to do with it. You have to be kind. But when you are in a battle, there is no room for kindness. Kindness in battle is weakness. Poor child. Born and raised by weak parents. We failed him." Jurnail was visibly agitated.

"Great Ashoka was kind."

"And ruthless." Jurnail picked the kahwah tea Rustam had just brought for him. After a sip, he continued with his disappointment, "I wish I could bring him back and raise him myself. I failed him, your father failed him, and you failed him."

151

"He is a child. He should be with us." At heart, Jai wanted him back. "But I know he needs education, a safe learning environment."

"He needs brothers and sisters. And he does not have any. Even if we bring him here, he will be a lonely child. I rather have him live at Gurukul with other children," Jurnail said.

After a pause, Jurnail said, "You know, Jai, one of the world's biggest problems is good and intelligent people make very few children, and evil and ignorant people make too many. The world only gets better if good people make more babies. So, Ali has how many? Twelve? And you have one."

"God's will, Baba-ji."

"Why bring God into the middle of this unnecessarily? God has no will. You should have married again. Hari deserved someone to call brother or sister."

After every visit with Hari, Jurnail got restless and disheartened. He would complain at long length on how Hari was being raised.

Bhole and Mary were not pleased with the frequent visits from Jai and Jurnail. Besides, Jai didn't like Jurnail's disgruntled outbursts during the visits. Instead, Jai asked that Hari visit Peshawar during breaks at his school. "That way, he gets to see the entire family and spent more time with us," Jai had told Bhole.

A few times a year, Hari was required to visit Dil Mahal. He paid longer visits around August, on the festival of *Rakhi*, and later in the year on Diwali. Every year on Rakhi, the family got together with Jurnail's sister, Sukhi, visiting to tie Rakhi to Jurnail; and Satwant's daughter, Raji, tying Rakhi to Hari.

Bhole and Mary had been married for more than a decade but had no child of their own. They were thrilled to have a child in their life and believed that even without making it formal, Hari was their adopted child. When Hari came to visit them from Gurukul, they both made sure Hari had their full attention. Bhole and Mary didn't want Hari to get too attached to Jai or anyone else in the clan. They would send Hari to Peshawar only after they received multiple requests from Jurnail and Jai. Jurnail worried about their intentions. "I think we made a mistake by sending the boy with Bhole."

"I was dying, Baba-ji," Jai whispered as they waited for dinner.

"Neither of you trusted I would do a good job raising him," Maher said to Jai and Jurnail.

"You can't even tie your *perahan tunban* properly," Jurnail joked as they laughed.

"Gurukul wants to do a *janeu* ceremony to initiate Hari into Sanatan Dharma," Jai said.

"Ah, how come he is getting away with janeu while I have to keep all five of my religious symbols?"

"Well, you can decorate him like a Sikh," Jai said with a smile.

"He will be a Sikh when he acts like one. What good are symbols if all you do is live a selfish and immoral life? Keep him a Hindu. His mother would have wanted him to be one. One day he will be able to experience by himself the love of God."

Every day at dinner, Jurnail waited for Jai and Maher. They talked about politics, religion, and family. And they mostly talked about Hari. They all missed him and wanted him back at Dil Mahal.

\*\*\*

For Hari, growing up in boarding at a traditional Hindu school was not easy. He constantly worried about his father and family. Accepting Mary as his mother was even harder for him. He subconsciously still believed the soul of his mother resided in the well in Dil Mahal. There was a pall of sadness on his face. Mary tried to cheer him up. Sometimes she was even successful in bringing a little smile to his face. She tried hard to play her role as a mother. Every week, she made sure she spent time with him. She taught him English and Western cultures. She introduced Hari to British families as her adopted son. They congratulated her, and she was happy and proud of him.

Bhole was one of the few Indian commissioned officers in the army. For Hari, living among the British felt strange. He was raised not to trust them. They were 'cunning,' 'savage,' 'dishonest,' and other bad things. But he liked Mary. To him, she was an appointed mother. Someone to take care of him in the absence of his real mother. Although for him, the distinction was very clear. Mary was not his mother.

He had vivid memories of Lakshmi, some real and some made up. He grew up believing Lakshmi was lost in the well. While away from Peshawar, Hari missed Dil Mahal. He missed the well. When he visited Dil Mahal, he spent a lot of time around the well. Mehar got so concerned with Hari's obsession with the well, he had it covered with wooden planks. On Hari's next visit, when he saw the well covered, he was distraught.

"I have never seen him this upset," Jurnail said after he saw Hari's red face.

Jai and Mehar explained to Hari a version of the truth. "Your mother fell in the well and died. It was an accident."

Hari showed no emotions, but his answer was reassuring. "I know that, but you don't have to cover the well. This is the only memory I have of her." Hari knew how his mother had died. He had seen her jump in the well.

"It is a sad memory," Jai whispered.

"It is a memory of my mother."

"Remove those planks, you idiots, and come see me in the drawing-room, both of you," Jurnail shouted at Jai and Mehar. "He has gone through so much. Be considerate and hear his side first. You will not cover that well."

Then Jurnail turned to Hari and said, "They think your mother's memory will make you weak. They are wrong. She died so that you and this clan could stay strong. That is what you should always remember."

About four years passed like this. Hari continued his studies at Gurukul. He split his weekends and vacations between Rawalpindi and Peshawar. Jai kept himself busy with his new business importing and trading industrial machines. The Dils' office in Qissa Khwani was not used anymore, as Jai had stopped mediating between tribal disputes. *Our Position* still hung there under Kalyan's portrait in the dark, as the office stayed closed for days.

Jurnail spent most of his day meditating and traveling to nearby temples and shrines. Mehar just hung out wherever he found affection. He would spend a few hours in the morning with Jai at his hardware store and the rest of the day just hung around at Dil Mahal and Qissa Khwani Bazaar. Things were slow and dull in the clan as if Jawar had taken the life of the clan with him to Jalalabad.

One such day, Ullas brought the sad news that Jawar had died in his sleep in Jalalabad. Jai was devastated by his father's death.

"I wish I had visited him earlier."

"There are always regrets. It does not matter how much you do. You would still regret something." Jurnail himself was sad. "First Dostan, now Jawar. When I die, which won't be too far off, what will you regret? Let us work on that."

"I will regret not being on the battlefield with you."

"Let's hope we never have to. I am seriously old."

All men in the clan went to Jalalabad to perform Jawar's last rites. On the way back to Peshawar, Bhole talked about his plan to retire from the British army and move to Belfast. "We plan on taking Hari with us."

This took Jai by surprise. "Bhai sahib, I have one son. You can't take him that far away from the family and me."

Bhole looked at Jai as if he had said something out of line. "Mary has been away from her family for so many years. She wants to go back. Hari is now our son, and he will go with us."

What Bhole said made Jai very upset. "Did you hear him? Hari is the only heir to the clan. You want to take him away from his roots, his family?"

Bhole was clearly disappointed with Jai. "Jai, you forgot, you were almost dead. You were worried about the future of the boy. The boy has been our son now for four years. We need to move to Belfast, and the boy will come with us. We are not discussing this."

Jurnail, who had been quiet so far, raised his hand. "Let's talk when we get to Peshawar."

Jai was upset, but he could not disobey Jurnail. So, he broke away from the convoy and trotted ahead.

"Daler, take some men and go with him," Jurnail said.

Daler followed Jai with a few other clansmen. At the town of Landi Kotal, Bhole separated from the caravan after seeing a convoy of British soldiers. Jurnail stopped the caravan and waited for Bhole, signaling him to hurry up. "Not a good time and place to show your attitude, Bhole, even I won't venture alone in Afridi areas."

Bhole came along but remained many yards behind the caravan. After the caravan reached Peshawar, Bhole separated and went on his own way. "Ullas, can you bring him back to Dil Mahal? Be gentle. Tell him I am asking for him," Jurnail said.

"What will I do with him?" Jurnail whispered as he shook his head, then he looked at the rest of the clansmen, who were waiting for him. "You all go on your way. I will be at Dil Mahal soon."

When Ullas and Jurnail arrived at Dil Mahal with Bhole, Jai was waiting restlessly.

Soon after their arrival, Bhole announced, "I have to go to Rawalpindi today. It is getting late. Mary is alone there, and she is not well." He bowed to Jurnail. "Do I have your permission to leave, Baba-ji?"

Jurnail put his hand on Bhole's shoulder. "Don't leave India. Your family is here. This is your land."

Bhole looked up. "What family, Baba-ji? We were never treated as part of the family."

"Don't you have any love for your country?"

"This place will never be peaceful. All people know here is to fight."

"Agreed. Sometimes they fight for honor, sometimes over stupid reasons, but men of these lands didn't start two world wars. And they did not take other cultures' lands, robbed them of their livelihood and brutalized them."

Jurnail walked closer to Bhole and, in a low voice, said to him, "If you have decided to leave, drop the boy off here. He is all we have."

Bhole now looked upset. "Jai gave him away. You know that. He is our son."

"Jai asked for help from his brother. Don't be foolish." Jurnail was still talking when Bhole walked out of Dil Mahal. As Jai followed him, Jurnail stopped him. "Wait. Think first. We need to follow the law here. He is a military officer."

Jurnail became very concerned with Bhole's intentions regarding Hari. "Daler, go to Chaman Talwar's haveli and tell him I need to speak with him right now. Go right away." Chaman Talwar was the family attorney. At his direction, two police reports were filed by Jai, one in Peshawar and one in Rawalpindi. Jai reported that his son, Hari, was being held without his consent by his brother and being taken to Belfast. Jurnail and Jai used their influence with the magistrate to order Bhole to produce Hari in district court in Rawalpindi the following day before 2:00 pm.

When Bhole received the notice to appear in court, he knew he had no legal basis to take Hari to Belfast. Mary cried all night as she watched Hari sleep.

For Jurnail, it was a painful day as well. He had reached the court early in the morning with Jai and Daler. There, he waited outside the court for Bhole to appear. There in the court, Hari identified Jai as his father. Since there had been no legal adoption, Hari was handed over to Jai. Upset over this, Bhole stripped Hari of everything he had given him. He even took away his shirt, leaving him in just shorts.

When Jurnail saw Hari walking out of the court shirtless, he laughed. "Here is my shirtless prince." He kissed him, hugged him, and picked him up. Then he removed his gold chain and put it around Hari's neck. "From now on, you stay with me till I die. Let's go." Jurnail walked with Hari as Daler and Jai followed them.

"Can I have a shirt?"

"Don't you worry about the shirt. Never think that you have to be in royal clothes to be royal. It is the thing of the heart and mind, a thing of aura."

Lal Singh opened the car door, and they all sat in and headed back to Dil Mahal. That night, they celebrated at Dil Mahal as if it was Diwali.

In a few days, Bhole and Mary left India for Belfast and were never heard of by the family again. Jurnail and Jai took Hari under their command. Hari was further trained in horse riding and gun handling and became a skilled shooter. By the age of nine, he would mount a horse with a revolver on his waist and make the rounds of Qissa Khwani Bazaar. The clan's fighters followed him on Jurnail's orders. Within a year, Hari started hunting in the Lower Swat mountains. When Hari rode with a hunting rifle on his shoulder and two handguns in the holsters, Jurnail could not take his eyes off him. In Hari, everyone saw the face and intelligence of Jawar, so much so that Jurnail called him "chotta Jawar," or little Jawar. Jai, however, was not as thrilled about Hari being out in the tribal area. He knew that Hari was only safe as long as he was not recognized.

***

Since Jawar's death, Jai would leave Dil Mahal frequently and spend his evenings on the rooftop of Preet House alone. In Preet House, he found the solitude he couldn't get at Dil Mahal. There, he looked at the sky, thinking about his past. Mostly, he thought about Jawar as he fought tears. *One by one, everyone is dying. The clan is shrinking.* Fear and worry about the future concerned him. The curse of Messa had always been on his mind. Now that Dostan, Jawar, and Bhole were no longer part of the clan, he worried. *If something happened to Hari...* As he stared into the distance at nothing, the sound of Jurnail's walking stick broke his thoughts. "Baba-ji, what are you doing here at this time?"

"You have been missing at dinner time more often. When I die, you will regret not spending time with me," Jurnail said and smiled.

"Sit down here. You could have sent someone for me." Jai pulled a jute cot close for Jurnail.

"What are you thinking?" Jurnail, who rarely came to Preet House, looked tired after climbing the stairs to the rooftop.

"Baba-ji, I am sad these days." Jai shared his heart with Jurnail, who had sat down on the cot next to the wall where Jai stood.

"Come sit down here with me." Jurnail pointed for Jai to sit with him. "Your sadness is understandable. The death of a father does that to a man," Jurnail said as he rotated his walking stick in the middle of his feet. "Sometime around the same age as you, I left my family to go serve in Guru's house. This age makes you question the meaning of life. But it will pass."

Then Jai hesitantly said what had been really bothering him: "I worry about the safety of Hari. I worry about the curse of Messa."

Jurnail looked at Jai to read his tormented face. "You know who is cursed? Our women. Preet died young. Lakshmi died too young, and Kirat — she was just a girl." After a thoughtful pause, Jurnail continued, "Strong clans are made by strong women. They produce strong children. They raise them well. They motivate men to do better and discourage men from doing dumb things. Like getting cursed by Messa. Look, I am not Messa. He was a great saint. Hari will be fine. I assure you that. Do you trust me?"

Jai nodded his assent.

"I will watch him. I will take care of him. Don't you worry at all. Now go back to Dil Mahal and sleep peacefully. I will just stay here a little longer. Daler is waiting for me downstairs. He will drop me."

As time passed, the political situation in British India deteriorated. Distrust between Muslims and Hindus widened. The Muslim League had built a strong organization in Peshawar. Ali became an active member and decided to return to Peshawar to lead the party. He claimed that after Jawar's death, the agreement to stay out of Peshawar was no longer binding to him. He also knew that after Dostan's death, Ullas would not bother to enforce anything. His presence worried Jai and Jurnail, but they thought conflict with Ali may not make Hari any safer and decided to wait and watch.

# Chapter 7
# [1946] Men of Khyber

## Oct 1946, Peshawar

Since his return to Peshawar, Jurnail had been presiding over all the important decisions in the clan. Under Jurnail's watchful presence, Mehar and Jai's lives had become a little easier, and both brothers had become used to a relaxed lifestyle. During his travels, Jai no longer had to worry about affairs back home, and Mehar did not have to cover for Jai in his absence, a burden Mehar was happy to forgo. The Dil clan's businesses had changed a lot as well. There were no dealings with tribal leaders. The family had closed its mediation business. There hadn't been many conflicts between the British and the Pashtuns since the *Mohmand campaign* of 1935. The pride and influence were less, but changing political conditions meant that the role of Hindus and Sikhs was changing in Muslim-dominated areas.

Dils had bought companies that imported machines from Europe and supplied them across British India. Business was good. Jai had also bought himself a Red Indian motorcycle, which he rode wherever the roads allowed him to. He rode it through Peshawar's streets on his way to business dealings, and he rode it to visit temples and Sufi shrines. The Dils also bought a new Cadillac. The family's old Packard was now driven by Bazam Lohana, a short young Sindhi man who did deliveries for Jai's hardware business. Jai found Bazam to be loyal and trustworthy. The Dil family was noticeably rich but stayed away from the high society of Peshawar.

With new trading businesses, there was more money and less hassle. With the political office closed, the Dils no longer needed the militia to handle tribal adversaries. The clan's militiamen went back to their villages to work on their farms. They had no safety, and clansmen were getting killed regularly. Jai had opposed any retaliatory attacks unless aimed at specific people.

Joga was worried. In their regular after-dinner meeting, he expressed his concern, "These attacks on our men are no random incidents."

Jurnail agreed but worried it made the family look weak. "We are deserting our people. This will embolden people like Ali."

"The ability to call in the militia when needed is crucial." Joga was worried about being unable to defend the clan when such urgency arose. "Great Kalyan used to say that these lands are damned. There will always be unrest and savagery here. Without militia, we cannot defend the freedom, our faith, our way of life."

"Centuries back, there was a flourishing culture here. Many temples and monasteries adorned these lands. Then these people from the desert and sand came here. They brought savagery, murdering and butchering people. That has continued for a thousand years. The souls of saints have cursed these lands," Jurnail said as he looked intensely at Jai and Joga.

"You wonder when it will end," Jai said. "Sufis and saints could help, but mullahs won't give them a chance. *Redshirts* are a hope, but they are being butchered. Pashtuns could control their own destiny if they could decide for Pashtunistan. But the League is vicious. Worse than any, even in Arab lands."

"Who are Redshirts?" Hari asked. He was now an active listener in these clan meetings.

"Khudai Khidmatgar, a Pushtun group. They wear red shirts. They are led by *Bacha Khan*. They want to see a united India. Your father is hoping that at least they could get a separate Pashtunistan," Jurnail replied to Hari in a low voice.

"Other than from the few of us here, there is no support left to form a militia. After Dostan and papa are gone, we will not muster any support in tribal areas. I have talked to Ullas. He has promised me he will protect our people in Tarnab, but he has been hesitant in committing his men," Jai said.

"I agree. We need access to a militia, a smaller militia. The problem is a smaller militia that only protects us is no good for our clansmen. They live deep in tribal areas, and they need protection there. With Dostan and Jawar gone, we cannot provide that protection anymore," Jurnail said as he looked around at everyone intensely and asked, "Why will they join our militia?"

"I understand there is practically no militia left that could fight the battles like before, but we cannot expect Joga and Daler to protect Dil Mahal by themselves. I am not even sure if we can trust Ullas' militiamen anymore," Jai said.

"I think we should plan to shift to Preet House in the cantonment if the situation worsens here in Qissa Khwani," Mehar suggested.

And soon, the situation worsened. By demanding a separate country for Muslims, Muslim League and its leader, Jinnah, had brought together the radicals and given them a voice and platform. In mosques, clerics like Mullah Arfan were giving outright calls to eliminate infidels. The Muslim League's influence grew by the day. Their modus operandi meant using hate as a weapon to grab power from Congress. And

hate was slowly, but firmly, creeping into and changing the minds of people.

As sporadic violence became more frequent,
the Dils worried more about the safety of Hari. There
were always men protecting Hari wherever he went.
Jurnail had assigned Daler the responsibility of Hari's
security. Daler drove Hari to school and picked him up
every day. Jurnail always had to know where Hari was
when he asked; otherwise, he would get anxious and
angry. If Jurnail ever left Peshawar to visit someone,
he would take Hari with him. Sometimes, he would
make Hari skip school to go with him on excursions.
If Jai and Mehar told him that was unnecessary, Jurnail became agitated. "Both of you are cowards. I
can't leave him in your protection. What face will I
show to Jawar, to my ancestors, if something happens
to the boy?"

Jurnail's obsession with Hari worried Jai.
"Baba has gotten old and senile."

"He is reacting to the reality outside. But look
at the other side, at how much Hari is learning from
him," Mehar responded.

"If he is so concerned, why not leave this
place? We can go settle somewhere in the East," Jai
had said this many times, but Mehar would not engage
on this topic. For him, it was foolish and unthinkable
to leave the land of their ancestors. Jai had been

watching the progress of the Muslim League and their alliances with the British, and it worried him. Recent Hindu-Muslim riots across India resulted in the deaths of so many people. The large-scale violence and deaths had disturbed Jai's peace of mind. He was privately exploring other options to protect the clan.

\*\*\*

As family meetings on the situation became frequent, Hari was confused about this lingering crisis. Every other time, he'd known the name of the enemy, but this time, he had no idea what the family was preparing to deal with. One evening, as he overheard the conversations about how to protect Dil Mahal, he decided to ask Jurnail, "Baba-ji, is there a bunch of tribal leaders planning to attack Dil Mahal?"

"No. It is a little complicated, son," Jurnail answered, debating if he should explain or not.

"Help me understand," Hari looked at Jai and Jurnail.

"There is a talk of dividing the country between Hindus and Muslims," Jai said as he looked for Hari's reaction.

"But that should be easy. Hindus are people who live around and east of the Sindhu River. So that side goes to Hindus, right?" Hari asked.

"Well, Hindus who were converted to Islam don't think they are Hindus anymore," Jai replied.

"Why?" Hari asked in surprise.

"Hindus include everyone who is open to the debate around the idea of God. Any religion that is radical believes that God exists only in a certain way and form as described in their books. So, they impose their limitations on God's existence and form, and they think other ideas about God are wrong," Jai replied.

"Why would they be upset with other ideas? At Gurukul, they taught us no one knows the nature of God, and everyone has to discover God in their own way."

"Radical religions survive only if they defend their idea. So, they force it on others using threats and violence. There is no other way to sustain an idea that is so limiting except by using violence and threats," Jai said as he intensely looked for expressions on Hari's face. "In Hinduism, all thoughts and ideas about God's existence and nature that are supported by reasoning are acceptable. That is a beautiful thing in the culture of the people who live on the other side of the Sindhu River."

"So why again don't Muslims on the east side consider themselves Hindus?" Hari asked, looking confused.

"I guess they don't know they can be Muslims and Hindus at the same time," Jai replied.

"So, what I have observed is…" Jurnail said as he took a sip of kahwah from his cup. "The more hardline a sect or religion gets in India, the more it claims to be separate from Hinduism. Primarily because Hinduism allows debate on nature and the form of God. The strict beliefs of hardline religions make it blasphemous to have independent thought around the nature of God."

"Your baba explained it well." Jai smiled.

"But Baba Jurnail only prays to one shapeless, formless God," Hari asked Jai.

"Sikh scriptures say you should pray to one shapeless God. But that does not mean Baba Jurnail is going to beat me for praying before idols." Jai smiled as he looked at Jurnail.

"I can beat you up for anything," Jurnail said as he raised his eyebrows and smiled back. Then he turned to Hari, "Your father prays to Lord Shiva."

"Tell me about Shiva," Hari asked Jai.

"Shiva is Adiyogi. The first Yogi. The founder of Yoga. He is the seed of cosmic consciousness. His wife, *Shakti*, represents the energy that brings that seed to life. Shiva is also called Mahadeva, or Great God."

"So, where do these gods go after their life is complete?" Hari asked as he looked at Jai, waiting for him to reveal the secret that he had wondered about for some time.

"What we call God in a general sense is supreme cosmic consciousness or ultimate reality. We call it *Brahman*. But just consciousness itself cannot do anything. To make a difference or to intervene, God must incarnate as a living being, build worldly relations, complete the work, and leave the body."

"So Gods die as well," Hari was astonished.

"Laws of Maya or material world are unbreakable. Even supreme consciousness cannot change those. If you are born, you must die. It is true for a tiny organism to the largest of universes," Jai said as he looked at Hari's expressions. After a pause, he asked Hari, "Why don't you tell us what they taught you about God in the Gurukul?"

"They said I can create or see God in any shape and form of my choosing because I am the one creating it. That no two people can experience God the same way, so, in certain ways, God is different for everyone. They also taught us that people who question God's existence are talking about the wrong God because you really cannot question the existence of consciousness," Hari looked at Jurnail and Jai, wondering what they thought.

"Very intense for your age." Jurnail raised his eyebrows as he nodded his head. Then looking at Jai, he said, "We should take him to *Pandit* Daya Shankar."

"Who is Pandit Daya Shankar?" Hari asked.

"A priest in Haridwar. He is our *purohit*," Jai replied.

"Ok. Tell me, what is the new worry about the family?" Hari asked impatiently.

"The worry is, will these Allah people and Waheguru people, and this shrinking group called Hindus that for long tolerated everyone else, will they get along, or will they tear each other apart?"

Jai was in thought and then turned to Jurnail and said, "I am going to take Hari with me to Haridwar."

"No, you won't. It is risky," Jurnail said sternly.

"He will visit the Golden Temple on the way, and then he will visit Haridwar. He will learn about God," then he paused and looked at Jawar and added, "from Pandit Daya Shankar."

"I just said it like that. I cannot allow it," Jurnail said, shaking his head.

"He is safer going with me than sitting here in Peshawar," Jai said.

"We are not discussing this." Jurnail refused to entertain the idea of Hari being out of his sight.

"I want to go," Hari whispered.

"Let us talk when the time comes," Jurnail said as he walked to his room to retire for the day.

***

Every year, Jai would take the ashes of the deceased and immerse them in the Ganges River. This year, it was special because Jai was taking the ashes of Jawar with him. The day before he was to leave, Mehar and Jai went to collect the ashes from the Dils' office. The office had not been opened for over a month, and the lack of ventilation made the place damp. "We should come here more often. This place is getting ruined," Mehar said as he covered his nose from the dust.

"Rustam, clean this place today. Let's clean it once a week. Get Hamdard to help you, if needed."

"I will do it myself, Lala-ji. It will be an honor." Rustam and his father had served the Dils with love and dedication since they'd come to Peshawar. Rustam had only been a young boy when his father died. The Dils had raised him as part of their clan.

Rustam's words melted Jai's heart. *Still, there is loyalty and love. I hope it lasts.* Jai was disappointed to see Kalyan's portrait covered in dust. He removed his turban cloth and started wiping the dust off the portrait with it. Then he picked up *Our Position*, wiped off the dust, and started reading it when Hamdard walked in with kahwah.

"*Salem Aleikum*, Lala. So happy to see you, Lala-ji. Why don't you open this office anymore? I was worried you'd sold it to someone."

"No. I wish I could. But my heart won't allow it. Besides, if I sold it, Baba Jurnail would kill me."

"I wanted to tell you something, but I don't see you anymore. Ali and Ajmal Khan were peeping in through the windows a few days back."

"Keep an eye on them for me, Hamdard. And you can always talk to Mehar, Joga, or even Daler, in my absence."

"I will keep an eye on Ali and his men. They visit our shop frequently. They are not good people. I must warn you," Hamdard whispered to Jai.

Jai patted Hamdard's back, saying in Pashto, "*Khad aw abad* ose," meaning to wish Hamdard a prosperous and happy life.

Hamdard was still a teenager. His father had been killed by a tribal customer over a small dispute.

Both his grandfather and his father were close to Jawar. Since his father's death, his old grandfather made kahwah, and Hamdard served customers. Their small shop was just across the street from Dil Mahal.

Jai took the pot containing Jawar's ashes. *Your time in Khyber ends, Papa. Let us travel on your last journey together to Haridwar.* Jai had done this for as long as he could remember. Even when he was a little boy, he would go on pilgrimage with Jawar. As a boy, he collected the urns of the ashes of those who'd died in the clan during the year. He kept those urns in the small prayer room in the family's office in Qissa Khwani.

His mother Preet would object to Jai collecting urns of ashes. "Jai is still too young to be so close to all this."

"He is nine. *Maharaja Ranjit Singh* fought his first battle at ten." Having sent his eldest son Bhole to London, Jawar had groomed Jai from a young age to be the leader of the clan. He could see Mehar was a loyal follower and a helper. "Mehar is a loyal and free-spirited boy. Jai shows responsibility, initiative, thoughtfulness, and bravery. He takes ownership. Mehar waits to be told what to do next. Mehar will be Jai's right hand."

Although Mehar was four years older than Jai, he was happy to follow him. Even as a young boy, Jai was aware of the affairs of the clan. At any time, he would know how many had died in the clan of sickness and war. In each urn he collected, he made sure to place a slip with all the important details of the deceased person. Taking these ashes to Haridwar was a heavy burden and a religious duty that Jai fulfilled with a great sense of responsibility. With each urn, he carried a person with him in his heart and mind; their life stories and the people they had left behind. He was very much aware of the costs of war, the mortality of humans, and the grief of losing a close family member. Another important purpose of the pilgrimage was to meet the family purohit. The family purohit was a revered man whose generations had kept the logs with all details of the deaths and births in the clan for centuries. The purohits maintained the details of the clans spread across the land. Through purohit, Jai would know who had died and who was born among his relatives across a vast swath of land from east to west across the Indian Sub-Continent.

A few days after Diwali, Jai left on *Frontier Mail* to Lahore with Hari. Jurnail had reluctantly approved Hari's travel primarily because Hari really wanted to go. Mehar and many other men came to see Jai and Hari off at the railway station. Many reminded him about important matters that they needed him to address during this visit.

After the train had left Peshawar, Jai asked Hari, "You know why I really wanted you to come with me this time?"

"You want me to meet *Pandit* Daya Shankar?" Hari guessed.

"True. But more importantly, I wanted you to be there for your grandfather's last rights. And I want to spend time with you. This may be our best opportunity to spend some time together. Now you are almost twelve, and we can discuss all kinds of things. So, ask me anything on this trip, and I promise I will answer it to the best of my ability and honestly."

Hari nodded his head.

Jai then lowered his head and voice as if he was telling a secret, "Hari, I would like you to understand this train route. It goes to Haridwar. If in future, you ever had to go alone, it will be helpful to get familiar."

"Why will I go alone?"

"Fathers don't live forever. One day I won't be there," Jai said.

Hari became sad on hearing this, and then he knew he had to change the topic, "What cities are we going to visit?"

"You know. Lahore, Amritsar, and Haridwar, and I have some other plan."

In previous years, Jai's travel plans were the same. He would go to Haridwar first and stop on the way back in Amritsar and Lahore to meet members of the clan in those cities. Unthinkable brutal riots in Bengal had stirred his mind. One of Jai's British friends, Major Brown, who was deployed in Peshawar, had warned Jai of the certain partition of India and impending consequences of political and ethnic unrest. He had recommended that Jai consider moving his clan to the east, to someplace where there was a Hindu and Sikh majority. Major Brown had also put Jai in contact with a Diwan of Patiala and a military contractor in Ambala to help him decide the location and property. Jai had planned to scout these towns to see the possibility of moving east in case of the partition of India.

\*\*\*

After Jai and Hari reached Haridwar, they stayed with their family purohit, Daya Shankar. The morning after their arrival, a priest ceremoniously performed the last rites of fourteen people who had died in the clan in the last year. One by one, the purohit and pundits chanted mantras, and Jai poured the ashes into the Ganges. First was Mangal Singh, the man who died in the gunfight when Pashtun tribes attacked his shop in Qissa Khwani, then a lady who had died a few days after childbirth, followed by Daler's grandfather, Tucker Singh, who died in prayers after a good long life, and then was a young man named Karam Singh, who had been shot and killed as he rode his horse on his estate outside Peshawar, and so on, and so on.

From the slip in each urn was read the gotra of the deceased, indicating their lineage and names of their closest relations, husband of a woman, parents, and wife of a man, if married. After the ashes were immersed in the Ganges River, an entry was made in the genealogy register by the purohit about each person in the section dedicated to his or her family. These entries contained details of his name, how, where, and when they had died, and anything else their family wanted to record. This way, any clansman who visited Haridwar could know what happened since his last visit by going through the entries in their purohit's registers. Jawar's ashes were the last to be immersed.

Daya Shanker's eyes teared up as Jai emptied the urn in the Ganges, "The dharma is saved by a few wise and brave men. Jawar was both a wise leader and a brave warrior. He was one of few Hindu leaders in Khyber that held the fort against radical and bigoted elements there. And he had earned the respect of wise

Pashtuns, who really knew Hinduism stands for everyone. It stands for humanity."

Then Daya looked intensely at Jai and Hari and said, "I hope Jai, you and your son, will step into his shoes. Although your work is almost impossible. New enemies of Hinduism are more dangerous than ever. They are neither British nor invaders. They come from within India. They are people of this land."

After completing the ceremonies, they took a dip in freezing cold water of the Ganges and left for Daya's place. During such visits every year, Daya Shankar would become Jai's host in Haridwar, just as Daya's father had hosted Jawar and Jurnail, and so on. Generations of purohit served the generations of the clan. During their stay at Daya Shankar's place, Jai and Hari discussed religion and meditated together.

On their last day of the stay, Jai told Hari, "I want you to ask any question that is on your mind to Pandit Daya Shankar. Consider this as a very special opportunity. Don't waste it. He is the greatest pandit we have known."

After meditation, Hari started asking Daya Shankar all the questions he had on his mind.

"Pandit-Ji, what is consciousness, where it comes from, can it be destroyed?" Hari asked as he wondered about the human experience from birth to death and beyond.

"Your state of consciousness is the knowledge about yourself, about reality and perception, your surroundings, and your time and place in the cosmos. A higher state of consciousness means you know yourself and your relationship to the cosmos. You are in peace with everything. Supreme consciousness is God's state. You should know that consciousness can't be destroyed because it is there even when you are not. You just operate at a certain level of that consciousness. The higher is your consciousness, the higher you operate in this cosmos. When you die, based on your karma, only a very small part of consciousness travels with your Atman."

Daya paused, closed his eyes, and said, "There is a never-changing, absolute consciousness that operates everything in this universe. We call it Brahman. This source of consciousness cannot be destroyed."

"Why do some people have a problem with idol worship?" Hari asked as he thought about Islam and Sikhism.

"Don't worry about people. People in this world have all kinds of problems," Daya laughed, "Let us clear our doubts first. Is Jurnail influencing you?"

"No. No. Baba Jurnail will never do that," Jai intervened.

Daya continued, "Namaste means the divine inside me bows to the divine inside you. When we bow in front of someone, even an idol, we are bowing to their Atman. The Atman is eternal, even if the person existed five thousand years back or more. People who have problems with this simple concept, I just doubt their ability to think and reason. They are slaves of their religious book. How can you raise your consciousness if you can't even think for yourself?"

After a pause, Daya smiled and said, "For Jurnail, I am not just a pandit. I am a friend. Once, he got offended by my answer. He wanted me to reason why *Guru Nanak* opposed idol worship. I told him because he was under Islamic influence, plain and simple. *Guru Nanak*'s father was on the payroll of an Islamist who was sponsored by Lodhi. Besides, *Guru Nanak* had Islamic education from Mullah. Otherwise, it is hard to believe a man as great as Nanak won't understand the reasoning behind idol worship. I think Jurnail gets my point of view. After all, stone and idol have as much similarity as common paper and *Guru Granth Sahib*. The value of both lies in the person that understands and believes in it."

"Believe me, Baba Jurnail understands your point of view," Jai said.

"I hope so," Daya said.

"But do we need an idol to pray?" Hari asked.

"In chapter twelve of the *Bhagavad Gita,* Lord Krishna tells of multiple paths to enlightenment. You can choose the one that works for you, and praying to a shapeless, formless one is there as well. But it is hard for most humans to comprehend the shapeless and formless."

"I would prefer to pray anywhere."

"There are lots of people with different beliefs that pray and meditate on the banks of the Ganges. Do you want to see them? We should go for a boat ride on the Ganges tomorrow morning."

"Sure. That will be great," Hari said as he smiled in happiness. A boat ride in the Ganges was something he really wanted to do.

"Any more questions?" Daya asked. "Because I have something important in mind."

"I think this is it for now. If something comes to my mind, I will ask," Hari said.

"Hari, you are leaving tomorrow. There is an important ceremony that I have done for your father, grandfather, and even your uncle Jurnail. So, when a teenager from Dil's family visits the first time, there is a custom to initiate them as a warrior," Daya said as he lighted the clay lamps and incense sticks.

Daya made Hari sit close to him, and then he started a *hawan*, an ancient Vedic fire ceremony, as he chanted the mantras. He tied a thread on Hari's wrist and asked Hari, "Are you ready to be initiated as a warrior?"

"Yes…" Hari said hesitantly.

"Why the hesitation?" Daya asked.

"Because Papa never told me," Hari said smiling.

"You belong to a fighting clan that has been fighting battles to protect dharma. You should have no hesitation whatsoever," Daya said.

"I am ready. Will I be fighting battles when I go back to Peshawar?" Hari asked Jai.

"As Dil clan warrior, you have a purpose, and you have to work hard to fulfill it. And if a battle needs to be fought, you fight it. That does not mean you pick fights. But you don't run away from it," Jai said as he looked at Hari.

"Sure. Let us do it," Hari replied.

"Hand over your weapon to me," Daya said with his right-hand open.

"I got it. Here," Jai handed over Hari's handgun to Daya, who put it in front of the idol of Krishna.

"Get up. We need to stand up," Daya said as he got up.

"As you stand here today in front of the fire and the idols and images of great Hindu gods, who fought to protect dharma, holding them as witnesses in your heart and soul, answer a few questions for me."

Hari stood there silently, waiting.

"As torchbearer against hate and bigotry, will you be willing to die and kill for upholding human dignity and everyone's right to pray and practice their beliefs? Are you willing to lose everything to fight oppression?"

"Yes, I am," Hari said.

"You promise not to take an innocent life for any personal reasons?"

"Yes. I promise."

"May life examples and words of these Gods guide you."

Daya handed over the handgun to Hari and said, "Here is your handgun, Today, you are officially a Dil warrior. Take some prasad." Daya smiled as he handed some sweets to Hari.

"Hari, ask any more questions you have. Tomorrow we will leave," Jai said.

"The kind of questions he asks at this age, only a few grown-ups have ever asked me," Daya said. Then he put his hand at Hari's head to bless him.

"He is twelve. Old enough to take control of his life. I worry about his curiosity, though. Too many questions make you weak," Jai said.

"Curiosity starts with observation of surroundings. He seeks the truth. He does draw some knowledge from his soul, which is great. But still, education is needed. Right education prepares you for knowledge; right knowledge leads to higher consciousness," Daya said.

"We sent him to Gurukul. We had to pull him out. The situation has been tense. Even within the family, there have been a lot of uncertainties," Jai said.

"You have to save yourself before you save the world. Inner calm is important. With continuous threats to life and property, it is hard to have an inner calm. Move east."

Jai expressed his frustration: "I feel so broken and helpless after the death of my father. No one listens. We will be dying there without any purpose."

"Don't surrender. Always fight, even if you have to die fighting, rather than surrender to the situation."

"The family does not want to move. I am very concerned."

"There were no two nations based on religion before. Buddhists, Jains, Sikhs, Christians, and even Jews and Parsi lived together on this land. So have Muslims for centuries. Why do you think they want to divide the country? So that they can rule it. Who rules? Just a few. Maybe two. Two want to rule the masses. They will divide this country. The partition will happen. They each need their piece of land to rule." The purohit closed his eyes and took a deep breath. "The clan should move, or it will burn in the firestorm of hate. A country built on hate will not thrive. So even if you live there, that land will have no future. Trees are grounded, attached. Don't be a tree in a forest fire. Move. Move east."

The next morning before leaving, Jai, Hari, Daya, and his son took a boat ride in the Ganges. They stopped at many places where Daya showed Hari sadhus and ascetics of various sects praying in different ways.

"Sadhus with various beliefs pray here side by side for thousands of years. Some pray to idols, some pray to Sun. Some pray to all-pervading shapeless, formless God, so many different beliefs here. They never attack each other. They will be fine even if Muslims come here and pray. But Muslims want to kill them. They call them infidels. I personally would have loved seeing Muslims and Christians pray here to their Gods or Allah or whatever they choose to call them. It will be beautiful if they pray side by side with all other beliefs. But they all need a God that is exactly as described in their book, and they can't allow anyone else to be any different," Daya said.

After they came back from boating, Jai stayed at Daya's place as if he didn't wish to leave.

"It is time to leave if you are going to catch your train," Daya said as he noticed resignation on Jai's face.

"Try to convince Jurnail. At this point, there is no reason to stay there and lose your life."

"I have been trying," Jai said. There was sadness in his eyes. "I want to thank you, Pandit-ji. If I don't see you again, our clansmen are forever thankful for your guidance," Jai said.

"I will be here when a Dil clansman comes next time," Daya said as he blessed them and smiled.

After leaving Haridwar, as Jai traveled around the country, he noticed the change in the air. The League was provoking Muslims against Hindus and Sikhs. Many Muslim League leaders were filling the hearts and minds of Muslims with hatred by giving provocative speeches. They knew that if the masses of uneducated Muslims were provoked, the circumstances could be created where the only viable option was the partition of India.

Secular and intellectual Muslims risked their lives both from the League on one side and the British Raj on another. Leaders like Allah Baksh were assassinated by League members in collusion with the British. This brutality of fanatics had silenced the voices of peace-loving Muslims. As a result of their influence, the hatred and rioting had spread across India, and people were butchering each other in the name of religion. Jai realized that his clan would no longer be safe in Peshawar. He was determined to try to save his clan from the impending partition and subsequent violence that he feared would be inevitable. On his way back from Haridwar, Jai stopped in the erstwhile princely state of Patiala. There, he gave a deposit to buy some land and a house near Baradari.

When he returned to Peshawar, Jai explained to Mehar his decision to buy land in Patiala and suggested that the family move there. "Mehar, for thousands of years, India welcomed everyone from all parts of the world, and people of the land accepted them as our own. The migrants and invaders alike fell in love with this land. But the British have been different. They just want money, at any cost to us." Looking at the painting of the Qissa Khwani Bazaar massacre that had been gifted to Jawar by Dostan, he continued, "For decades, the British have stood on the corpses of our men, Hindus or Muslims, and made money. Now, they are bitter as we are forcing them to pack and leave. Since they are few in number, they will just have us kill each other."

While Mehar listened intently, he did not take it seriously. As a man without a wife or any children of his own, he had a different perspective on this than Jai. "I do not believe that Pashtuns will just go about butchering people as these Bengali have done."

Jai disagreed. "It is very easy to use religion to provoke people to kill someone. And the Hindus are rich, and the Muslims poor. There are additional incentives to riot. If Khan sahib could muster enough courage and break from Congress and Gandhi, then, and only then, is Pashtunistan possible. But he won't."

"He is the only one who stood for the rights of Pashtuns and Hindu Muslim unity, but he strongly opposes the partition, and partition will happen, so he will have nothing," Jai whispered to himself as he walked around the living room.

Inside his heart, Mehar agreed with Jai's concerns, but uprooting the family, to him, seemed such a drastic idea. "If tribesmen come to Peshawar to kill people, the British Army will protect the city."

Jai retorted, "My brother, I am not worried about the Pashtuns. I am worried about the British and the League. I am convinced that the governor, Olaf Caroe, has colluded with the League to support the attack on Hindus and Sikhs in Peshawar. Jinnah and British are together on the partition of India."

Jai tried passionately to influence Mehar. "These British are no one's friends. But somehow, they have convinced the League that they are their friends. Mehar, we must have a plan. Otherwise, this clan may not survive." On Mehar's lack of reaction, he stepped closer to his face. "And as far as I know, other Hindu clans have already started working on migrating east."

"Let's discuss this on Saturday." Mehar wanted to avoid the topic. On Saturday, everyone in the clan was gathering at Dil Mahal. This family gathering happened every year on Jai's return from pilgrimage and was an important family event.

Jai provided detailed information that he had obtained from the family purohit and conveyed messages from family and friends he had visited. Jai also handed out gifts bought by him or given by friends and relatives. After the dinner, as had been decided by the elders, children and women of the clan had to leave. The adult men sat in the drawing-room to discuss matters that better-suited men; matters of wars, politics, religion, alliances, and dominance. Matters that were supposed to be kept secret. Although, at night, while in bed, most men told all the secrets to their women.

Jai looked around the room and noticed that the clan had shrunk considerably. A picture of all the people the clan had lost ran through his mind. He missed his father, Jawar. He knew his father would have moved the clan to the east. He looked at Hari sitting with Jurnail, and a smile ran through his mind. There were only a few elders left in the clan. The room that used to be filled for such events was barely half full. Out of four sons of Kalyan, only two had survived into adulthood. Only Jawar had married. And then Jawar had three sons and only one grandson. The family tree had been shrinking for the last three generations. Then there was the Trehan family, which was rather large, but they were farmers with little interest in politics or tribal affairs. Many of the Trehan clan elders had stopped coming after the militia was disbanded. Many others who fought alongside them had stopped coming, as Dils offered little protection, if any, to families living in tribal areas.

In the drawing-room of Dil Mahal, the clan gathered to hear stories from Jai. Various kinds of food, dry fruits, and hot kahwah were served to the guests. Jurnail sat under the portrait of his father, waiting for everyone to settle. His long silver beard matched his white turban. His white shawl gave him a saintly look.

Jai took a cup of kahwah and served it to Jurnail, stating, "Should we start, Baba-ji?"

Jurnail raised his hand, and there was silence in the room as he started speaking in his old but firm voice. "We are in our fourth generation now in Peshawar. Before settling here, as I was told by elders that we had been walking on these lands as fighters and merchants for hundreds of years, if not thousands. Our ancestors protected these lands from invaders and lived and died on this land. My father Kalyan and all my brothers of blood and mind died here. I was born here, and I can't imagine dying anywhere else."

Then he took a sip of tea and continued after clearing his throat. "My father, Kalyan, had seen the most difficult times after the collapse of the Sikh empire. He lost his entire family. His first wife and their two sons during the battles in the mountains of Swat. But he did not run away. He married my mother, a Kalash woman. If you look at Jai, he will pass any day for a *Hunza*. That is because his mother, Preet, was from Gilgit, where Hunza people live. Jawar's close friend, Jung Singh, is an Afridi Sikh."

He paused and took a sip from his cup of kahwah, and continued, "We are men of Khyber. We have been here for a long, long time. Irrespective of what religion we follow, people of this land have always kept their relationship with God. Their relationship with God is as pious as God himself. How can that relationship be used to spread hate? We will fight against this philosophy of hate."

"It is the politicians. They want to divide and rule, and stupid people don't understand this," Jai added to continue the topic.

"You know my parents decorated me as a Sikh. Hindu parents happily changed the faith of their son. I love the word, *sajaya*," he said and smiled with a sense of pride. "My father named me Jurnail. I felt like an army general. I was not born a Sikh. No one is born into a religion. It is a false concept. As false as casteism. How can you be born a Sikh? You are decorated, given a purpose. I was told by my mother to stand up to injustice. This is injustice. What has happened in Hazara is injustice. Attacking innocent people just because they have a different religion, taking their property, raping, and killing their women and children. It is a gross injustice. We will fight against it to protect the lives of innocent and peace-loving people."

Then Jurnail stopped to sip his kahwah.

"Forcing young girls to change religions. Abducting and dishonoring the little girls. If your religion is better, if your beliefs are better, then let them show up in your character and actions. But people who hate don't have a relationship with God. They have a relationship with religion, politics. They don't want God. They want women, money, and power. Stay close to God, who lives in you, and don't hate. That is dharma. Not these turbans and beards. They have been there for thousands of years, on the heads and face of saints and thugs alike."

Then Jurnail paused for another sip of kahwah as he ran his grim sight across every face in the room. "Jai has returned from pilgrimage, and he will discuss matters that he discusses every year. This year, he has been concerned about the situation in many parts of Khyber. He thinks the clan should move east. He suggests we move to Patiala. This is a serious matter. I would like Jai to explain his thoughts to everyone here, and then we will make a decision together."

Jai stood up and bowed to Jurnail and then stated, "We are here in this room, three generations. These generations have seen a lot of battles and wars. Wars not against people or religions but against the bigoted ideology and against those who force it on others. These battles have never scared us. Irrespective of their beliefs or religion, our men have rallied against injustice even when outnumbered and out armed. And we know that our gurus fought against the oppression, and we saw our elders stand like a wall against the forces of evil. Those fights were hard but also easy in the sense that we could identify our enemy. It usually was a king or one of his generals or a fanatic tribal leader or some mullah preaching hate.

"While our elders, like Baba-ji, fought with armies and militia, they have never fought with a crazy mob, a mob of thousands of people. This is different. The minds of these people are weaponized by politicians to achieve their evil goals. These fools will just follow blindly. We don't know how to fight mobs. They are like a very large pack of wild dogs."

Jai paused as he paced himself, and then he continued, "For the last few months, I have been worried about something that this nation has never seen before. A recent phenomenon." There was silence in the room as everyone intensely waited to listen. "A hate-filled mob willing to kill other humans, innocent people. People of their own town or village, or the one nearby. People they have lived and worked with, traders and shopkeepers who serviced their community, even nurses and doctors who served them, for no particular reason other than just because they are not Muslims.

"Across India, every day, hundreds of people are dying in riots. Khyber has just started seeing this. You are aware of what happened in Hazara. These riots will happen here because it is being planned at the highest of levels by League leaders who intend to control the power of the people by using religion to create a country for Muslims, so they claim. And they have British support at the highest level. They say they are fighting for Islam. But all they are doing is exploiting innocent Muslims, using them as tools of hate to achieve their goals. Jinnah is no practicing Muslim. He just wants to prove something to Gandhi. To win the game, they are willing to divide India and let millions die for it," Jai said as clansmen nodded in agreement.

"I have every reason to believe that within the next few months, this place will not be safe for Hindus and Sikhs. I believe we should move out of Peshawar to the east. I have bought some land and shops in Patiala for us to resettle. I did what I believed was the right thing to do to protect and flourish this clan. Now the decision is in your hands."

Jai's speech was well delivered, but his closing was unexpectedly extreme for the clansmen who could not imagine leaving their homeland to settle on distant lands.

"*Khanna* sahib has assured us that they will protect us," said Sarup, referring to a renowned politician of Peshawar, adding, "We have support here. Why leave our land, businesses, friends, and go to unfamiliar places?"

Jai turned to his uncle, Balwant, and his sons, who were all sitting together on the benches nearby. "The British want India to be divided. They will support the violence and Muslim League butchery. The idea that their police or army will defend us does not make any sense."

"We can move to Chitral or Upper Swat. We have friends there," Satwant suggested.

"Mehar, what are your thoughts?" Jurnail asked.

Mehar did not want to oppose Jai's proposal, but he did not believe that the family should move. "We can live in the cantonment. There is a large presence of the British army there. We have a great standing in the city. I don't believe we are in danger. And if it comes to it, we will fight. No one in our generations ever left because of fear."

Jai shook his head at Mehar's response, but it made Jurnail very happy. "What do you think, Satwant?"

Satwant, who had created his own militia on his farm, was happy to stay and fight. "Trehans and us together have more than fifty mounted men that we can gather within the clan. There are a lot of people we know here. Even without Ullas, we can gather more than a hundred fighters."

"Out of a hundred or so militiamen we are counting here, more than half of those mounted men are Pashtuns. The only reason they support us is that the words of hate have not reached their ears. But efforts are on to incite them and break them away from us. Some have already left and joined the ranks of Haji Khan," Jai said, agitated.

Jai looked around the room and saw little support for his proposal. The reaction of his fellow clansmen ranged from outright denial to widespread surrender. In his last attempt to influence the elders, he spoke up again: "When India is divided, equations will change. I am afraid we will be left here alone, with no one to protect us or fight by our side."

Jurnail raised his hand, "We won't be scared by anyone. This land from Hindukush to the oceans of Saurashtra, and from Gilgit to Deccan, belongs to the great country defended by people who love this land and its values. For generations, people, irrespective of their religion, have taken pride in defending the culture and ways of this land. We are men of Khyber. We will stay on the land we were born on, and we will die on this land."

Jurnail looked around the room. His face had become red and his eyes brighter. "If you go anywhere in Swat, you will find ruins of Buddhist monasteries and Hindu temples going back thousands of years. Pashtunwali was here before Islam. We have been here for a long, long time. We will be here even if we die. Our remains will fall in this soil when our bodies are gone, and our spirits and souls will continue to fight for our values and principles. We are not going anywhere."

The room was filled with the noise of excited approval of Jurnail's decision.

"So, what will be our response when the partition happens, and riots start?" Jai asked helplessly.

"There are three types of people in this world. Ones that rule — people like the British Royals, Ashoka the Great, Akbar, wannabes like Nehru and Jinnah. The second type includes perpetrators and victims. They include people that are ruled. The ones that get used by rulers to achieve their goals. These are spineless people, the ones Jai calls mobs or rioters. Those who will follow the darkest ideas to serve their dark inner desires. That second type also includes the victims of these mobs, people who will die on the street helplessly, begging for life. Then there is the third type of people. They are free. People like Bacha Khan, Kalyan, Dostan. People like us. Dils and our brave fighters. We will live free on our terms and die free."

This time, the noise of approval was even louder. Balwant, Satwant, and their sons stood up to clap.

"Okay. Agreed. We are not cowards. I have a question for you all. Jinnah is creating Pakistan by using hate. Do you want to live in a country built on hate? Will it be a great place to live?" Jai asked the elders.

Then Jurnail stood and wrapped his white throw around himself. "Hate is not a new concept.

Hate was the reason Hindu mothers gave their sons to Sikhism — to fight hate — and we will fight hate, right here in Khyber." Jurnail pointed to the ground. Then with a pause, he looked at Jai. "Jai, you have to dispose of the land in Patiala. I am not happy that you made the decision to buy the land without consulting with the family."

Jai, with the unrest in his mind visible on his face, said, "It will be disposed of, Baba-ji. I do have two requests to make. I hope you all will see no harm in accepting them."

"I am listening."

"One, I request that we move the family to the cantonment haveli as soon as possible. I will continue to stay in Qissa Khwani, at least during day times. Second, I request that families with women think about safety carefully. These people are vicious, and you must protect your women and children and make your decision based on that. Maher and I don't have women to worry about. You all decide for yourselves what is right for you."

"I agree. The Trehan family can make their own decision. You live deep in the tribal area. Daler and Lal, you can decide your own course. Regarding moving to Preet House, I don't see any problem with that as long as the business stays open in Qissa Khwani."

It was a relief to Jai, as he feared the situation could get worse in Qissa Khwani Bazaar anytime.

As soon as Jurnail stopped speaking, Sarup slammed the wood floor with his rifle butt. "I would like to add something here. Again, with all respect to Baba Jurnail and Baba Balwant. I agree with Jai that we should move east. I also agree that we should not leave this place without a fight. My thought is that if you have the ability to send your women and children, you should do that while the men stay here and fight, and if all turns out well, which I highly doubt, then the men can bring their families back here."

"You have large families, and you need to do whatever is needed to protect them. Helpless children need us to protect them," Jurnail said in a low voice as if realizing he had not really considered women and children in the equation.

The annual jirga of the clan was over, and the clansmen dispersed to their villages. Even with the show of bravery, they were more worried than ever before.

\*\*\*

On Jai's insistence, Dils started preparing to shift to Preet House from Dil Mahal. Jurnail and Mehar moved there first, and Jai stayed behind at Dil

Mahal to enjoy solitude and to heal his bitterness about the decision against his plan to move east.

Mehar was sad about having to disagree with Jai on this important issue. He had been feeling guilty for letting him down and was looking for an opportunity to explain his position. He had not seen him for two days and decided to visit Dil Mahal. When he reached there, Jai was reading the newspaper with his morning tea. Mehar walked in, removed his gun from his shoulder, and put it against the wall close to him. Rustam brought the kahwah tea as Mehar sat on the wooden chair next to Jai. After customary respectful greetings to his elder brother, Jai continued reading the newspaper.

"What is the news?" Mehar looked with curiosity at Jai, who pulled out some pages of the newspaper and offered them to Mehar, muttering, "The evil Jinn is going to get a lot of people killed," referring to Jinnah, the president of the Muslim League.

Mehar looked at Jai with eyebrows lifted. "What I have read and heard is that he himself is not bad. It is always the second in command."

"That is the art. Use others to do your dirty work," Jai said as he continued reading.

"Some people say he is not even a practicing Muslim. That he does many things that go against Islam," Mehar said.

"He is as much a Muslim as Nehru is a Pandit and Gandhi a Mahatma," Jai replied without looking up from the newspaper. "They are cheats, looting people of their livelihood, homes, even life to win whatever game they are playing."

He had not looked at Mehar so far since he had arrived. Mehar started reading the newspaper. "What is happening across the country is such a shame. Considering that it is pretty much peaceful around here, I believe that the decision to stay here was the right one." It was as if Mehar was trying to provoke him into the discussion. Jai stayed quiet.

"Here, with Pashtuns, I am fully confident we will be safe. Until we know where the border will be drawn, we can't decide anything. Maybe there will be no partition. Maybe there will be a Pashtunistan."

Jai, who was trying hard not to engage in discussion, got irritated and uncomfortable. He looked at Mehar. "We need to use a little common sense. These are Muslim-majority areas. They will not go to India. Only if the Muslim League stops spreading the message of hate will we all continue to live peacefully, but it will not happen. There will be no support from anyone once the violence starts. I dread the times we will soon be in."

Mehar could read the discomfort in Jai's heart with the clan's decision against his recommendation.

"Don't worry too much. We are better here than any-where."

Jai dropped the newspaper on the table. His frustration was open. Mehar was a few years older than him. Normally, he would restrain himself, but Jai believed since he was the most traveled, he knew things that the rest of the family did not. He looked into Mehar's eyes and said, "Bhai sahib, the winds are changing. The day is not far when these winds of hate will burn this town. And when that day comes, it will be bad. I have one boy, a little boy, and I would like to keep him safe." Then he picked up the newspaper and pointed at the picture of Jinnah and Nehru. "I dread these men. They will get a lot of people killed. They both want their world to rule, and for that, they could get us all killed." He paused and looked away for a moment in anger, then turned his face back.

Mehar was lost in his thoughts. *My brain agrees with you, but my heart doesn't want to leave the land of our ancestors. I know that I would rather die here in Khyber than move someplace else.* Then with sadness eminent in his eyes, he looked at Jai and said, "Sometimes, we have to leave it to God." He consoled himself this way on his dilemma. "Think about sending the boy to Haridwar to our purohit for a few months till things settle down here," Mehar said as he took a sip of his kahwah tea.

Jai got up, asking for his sherwani, which Zahir brought quickly. After handing it over, he moved away. Servants knew not to listen to the conversations of their patrons.

"Will you come with me to the office?" Jai asked. "I don't feel comfortable going there alone anymore."

Mehar looked at Jai in surprise. He wondered what was happening that made Jai so concerned. Then Mehar got up and said, "Let's go. Is anything in particular bothering you?"

Jai put his double-barrel on his shoulder, which Rustam had readied for him.

As they walked to the door, Mehar said, "Hari is twelve. He is brilliant for his age. Great marksman that handles the horses well. He learns quickly. He can be a great leader, as was our father."

"Our fathers fought wars, not hate and treachery of the masses. Leaders like our father are not needed anymore. It is the time of politicians who hide behind mobs and use hate to grab power and rule the masses. The time of clans like ours is done," Jai retorted. "Now the question is what to save and what to sacrifice. Our lives — those can be sacrificed. Hari can't be sacrificed."

From Dil Mahal to the office in Qissa Khwani was only a five minutes walk. The office was more of

a political office, a power center for Dils, where Pashtun leaders used to meet with the British to negotiate.
Both parties needed the Dils' influence to settle conflicts. Until a few years back, the fate of big tribal
landlords had been decided there. Alliances were decided, money was exchanged without any interest.
These days, however, Jai was spending less and less
time there. It had become only a symbol of the Dil
clan's past glory and shrinking existence.

As they walked towards Kabuli Gate, they saw
Ali and his men outside on the street. Ali had shown
flagrant disregard to the verdict at the jirga, claiming it
did not hold after the death of Jawar. He had joined
the League because it made him more powerful. Any
action on Ali by a Hindu would be treated as a religious attack. In the past, Mehar had warned Jai to do
something about him. But Jai had been avoiding conflict. Now, as an active member of the League, Ali had
been part of meetings with Governor Olaf. It was
known that Olaf was very close to Muslim League
leaders in Peshawar.

As they walked towards the office, they saw
Haji Khan's key men standing in the street. "*Salam
Walekum*, Lala," said one named Fateh Khan, as he
adjusted his gun on his shoulder. He had helped Ali
and Masood Khan negotiate the settlement with Bhole

when Jai was sick. His greeting had an insinuation of trouble that Mehar could see.

"*Wa alaykumu salam*, Fateh," Jai responded as he looked into the eyes of each of them, reading their faces. As he passed them, Jai turned his face towards Mehar's ear, whispering, "They've been camping here for the last couple of days. They are hosted here by Ali. His activities are bothering me. Sometimes, they are sitting outside our office steps, and they have been passing mild taunts."

Depending on the taunt you use with Dils, it could cost you your life. Jai was trying to avoid conflict and, in the process, Mehar was worried that he was looking weak. "We have to address this Ali affair. He is cunning and evil, and you never leave an evil man around, especially when his intentions are to harm you."

Jai knew winds had changed. "We had relationships in the governor's office. But since Olaf's appointment, things have been different. Ali is a League leader in Peshawar. If we do anything here, we will be in trouble. The odds are against us."

"He knows he has the upper hand." Mehar looked concerned. "We have no obligation towards Ali. I don't care who he is. We must address this."

Rustam, who was ahead of them by a few yards, opened the door of the office. They went inside and sat on the floor against cushions. "Rustam, you have been doing a great job with the upkeeping of this place."

"I clean it every day, Lala-ji."

Jai looked around the room. "It has never looked this clean."

"This Ali problem will only get bigger as we wait. We will only see it grow," Mehar said as he looked at Jai, trying to elicit his response. But Jai stayed quiet. He knew that the clan's militia had been practically disbanded. With Dostan's death, there was no reason for Ullas to risk his men and trade hostilities with other tribes. The League had been very successful in inciting the Muslims against Hindus and Sikhs. British support of the League in Northwest province had broadened their reach and weakened any political influence of Hindus or Sikhs in the area.

"The reality is that in politics and power, when you are falling down, there is no one who comes to save you," Jai responded as he looked through the old seals and documents.

"We can't align with Pashtuns too much unless Pashtuns want their own country. Then we stay here, or we move up into the mountains to live with one of our friendly tribes, or maybe move to Kabul," Mehar said.

"Moving east is the only way out. Kabul is going to be the same situation as here," Jai said as he scratched his head. "I don't even know. My mind is not working. But I know we are doomed here. I won't be able to protect anyone here."

"I owe you an apology for opposing your plan. I just don't want to leave this place," Mehar said, rolling the family seal on the table and looking into Jai's eyes.

"Baba-ji wants to live and die here. You want to live and die here. Why would I go anywhere else?" Jai tapped Mehar's shoulder as he looked outside the window at two Pashtun militiamen rubbing tobacco.

"The time is getting near for conflict. The time is approaching to finish things in glory, to fulfill our duty to protect our land and way of life. Since we choose to stay, we better make it worth the price of our lives. Our ancestors will be watching," Jai said as he looked at armed tribesmen outside in the street.

# Chapter 8
# [1947] Ali's Whisper

In December 1946, large mobs of armed Muslims attacked villages in the Hazara division near Peshawar, plundering, burning houses, and murdering their non-Muslim owners who had lived there for many generations. Women were raped and murdered or sold off. Attacks in Dera Ismail Khan, Multan, and other places became a regular occurrence. These attacks were well organized by the Muslim League, and the local British administration did little to stop them. In early January 1947, a pregnant Sikh woman, Basanti, was abducted in Hazara and forcibly converted to Islam after her family was killed. After unbiased intervention by Chief Minister Dr. Khan Sahib, Jinnah influenced Governor Olaf to dismiss Dr. Khan Sahib's government, and Gov Olaf recommended the dismal to Mountbatten, the then viceroy of India, who disagreed.

Despite the terrible situation, assurances kept coming from the key Hindu-Sikh leaders in Peshawar that there was no reason to migrate east. Given these assurances, some in the Hindu-Sikh community in Peshawar ignored the seriousness of the situation. Organized attacks on non-Muslims in villages and towns of frontier province continued. Muslim League, through well-organized channels, collected arms and gave speeches to incite the mobs. The planning was done with the covert blessings of local officials who didn't do anything to protect Hindus or Sikhs.

The Dils stayed within Peshawar. They decided Hari would spend his days either at school or at Kabul River under Bazam's or Rustam's watchful eyes.

Jai now only went to the office in Qissa Khwani two days a week, just so it did not seem abandoned. Ullas had helped with a few militiamen, who guarded Dil Mahal day and night, but warned not to count too much on their loyalty. Dil Mahal mostly stayed vacant. Even Rustam and Zahir had moved to the Preet House. Lal and Joga would still sit outside the entrance during the daytime or when Jai was visiting.

In March, large mobs organized by the Muslim League marched through the streets of Peshawar, attacking Hindu and Sikh houses and businesses. Ali was actively involved in the organization of these mobs. He marched them through the streets of old Peshawar, eventually directing them through Qissa Khwani Bazaar. During these marches, there were several stabbings of Hindus and Sikhs. Ali had his eyes set on Dil Mahal. He thought it was only a matter of time when he would occupy the elegant mansion.

In May, Jai was shot at while riding his motorcycle with Daler from Dil Mahal on the way to Preet House. It was nighttime when the sound of gunfire started. The bullets hit the motorcycle, and Jai fell and was hurt. Daler had bravely returned fire and helped Jai to safety by pulling him in the side street. Then they exchanged gunfire with a few tribesmen for some time before tribesmen left on their own. Jurnail was not told about the details of the incident.

June and July were very tense, with numerous organized attacks in Qissa Khawni Bazaar. Muslim League leaders were using every reason and opportunity to cause unrest and violence by provoking marches and agitations to build mobs and then leave the fate of Hindus and Sikhs in the hands of those violent mobs.

Hari was told not to go outside Preet House except for school or to spend time on the riverbank. He was always to be accompanied by Bazam on the riverbank. "Hari, listen carefully, child. The situation is getting worse. Always be on alert. Wear your school uniform only when you are going to school, otherwise wear our dress, the dress of Pashtuns, and cover your head with a cap," Jai instructed Hari.

As the situation worsened, many Hindu and Sikh families decided to leave Peshawar. Jai asked a few prominent Hindu family elders to meet Jurnail and explain their reasoning for leaving for the east. Jurnail, however, was still in denial and did not change his mind, even though he was convinced there would be unrest and violence. It was unfathomable for Jurnail that India could be divided. On June 3, the partition of India was announced, and Jurnail realized that Jai's warnings had not been baseless.

"So, who benefits from this?" Jurnail said angrily.

"Jinnah is happy. He got Pakistan to rule. Nehru is happy he will be Prime Minister of India. Both of their schemes worked. Hopefully, that answered your question," Jai said with a pinch of sarcasm.

Jai paced himself around the drawing-room as Jurnail sat in the chair, looking around with apparent anger on his face.

"Gandhi is still working to win sainthood from Muslims. Besides, he stays as the de facto ruler of India. All three were playing for the British, and now they are getting their payoff," Jai added, "and Hindu is made a total fool by this Pandit from Kashmir and this saint of Sabarmati," Jai laughed.

"Why are you laughing?" Jurnail said with irritation on his face.

"Well. I am laughing because things are going as expected. There is no uncertainty. Next comes a storm of violence. Let us get ready," Jai said.

As everything Jai had said was turning out to be true, Jurnail started to worry about the safety of his clansmen. By August, most of the rich and influential merchants from the community had already left for India with their families. As the situation became worse and authorities colluded with rioters, Jurnail became very concerned about Hari's safety. In doubt about his decisions, he asked Jai if they should migrate or stay put.

"We cannot go now. There is too much violence outside. Amritsar is far. I don't want us to die in vain." Jai had long given up on his push to migrate. He had mentally prepared himself for a certain conflict in the near future. He, however, was deeply worried about Hari and was thinking day and night on how to protect him.

In early September, large armed mobs of tribesmen marched in the streets of Peshawar, attacking and killing non-Muslim men, women, and children. On September 7, Pashtun tribesmen raided Peshawar, killing any Hindu or Sikh men or women they could find. They did not even spare Hindu nurses in the hospitals. After learning about the butchery and murder of many of his friends and acquaintances, Jurnail was out of his wits to understand why people who had lived together for centuries had suddenly turned on their non-Muslim neighbors. He had fought battles with armies, but he had never fought with rioting mobs.

On September 12, Balwant, Satwant, and Lakhbir showed up in the middle of the night at Preet House. Mehar woke Jurnail from his sleep and said, "I have very bad news. The Trehan family farmhouse was attacked by a mob of tribesmen."

"Did they survive?"

"Only two," Mehar said with tears in his eyes.

Outside in the yard, Jurnail could hear sobbing. He walked out to the yard and hugged Balwant.

"My family is all gone, Jurnail. They killed everyone mercilessly," tears from Balwant's eyes rolled down and were soaked into Jurnail's kurta.

"Did they fight back?" Jurnail asked as he fought tears.

"They did. Very bravely. They all died fighting. It was a surprise attack. Hundreds of rioters. Baba Balwant and Lakhbir were out in the town. They survived," Satwant said.

"My sons and grandsons…." Balwant broke into wailing, and then he controlled himself.

"Balwant, it is very difficult to lose one family member, and we have lost so many today. Your grief is beyond imaginable. But they were not victims. They were martyrs. Brother Sucha and his sons, your sons, Nek, Amar, and their boys, fought bravely. Our respect for them is that we fight like hell against our enemies. That is our respect. I won't cry for them. I will bleed for them," Jurnail said as his eyes teared up and he consoled Balwant, who wept with hands on his face.

"We were out for the evening in the town when the mobs of tribesmen descended. When Satwant came looking for us, it was all over," Balwant said.

"Ullas learned about the attack. He sent some of his militiamen with me to check. They escorted us here," Satwant said.

"No help came from anywhere? Nothing from the British?" Jurnail asked.

"Who is going to help? The British are probably enjoying all this. Jai was right. We are not safe here. We can't fight thousands of people. There are mobs of Muslims looking to kill and loot us everywhere. Even Ullas' militia can't be trusted," Satwant said.

"There is a lot of violence in the town here. How come you have not prepared to leave?" Lakhbir asked Jai.

"The violence has been raging for more than a few months now," Jai said without expression on his face.

"Rustam, go call everyone. Joga's family. Lal's family. Get them all here." Jurnail looked distressed. He opened a bundle of his battle gear and started dressing.

"Who are you going to battle with, Baba-ji?" Jai asked.

"Not going to die without fighting. Battle is about cost. I will make sure I cost them more than my worth." Jurnail looked around the room, then said in a firm voice, "Get dressed. I hate crying, helpless people."

"Gandhi, Nehru, and Jinnah — they destroyed the lives of so many people." With his eyes intense with pain and anger, Jai turned to the grieving Balwant. "Mahatma? How can he sleep when so many are dying because of his decisions?"

Jai pulled an arms chest from the storeroom. "I had some hope for Pashtunistan. But that is gone as well. Congress betrayed Doctor Khan and the Pashtuns. Sometimes, it feels like Gandhi, Nehru, and Jinnah are working together to divide and rule India, even at the cost of millions of us."

"Where is the non-violence in Gandhi's plans now? Didn't he think about how to partition without violence? He is all-powerful, so convincing, he turns the tides with his satyagraha," Jurnail angrily said as he opened the second chest of arms.

"Non-violence is just Gandhi's means to deprive Hindus of any means to protect themselves. Muslims will never care about non-violence. Hindus will practice it, and they will be butchered. And if they react, Gandhi will go on a fast until death to stop them," Jai lamented.

"There is no non-violent Gandhi. It is a farce. The man recruited Indian boys to fight for the British. Mothers here never saw their sons who lost their lives in the battles of the World War in Europe. He supported the Islamic Caliphate of the Ottoman Empire, the most violent regime the world had ever seen. He uses non-violent strategies only when it serves him and the British," Jurnail said as he put three daggers on his belt. "This inferno of hate that Jinnah has started will burn everyone, even Muslims."

"They have damned these lands forever. There will never be peace here. Even after they have killed all Sikhs and Hindus, they will be killing each other. They are forever cursed by this," Balwant said as he wept. "Mark my words. They will never see peace and prosperity."

"Jinnah and the League fooled Muslims in the name of Islam, just as Gandhi and Congress fooled the rest of the people," Jai said.

"Jinnah and the League better worry about what comes next. They should be fearful of people who are brutalized here and what they will do when they reach the east. We don't want to be the ones harboring revenge and anger and then doing unjust things when we go there. We should settle it here with those who are inflicting this upon us," Jurnail said as he dressed for battle.

"I keep telling you, Baba-ji, you can't fight with mobs. It is nothing like fighting on the battlefield. We can't fight with thousands of people wielding swords, axes, and guns who are full of hate. They are moving house to house. They are killing men, women, and children. You can't fight them."

"We can. We kill as many as we can till we are dead, and then if they want to pull our hearts out, so be it," Jurnail said angrily, then he calmed as he looked at Jai's helpless face. "Well, what do I know, Jai? You were right last time, and you are right now. Tell us the plan. What should we do?"

A knock came at the door; Joga, Daler, and his wife and their two children had shown up.

"Thank God, you are all safe." Jurnail pulled Joga's arm. "Joga, come here. Sit with me."

"We need Ullas' militia. His presence is critically important in these circumstances," Joga said as he worriedly looked around the room to see who else was there.

Jurnail nodded in agreement. "Rustam, go to Lal's house. If he is there, ask him to come here with his family. Then you can both take the car to Tarnab to meet Ullas."

"I doubt he will spare his militia for us," Satwant said. "Hate has spread like a forest fire on land with a drought of love and compassion. Gandhi, Jinnah, and Nehru have fooled the world. These agents of the British have made their name, fame, and empire on the dead bodies of the innocent people of India. The disease of hate and trickery they have unleashed is beyond anyone's ability to help."

"There were already five men that Ullas had provided guarding Dil Mahal. I don't know if they are still there or if their loyalty can be trusted," Joga said.

Jurnail got up and walked over to Rustam, who was still not sure what to say to Ullas. "I have a message that you need to give to Ullas at Tarnab. Lal will take you there in the car. Tell him we need protection. Tell him I sent you. You understand? Say my name."

As Rustam hurried towards the door, Jai stopped him. "Wait. If you don't find Lal, go to Tarnab on the horse. Also, on your way back, stop by Dil Mahal and check if it is still protected. If you see Hamdard, ask if he has any information for me."

Rustam left in the dark of the night.

"Anyone know how things are in Tarnab?" Joga asked, worried about his brothers and their families.

"Any news about Sukhi and her family? Satwant, was it all peace there?" Balwant asked.

"It was tense. We had barricaded the farmhouse," Satwant said.

"We can only hope they are safe. We can count on Ullas to protect them," Jai said as he lined up guns against the wall.

"What will Ullas do? Keep the hope alive but don't be so sure of his help," Satwant said as he shook his head. "I hope my family has left for Jalalabad. They were preparing for it."

Someone knocked at the door, yelling, "It is Zahir. Open the door."

Daler opened the door, and Zahir walked inside the house, breathless. "Don't go out, Lala. Don't go anywhere," Zahir said with his trembling voice. "There are a lot of rioters and tribesmen on the streets. Lots of killing happening. You should leave Peshawar tonight. Tomorrow morning, they will be back at killing again. Please leave this place. Move to safety."

Daler gave Zahir some water to drink. "Relax, Zahir. You know Bazam? He lives in the shop." Zahir nodded.

"Ask him to come here. Tell him it is urgent."

"Jai, will you say something about what you have in mind? Let us ensure that at least women and children are safe," Jurnail said as he looked at Jai and then continued in a low voice, "I don't worry about the men. We will fight and die fighting."

Jai looked grim, and with his face fixed on the ground in front of him, he kept silent.

"Jai, the elders are asking how we can leave the area. Please propose a plan," Mehar said. There were fifteen or so men, women, and children in the room.

"We are late. We don't have the same options anymore that we had three months, or a month, back." He looked into Mehar's eyes. "Most families have already left Khyber. Others, unless in the protection of a tribe, could be already dead," he said, then paused to look at Joga and Jurnail's face. "Every place between here and Amritsar is unsafe. Going east is not an option. It is not safe anymore. Trains are being attacked, caravans slaughtered," he added.

Balwant, who was the eldest member of the family, looked at Jai. "I agree with your concern. We need a plan. I don't think we are going to find any help sitting here."

Jai looked around the room. "We have to split up. Some of us who believe it may be safer here can stay in Peshawar, but I warn that you may run out of luck. Those who wish to leave should head out to Amritsar and wait for us there. If the situation improves, you can come back from Amritsar to Peshawar. And if it becomes worse here, we will try to reach Amritsar."

There was quiet for some time, then Jurnail got up and refused to give his approval to splitting up the family. "We need to stick together."

Mehar walked over to Jurnail. "You know, Baba-ji, I opposed Jai's original plan to leave in January. I regret that, and the decision has put the family in this dangerous situation. Let us follow what he is suggesting."

Jai was looking at Jurnail with folded hands. "Baba-ji, I would not have asked to split up if the situation was not dire. Splitting means a higher chance of some of us surviving."

Jurnail, his hands on his face, mumbled, "I never thought I would see this day." His hands went around his long white beard as he nodded his consent.

Mehar turned towards the gathering. "What Jai is proposing will let us work on two plans when there is no certainty of any one plan succeeding. My take is that we will certainly all die here if we stay here. I will say, those who have families, women, and children leave for Amritsar. Jai and I will stay here."

"Hari can easily blend in with the local population. We need to make sure we have a plan for him to escape from Preet House," Jurnail said to Jai.

"Hari, Baba-ji, and I will stay here along with Daler, Satwant, and Lakhbir." Jai looked for their reaction and then continued, "Baba Balwant, you should join Mehar and others and leave for Amritsar on the train tomorrow morning. Please bear arms and carry the least amount of things," Jai said as if counting people at the same time.

Mehar objected, "Jai, I can't leave you alone here."

"Mehar, you are needed to escort this group to Amritsar. We will stay here till you send us the message after reaching Amritsar."

"You want me to leave you here, alone?"

"I will not be alone. There are six of us here," Jai said. Then turning to Jurnail, he added, "Baba-ji, are you good with this plan?"

"I trust you, Jai. Please keep Hari safe. I agree that sending him by train could be very risky." Turning to the families who were to leave for Amritsar, he added, "Remember, arm yourself. If you are asked to part with your money, do so without hesitation. If you are asked to part with your guns, don't do that. They will give you all assurances, but in the end, they will kill you, or even worse, they will try to forcefully convert you."

Jurnail now looked distraught. "I know it is hard to leave your friends, your land, your house, your rooms, your neighborhoods, streets, friends, but we have to leave. Please hurry up and pack the least, the most valuable, and meet here before sunrise. Lal and Daler will drop you at the railway station. When on the train, stick together."

One by one, Jurnail put his hand on the heads of everyone and hugged them, "Protect your women and children till death. Fight mercilessly. *Waheguru-ji the Khalsa, Waheguru-ji ki Fateh*," he said, meaning God's pure warriors' victory will belong to God. Jurnail picked out a gun from the line of them against the wall. "Jai, we need to go visit Dil Mahal. We need to get some important things from there.

"Get yourself armed as if we are going to battle," Jurnail said.

Jai opened the third chest for all to arm themselves. All the men filled their bags with rounds.

"Dil Mahal has the family safe and lots of guns and ammunition. We don't need to carry a lot of ammunition with us from here," Jai said.

"We need to get as much as gold as we can without being too greedy. Also, there are some papers, family history," Jurnail said discreetly. Although Dil treasure belonged to the Dils, Jurnail knew that many had come empty-handed. Also, he knew there was so much treasure that it was practically impossible to take it all without getting noticed.

The sound of the car alerted everyone. Daler rushed to the door. It was Lal Singh with his family and Rustam. "Come inside quickly," Daler said.

Lal, his wife, and their three children ran inside.

"Lal, you and Rustam go to Ullas as soon as possible and tell him to rush for help. Try to get some help with you. Check on Dil Mahal on the way back. Once you deliver the message to him, rush back here and drop everyone off at the railway station. Stay safe," Jai reminded them.

Lal and Rustam left the door as Lal's helpless wife looked on.

"Daler, Hari is your responsibility. We are going to Dil Mahal. Considering the situation, we may not be back," Jai said to Daler.

Daler nodded his head.

Jai looked at Hari with a smile, worried if he heard what he told Daler. Then he sat in front of him and said, "Don't you be afraid of anything in life. You are an amazing boy. Stay safe. Stay alive. Even if you don't find me."

Hari's eyes were full of tears, but he didn't let them flow out. He nodded his head.

Jai got up and hugged him. "Where is your handgun? Go get it. You don't use a handgun on the crowd. Okay? You just run away."

Hari kept listening without expression.

Jurnail pulled Hari close to him. "Son, if ever in life this question came to your mind about how and why this happened, always remember that we chose to fight the evil. We fought for our rights and our land. We would not have done it any other way. Now, give me a hug," Jurnail gave Hari a long, tight hug.

"Bazam, drop us off close to Kabuli Gate. We will walk from there. Drop Hari and Jigar off at the river. Then come back here and let Daler know where you dropped the kids."

Bazam drove through the dark streets of Peshawar. There were fires burning the houses and shops along the way.

"It does not look safe around here. Are you sure, Lala-ji?" Bazam asked.

"Keep driving till Kabuli Gate," Jai said.

Bazam dropped off Mehar, Satwant, Lakhbir, Jurnail, and Jai in Qissa Khwani Bazaar. As he was driving away with Hari and Jigar, tears rolled down from Jai's eyes. Satwant pressed the hand of his son through the window as he let him go.

"I didn't know you cry," Jurnail said as he wiped his tears. "I have told you he will be fine. Trust me."

Then they walked into Dil Mahal after midnight. There they spent a few hours going through the family safe and reviewed every artifact, photograph, and painting.

"This is too much stuff. We can't take any of it. Just take a souvenir and important papers." Jai was distressed as the clock ticked on the wall. He and Mehar sat around the table in the drawing-room of Dil Mahal. Jai looked at the walls of the haveli that their father had built.

"It is so hard to leave this place," Mehar said as he looked at the woodwork on the pillars. "Remember we used to run around these when we were little?" He smiled.

"I remember. There are so many memories, but, you know, the thing that hurts me the most is that we will not be together," Jai paused to control the tears in his eyes. They would have rolled out had he not looked away. "Mehar, we may not see each other again after tonight."

Mehar put his hand on Jai's shoulder and said, "Let's not be that pessimistic. I have seen that you have become a little weak. I want the old Jai back. If they come to attack, you promise me that you will kill more men than they can count with their hands."

Jai looked at Mehar, "You can count on that."

"Keep Hari safe," Mehar whispered as a tear rolled down his cheek.

"Someone will take Hari to the river every day and not bring him back till late after dusk. I have read in the news that most of the time, they are attacking after daytime prayers at the mosque," Jai said.

Jurnail was quiet. He was burdened with the guilt of not listening to Jai's warnings. He was impatiently waiting for Ullas to come with his men.

Mehar looked at Jai, "I think you can trust Rustam and Bazam."

Jai opened the wooden box in the corner of the room and picked up a dagger with an antelope-horn handle, and presented it to Mehar. Then he pulled two handguns from the bag, "Keep these two handguns and this dagger. Take them with you to Amritsar." Then, with a smile on his face, Jai continued, "This was gifted by Father to me. Remember last time he went to Kabul? He got this for me."

Mehar took the dagger and looked at the carving of Jai's name. "I remember that. I was very jealous." Mehar smiled as he pulled the dagger out and inspected the sharp edge. "You should keep it, Jai."

Jai put his hand on Mehar's shoulder. "Mehar, I want you to take it to Amritsar and present it to Hari if I cannot make it."

Mehar looked at the clock. "It is getting past four o'clock. I don't feel that we are safe here in Dil Mahal after daybreak."

"Why is Ullas not here yet?" Jurnail asked desperately and then climbed on top of the Dil Mahal roof to look for Ullas and his men.

\*\*\*

In Tarnab, when Rustam and Lal reached the farmhouse to meet Ullas, he was asleep. After a wait, he came out and heard the message from Jurnail.

"I am in immense pain about the situation the partition has created. My father dreamed of Pashtunistan till his last breath. Never he would have thought Pashtuns would forget their heritage and history. It pains me to acknowledge that some of my own militia is involved in the rioting."

"Khan Sahib, the situation is hopeless. Without your support, the lives of the Dil clan are in immense danger," Lal said.

"I have terrible news, Lal. Last night, the Bedi farmhouse was attacked by tribesmen. The attack was led by Haji's men. When I reached there with a few of my men, it was too late. I, however, was able to save a girl. She is extremely traumatized. She says her name is Raji."

On hearing the news, Lal Singh sat on the ground. "Can we please take the girl with us?" he said as he rubbed his hand on his face.

"Are you sure? The situation is dangerous outside," Ullas said.

"We can't leave her here. She will come with us." Then, turning to Ullas, he added, "Khan, what should we say to baba Jurnail?"

"If I could not save the Bedi farmhouse right outside here, I have little capacity to march with a militia to Peshawar. Tell him I am helpless. Their best option is to stay out of Peshawar for some time. The safest place will be Jalalabad or Chitral."

Ullas knocked on a hut close by. An old woman opened the door.

"Hand over the girl to her family," Ullas told her.

As Lal Singh waited outside the door, he could see a scared, bruised girl in a corner.

"I am coming from Dil Mahal. I will take you there," Lal said as the girl cried uncontrollably.

"We have a car. We will take you safely. I am Lal Singh. You know me."

"She is in shock," the old woman said.

"Here. Take this message for baba Jurnail," Ullas handed a note to Lal.

\*\*\*

In Dil Mahal, Jurnail and Mehar continued to hope for support from Ullas. Early in the morning, someone knocked at the Dil Mahal door. Jai and Mehar went in anticipation of seeing Ullas. But it was Ali.

"Salam, Bhai Jaan," Ali said.

"Salam, Ali. What brings you to our door this early in the morning?" Jai said.

"Bhai Jaan, I know you don't trust me. You know the atmosphere. I came here to alert you that you should not delay leaving the area. Riots can happen anytime."

Mehar walked up to Ali. "If only you stopped making hate-filled speeches, Ali, there may be peace."

Ali stepped back into the street, "Leave within a few hours. You all will survive."

Mehar stepped out of the door into the street, gaining a view into the street, where Fateh Khan and other armed tribesmen were standing. "Are you threatening us, Ali? I can't tell if it is a recommendation, suggestion, threat, or a demand."

Jai had also come out and was standing at the door.

Looking at Jai, Ali turned back. "Jai-Bhai Jaan, talk some sense into him. I will leave now. I won't be able to do anything to help you when the mob assembles. You know the situation. These mobs are frenzied. They will kill you and burn Dil Mahal. I would hate to see it burned." Ali walked away and then stopped, turned back, and said, "Also, when you leave, don't take anything with you. I need it all in here. We will be watching." Ali and his men laughed as they walked up the street. After taking a few steps, Ali turned back and walked to Jai. "Lucky for the both of you, you have no women to worry about." Then he left with his cohorts towards the bazaar.

Jai tapped Mehar's shoulder, indicating for him to come inside, as he walked back into the drawing-room.

Mehar sat down in the chair and whispered, "I told you to take care of him. He wants to scare us away. I can tell you the moment that we leave, they will attack us."

"Ullas should be here anytime. Why is he so late?" Jurnail said as he paced restlessly.

Jai got up from the chair, where he had been sitting in deep thought. "Mehar, you must leave. Go ask everyone to pack whatever they can and leave for Amritsar. Take that bag of gold and jewelry. Distribute it among the family. It is not safe for one person to carry it all. Also, take Baba-ji with you to the haveli."

"I am not going anywhere. And don't even try," Jurnail said firmly.

"Leave your gun here and change your shawl and wear a cap. Please leave right away," Jai hugged Mehar.

After covering himself with a gray shawl and a white cap, Mehar picked up the bag of valuables and gave hugs and kisses to all as tears rolled down his face.

He then touched Jurnail's feet. "God bless you! Live for a hundred years. We will meet you in Amritsar. Tell Hari we chose to stay here to fight. Tell him we fought well," Jurnail said as he removed the chain around his neck and put it around Mehar, "Try not to lose it."

Mehar then left as Jai and Lakhbir escorted him to the street corner. Jai's mind was restless as he saw Mehar leave. "How times change," he whispered.

As Jai and Lakhbir walked back into Dil Ma-hal, someone at the door startled them. For a moment, they expected Ullas, but it was Hamdard. He was hurt and bleeding. "Lala, it is not safe here. You need to leave now," he said, then collapsed in the doorway. "Lala, there are going to be riots. They are gathering outside the bazaar."

"Tell me more, Hamdard. What did you hear?" Jai kneeled close to Hamdard to check his bleeding. He had been stabbed below the left side of his ribcage and was bleeding profusely. "I overheard Ali talking to Fateh outside my shop." Jai pressed his wound to stop it from bleeding. "Lala, you should leave now."

"Hamdard, what did you hear?"

"Pull him inside and close the door," Jurnail warned.

Mehar and Jai helped Hamdard inside.

"Ali told Fateh to kill you all if you are still here after *zuhr* prayer. He also said there would be hundreds of Pashtuns descending from the mountains. They are planning lots of attacks."

Shortly, someone knocked on the door again. Jai opened it, and it was Ali again.

"Where is your informer?" said Ali, and then he shot at Hamdard as he tried to escape, but he could not go far. Fateh shot him in the middle of the street and then fired at Jai, who closed and bolted the door. Lakhbir and Satwant stacked furniture and storage trunks to block the door. They ran around Dil Mahal closing and locking all the doors and windows. Jai ran to the roof of Dil Mahal and fired two shots at Fateh. He was hit in the chest and fell in the street.

Soon, a mob of tribesmen and locals had gathered outside Dil Mahal, and intermittent gunfire started with the tribesmen. Some in the mob tried to burn Dil Mahal, but Ali stopped them. Gunfire continued for an hour, with Jai moving between the first and second floor and Lakhbir and Satwant covering the firing from the roof and windows of Dil Mahal.

"There are enough guns and rounds in Dil Mahal's gun chests to last a long time," Jurnail said. He took the guns lined up against the wall and loaded them as he passed them around. Then he handed each of them a bag full of rounds as the gunfire intensified.

"The great Kalyan said in *Our Position*, we can happily kill and die for those simple ideas, ideas like the people's right to live their life. We live by Pashtunwali. So today, we will do as is said by the great Kalyan. Today is the day, my sons," Jurnail said as he tossed a gun to Jai, who ran upstairs to the second floor.

"Jai, don't miss an opportunity to kill that snake, Ali," Jurnail yelled.

"I don't see him. He disappeared or is hiding behind a wall," Jai replied.

Ali knew the Dils were well-trained fighters and excellent marksmen. As per the arrangement with Haji Khan, he had more than fifty fighters available to him in Qissa Khwani to capture Dil Mahal. Tribesmen in Qissa Khwani were roaming unorganized, attacking any Hindu or Sikh family they could find, and looting their property. Ali had to go around and gather the unorganized tribesmen towards Dil Mahal. As Ali turned the corner from Jehangirpura Road towards Dil Mahal, Jai saw him coming for a moment before the shops blocked the view.

Jai rushed downstairs and yelled at Lakhbir and Satwant, "Ali is here. I'm going into the street. Cover me from the roof. I will die happy if I kill him." He opened the door, rushed into the street, came face to face with Ali, and shot him twice in the chest.

Satwant and Lakhbir covered him with a barrage of gunfire. They shot at least twelve tribesmen dead before Jai rushed back inside Dil Mahal.

"He is down, bhai sahib," Satwant yelled.

"Should have done him in a long time back," Jurnail said as he loaded magazines into .303 rifles. "We may run out of bullets," he yelled.

"As long as they are put to good use," Jai said as he ran back to the roof.

"Jawar built Dil Mahal like a fort. They won't be able to win this one while Dil Mahal stands." Jurnail kept loading the rifles and passing them around. The sound of intermittent gunfire continued for some time.

"If we had a few more men, we would have descended on them and likely taken over the street," Jai said as he fired on a tribesman who had taken position behind a dried-fruit stall. "There is no clear shot from here."

"It is the same for them. Let them shoot. Don't fire till you can take someone out. Also, watch the other rooftops around. There may be shooters. Lakhbir, go up to the roof and watch Jai's back," Jurnail yelled.

"And take a shot if you see any men on rooftops," Jawar said as he handed him the loaded gun.

Jurnail took Lakhbir's place near the broken window and started taking shots.

"They are burning the gate," Lakhbir yelled from the roof.

"That gate won't burn. They will have to blow it up," Jurnail said. "And they will," he whispered to himself.

"Lakhbir, quickly jump on Wazir's roof and check the situation. You will have a better view of the street from there," Jai yelled.

Lakhbir did as instructed. "There are many tribesmen. Like, forty or fifty. Also, I think there is military. We need more bullets," he yelled and ran back to join Jai.

"If we run out of bullets, we will fight with swords," Jai yelled as he inspected the mob from the window.

"That's my boy," Jurnail yelled back.

"They have to blow up the gate to get in, so we should have some time. I hope Ullas will arrive soon. Jai, what do you think?" Jurnail waited for a response.

"I wouldn't count on that too much. Actually, I don't think he will be able to come," Jai said as he looked at the disappointment on Jurnail's face.

Jurnail was not expecting that answer. He froze for some time. Then he whispered to himself, "So, this is it. Today is the day. I hope I have made you proud, Raye-ma." With that, he started shooting at the tribesmen who were pushing forward despite taking casualties.

"We have seven loaded revolvers, five dag- gers, and eight swords. High possibility of breach anytime," Jurnail yelled. "Take your weapons when ready."

Rustam and Lal reached Qissa Khwani with Raji in the car and saw a large number of tribesmen surrounding Dil Mahal and exchanging gunfire. "Lal-bhai, you take the girl to Preet House. I will stay here to watch. It is dangerous here for you," Rustam said.

Outside Dil Mahal, Rustam stood behind the crowd watching it all unfold in front of them. Written on Rustam's hand was the message from Ullas. *Jai-Bhai Jaan, strange are the times when a Pashtun forgets about Pashtunwali and kills innocent people for all the wrong reasons. My tribesmen are gone to escort Sikhs in Tarnab to safety. It may be too late before I can get you the help. Please stay out of the old city. Haji khan is planning to attack Dil Mahal.* Then it ended with *Allah de obakha*, meaning, *May God bless you.*

\*\*\*

Lal Singh rushed to Preet House and informed Daler of the situation at Dil Mahal.

"Don't tell anyone inside about Dil Mahal's situation," Daler said to Lal.

"What is the direction for me," Lal asked.

"Take the women and children and drop them off at the railway station. You go with them to Amritsar. Bazam will drop you all off," Daler said, then turned to Bazam, adding, "After dropping them off outside the railway station, go to Dil Mahal and see if you can get them safely out. It is unlikely, but just go there and check for me. I have to make sure Hari is safe at the river."

Then, as instructed by Jai, Daler rushed to the banks of Kabul River. On his way, he decided to check on Dil Mahal. Daler saw wild crowds of Pashtuns rampaging through the old city. Many houses and shops had been set on fire. As he reached Qissa Khwani, he found it invaded by tribesmen who were shooting and butchering people and burning houses and shops of Hindus and Sikhs. A bullet shattered the left window of the car and narrowly missed Daler. He turned onto Cinema Road and saw Rustam running.

"Rustam! Rustam!" Daler slowed down the car and waited for him.

"Oh, my god, Daler-Bhai Jaan," Rustam jumped in the car as they sped away.

"What is happening there?" Daler asked.

"They are blowing up Dil Mahal. There are hundreds of tribesmen and some military. They have big guns. Canons." Rustam looked very distressed.

"What did Ullas Khan say?" Daler asked.

"Ullas Khan won't come either. I think he knew that Qissa Khwani would be attacked. He wrote in a note to stay out of the city."

"Our Baba-ji is there. It won't be easy for them to take Dil Mahal," Daler said.

"Well, they killed so many tribesmen. That is how the military got involved. It won't end well. This is so bad," Rustam started crying.

"Is anyone there? Someone should have stayed outside Dil Mahal."

"I have asked Zahir to stay there," Rustam said.

"We need to save Hari and Jigar. Let's pick them up first. There is no point in assuming things will improve." Daler turned back towards the river. "Jaibhai sahib was right. He knew this would happen."

On seeing Rustam still crying, Daler told Rustam, "Don't cry in front of Hari. We need to keep it all secret from him."

Soon, they reached the river. Hari and Jigar were sitting there just watching the water, completely unaware of the tragedy that had struck the clan. Daler ran towards them, shouting, "We need to go now."

Hari was confused. "What happened? Bazam just dropped us off."

"There is bad rioting. We need to leave the area."

"For where? What about everyone else? Papa? Baba-ji?"

"Well, I am going to go find out how they are doing," Daler tried to remain calm.

Hari noticed Daler's face was pale. As they reached the car, he saw Rustam crying. "Rustam-bhai, what happened?" Hari asked.

"Get in, boy. We need to hurry," Daler said.

"No. Tell me first!" Hari yelled.

"I will tell you. First, please get in," Daler said. As Hari and Jigar sat in the car, Daler sped away towards the railway station. He noticed military trucks with *Gorkha* rifle regiments. He stopped the car and ran to talk to the officer. "These boys are without family and need protection. They belong to a military officer's family. Their uncle is Captain Bhole Nath. Their haveli got attacked."

"The next military truck that comes here will go to the railway station. You can put him on the truck. They will put them on the train to Amritsar."

"Can't they just stay in your protection till I check on the rest of his family, officer?"

"The truck is coming. Just wait in the car," the soldier said.

"Please give me a sign when the truck is here. Please," Daler said with folded hands.

The officer nodded and told him to sit in the car.

Daler ran back to the car and yelled, "The military truck will drop you two off at the railway station. You get on the train to Amritsar. You must protect yourself." Then he looked into Hari's eyes, "You are the only child of the Dil clan. I gave my word to your father to protect you."

"I am not going till I go to Dil Mahal," Hari said.

"No one is there. Believe me," Daler replied.

"I won't go without seeing Papa and Baba," His face was red.

A couple of military trucks were seen approaching. The officer signaled Daler to bring the boy over.

"Where are we going?" Hari asked.

Daler hugged him, "You are going to a better tomorrow. When you get to Amritsar, try to find your family. Look for us there. Look for Raji. She will need you there."

"Raji? Where is she? Where is everyone else? Where will I go in India?" Hari asked.

"Nothing will happen. You will reach Amritsar, and I will see you there, and someone will meet you there. I have to go check on the others," Daler yelled as he left.

"Never lose hope. Never give up. You belong to the Dil family of Khyber. You can survive in the east. Remember who you are, and never give up," he said, wiping tears from his eyes. Then turning to Rustam, he said, "I need to go to Preet House. Balwant-baba and his family are there, waiting for Jai and all. Watch these kids until the truck leaves."

"I am so afraid for them." Rustam wiped tears off his face as he trembled.

"Are you two coming?" the officer asked as the truck started to move.

"I am going to stay here with you," Hari said to Rustam.

"No. It is very dangerous. Go with the military. Jigar needs you."

"I will go myself if you don't take me."

As Hari started running away, Rustam said, "Wait. Don't run away. They will kill you. I will take you there. Stop. Please!"

"You have to promise me you are taking me to Dil Mahal," Hari said.

"You are the only child of the family. They would want you to live," Rustam begged.

"I can't leave without seeing Papa and Baba-ji," Hari wiped tears off his face, his heart and mind gripped by intense fear. "Tell me how my father is. And how are Baba-ji and Uncle Mehar?"

"The trucks are leaving. Officer? Are there more trucks coming?" Rustam was frustrated.

"There is a refugee camp on the other side of the bridge. But you have to hurry, because who knows how long it will be there. Things are very bad here. You don't want to be left behind here." Then a military officer gave orders for the trucks to leave.

Rustam yelled at Jigar, who was trying to get down from the truck. "No. Go to the railway station. Everyone is going to come there. But don't wait for anyone. Please catch the first train to Amritsar."

Jigar sat back.

"Look, he is alone now," Rustam said and then turned to Hari. "Okay, I will take you to Dil Mahal after dark. Daler-bhai will kill me," Rustam lamented.

"Why not now?"

"Because there is rioting in the entire old city. You stay on the river, right where we picked you up. I will come and pick you up when it is safer. Do you trust me?"

Hari nodded.

"Don't ever leave this place, even if I am late," Rustam said as he ran towards the city.

\*\*\*

At Dil Mahal, tribesmen were unable to take the Dils out. The sun was already beginning to set. They had set the wooden entrance on fire a few times, but the metal structure of the gate was still standing strong. Many tribesmen had been killed by Dils, and Haji Khan's anger was boiling. A military officer, a Punjabi man, inspected the haveli from all sides. He asked that the back wall of the haveli be blown up with dynamite. As dynamite was placed on the wall, he asked the tribesmen to line up to charge in.

Haji Khan was yelling, "Fifty rupees if you catch the old man alive. Zero for dead."

There was dead quiet as the mob waited in anticipation. Then the soldiers lit the dynamite. As a powerful blast blew up the back wall of Dil Mahal, the army fired two mortar shells through the opening before the tribesmen stormed in. There was a battle inside Dil Mahal, and shouts of, "Jo Bole So Nihal," meaning, "Who so ever says God's name will be saved," echoed from Sawant, Lakhbir, Jai, and Jurnail. The battle didn't last long, as scores of tribesmen and a mob invaded Dil Mahal. The Dils had no plan to surrender, and they all died fighting until the bitter end.

After the owners of the Dil Mahal were killed, Tribesmen and mobs started clearing everything out from Dil Mahal. There was more treasure inside than they had imagined. For hours, they knocked on the walls and ground, checking for hidden treasure. As darkness fell, they picked up their dead and left. Jai had fulfilled his promise a few times over by killing more attackers than *they could count on the fingers of both hands.*

Jurnail lay dead, sitting against the wall with numerous gunshot wounds and a dagger pierced through his chest. Haji Khan stared at Jurnail's dead body and then pulled his revolver and pointed at his head. Then he noticed, Jurnail's right hand still was holding the .303 with a bayonet. For a moment, he was scared, and then he smiled and fired the shot.

\*\*\*

When Bazam reached Dil Mahal around midnight, the crowd had already dispersed. The tribesmen had mostly left with their dead and their loot. Zahir was still there, sitting outside in the street.

"They are all dead," he announced to Bazam. "They fought bravely. There were dead bodies all around. They killed so many tribesmen."

"I couldn't do anything to save them. I am old and…." Zahir started crying. "What good is this Pakistan? So much hate…."

From the burnt gate, Bazam entered the front yard. The moonlight was enough for him to recognize Jai's dead body on the floor. Not too far from the kitchen was Jurnail with a knife in his chest, his body sitting against the wall.

Bazam's breathing became heavy. He felt suffocated and ran out and drove towards Preet House. When Bazam arrived at Preet House, sensing bad news, Daler came out to talk to him.

"I came from Dil Mahal. I have terrible news. It is all over. No one at Dil Mahal survived."

"No one?" Daler asked as Joga, who was listening, also came outside.

"No. I saw Lala Jaan, baba Jurnail, and two others. They were down on the floor. They died fighting."

Daler was frozen for some time when Joga shook him, "Son, come inside."

Daler composed himself as he wiped a tear rolling down into his beard, "Bazam, can you go drop everyone here at the railway station?"

"Anything Daler Bhai," Bazam said as he felt terrible for the situation. Then in an attempt to console them a little, he added, "Lala-ji took out Ali."

"Should have done it a long time back. We have this problem in our community of tolerating these types of people too long," Joga removed his turban and scratched his mostly bald head. Then, he leaned against the entrance door and sobbed for a moment before walking inside as he wiped his face.

"Go back there, Bazam. Stay with Rustam at Dil Mahal. I will join you shortly," Daler said. Then he walked inside, sat on a chair, and burst into tears.

"Get up, son. Get up. This pain will be there till we live," Joga said.

"Balwant-ji, we need to leave for Amritsar now. There is nothing left for us in this wretched land," Joga stood in the door as if ready to leave.

"Where are the boys? I won't go anywhere without Jurnail and the boys," Balwant said.

"They are martyrs. The warriors who did not run away. Like us," Joga said as he cried and consoled Balwant, who looked confused.

"What happened? Tell me," Balwant started shaking Joga.

"They died fighting in the attack on Dil Mahal," Joga said as he wiped tears from his face. "Daler, son, let's go. Get the car. Let's all go. Move. Move, everyone. Unless you want to get slaughtered. We won't be able to fight like them."

"Tell me what happened," Balwant followed Joga restlessly into the car.

"Bazam, drop them off at the railway station and then go back to Dil Mahal. I will join you there shortly," Daler said.

Bazam sped the car towards the station.

\*\*\*

Rustam walked all the way to Dil Mahal and entered from an opening in the back wall. Zahir was still there. There were few people scavenging.

Rustam pulled out the revolver and yelled, "Get out. Get out."

The place was ransacked, and the mortar shells had razed the drawing-room. Kalyan Dil's portrait was on the floor. Rustam picked it up, wiped the dust from Kalyan's face, and leaned it against the wall. Lakhbir and Satwant were on the veranda face down on the floor. Rustam turned them face up and leaned them against the wall. They were both cold and soaked in their blood.

Jai was in the front yard with wounds all over his face and body, likely from a mortar shell and bullets. Jurnail was in a sitting posture against the kitchen wall. With a dagger in his chest and a gunshot wound to the head, he was still holding a .303 in his hand.

Rustam removed his cap and cried as he sat on the floor in front of Jurnail. Then he got up as he heard the footsteps.

"Rustam?" Bazam had just arrived from the railway station.

"Yes. Who is there?"

"This is Bazam," Bazam walked and saw Rustam was crying. At a loss on what to say, he looked around. Then said, "They were very good people. It is sad and shameful what is happening."

Rustam stared around helplessly wondering how he could help. Then he gave up the thought.

"Did you bring the car? We need to go to the river to pick up Hari."

Bazam looked around at the bodies. "We can't leave them here like that. We must do something."

"Daler-Bhai Jaan will be here soon. He will take care of it," Rustam said, and then he walked out, "Let us go, Bazam. We need to take Hari to safety. There is a refugee camp across the bridge."

# Chapter 9
# [1947] Strangers in the Story

It was September 13, 1947. A little boy peeped through the broken window of the third floor of a burnt house. He had been looking at the drowning sun to the west. His mother had told him to hide until dark. The narrow lanes connecting Qissa Khwani Bazaar were already consumed by darkness. The boy could still see the smoke coming out of burnt houses, disappearing into the darkening sky.

He remembered what his mother had told him as the mob organized by the Muslim League had broken into their house: "Hide, son. Run upstairs. Escape through the window to the roof of Afzal's house, stay there till dark, and then run away wherever your soul takes you. Lord will guide you." Then she had doused herself and his sister with kerosene and burnt themselves to death — a common way for Hindu and Sikh women to save themselves from rape and forced conversion to Islam. He did not hear any screams among the deafening shouts of the crowd. It lasted a few minutes. Then it was all over. The boy's father was nowhere to be found. *They must have killed him as well*, the boy thought as he hid there waiting for darkness.

Earlier in the day, mobs of rioters and tribesmen, provoked by mullahs, had attacked Hindu and Sikh houses and shops in the city. In Qissa Khwani Bazaar, smoke was still coming out of the shops that were set on fire during the second day of continuous rioting. From the window of the second floor, the boy had crossed over to the other haveli and hidden on the top floor of a dilapidated old house.

Although the bazaar had already been cleared of most corpses, some stayed there on the roadside for a second day. The bodies of rich, educated, and well-established people who would only ride the finest horses and cars were collected and piled together on the bullock carts with the not-so-rich and illiterates. Dead people don't mind company. Neither caste, religion, status, nor political views matter; there are no disagreements among the dead.

There was the smell of death in the air, but there was no wailing, only celebratory laughs, and smiles of a few men standing at the entrance to Shah Wali Qataal. They had just killed a Sikh family. There were men pillaging inside the house, loot was still getting moved, and the dead were still dying. The blood of the victims was still fresh, and their wounds were still open. Two young women were sitting in a corner shivering with fear, staring at their dead guardians. They had screamed enough; now it was futile. They were now owned by the perpetrators.

A young Pashtun boy hastily walked past these men. He knew the victims well but hid his face in case the women called to him for help. He quietly walked towards Jahengirpura Road. He had a stack of naan bread that Rustam had given him as part of his disguise under his arm.

His face was red with emotions; anger and sadness had mostly swallowed his soul. He shivered as if cold, though his brisk walk had warmed his body, and he felt feverish. A few tears rolled down his right cheek, but he quickly wiped them off. His eyes were fixed a few feet ahead on the ground as if he was looking for something he had lost in the street. He kept his eyes down so as not to face anyone. Leaving the chit-chat of a group of armed men behind him, he kept walking towards Dil Mahal. He knew if these men found out that he was a Hindu, they would kill him. For a moment, he wanted to scream at them. *What could death take away that I have not already lost?*

Earlier, Rustam had begged him not to go to Dil Mahal, but he had insisted. He had to go. "How can I leave my mother behind? I would rather die," he had told Rustam. The situation was unbearable for him. "I have to see Papa." He could not believe his father, the head of a powerful clan, was dead. Hari, the prince of the clan, as Jurnail called him, had lost everything. Rustam knew the misery he was going through and had to help him. Rustam had dressed him as Pashtun in an attempt to protect him. He would not have looked any different, even without the disguise, but Rustam insisted with tears that he hide his identity as much as possible. "Please go from the backside. No one should see you there at this time. The back wall is broken. Enter from there."

Hari kept walking in the back streets. He knew the people who lived in every house on each side of the street. "How could they?" he had asked Rustam, who turned away and could not answer. Hari could not understand how it all happened. *We treated them so well, always helped them. They called Papa their chacha.* His body shook, his heart pounded, and his walk became faster and faster.

He tried not to look at the dead man lying at the doorstep of a familiar house, a Sikh man whom he had seen many times in the bazaar. His arms had been cut off. He wanted to stop, but then what was the use? No one came to help these men, women, and children. Not the British; they had no reason. Not the politicians; they did not care; they got their part of the land to rule. Not Gandhi. He was fasting to protect Muslims in India. But no one was fasting for Hindus and

Sikhs. Jinnah seemed to have achieved his goal of ethnic cleansing. There was no message of peace and protection for Hindus and Sikhs from him. And now it was too late. The hate had broken all the bonds that had tied these men who had lived together for centuries.

As he neared the haveli, he saw that Dil Mahal's big strong wooden gate was burnt but still standing. He wanted to run to the gate, but then he remembered that Rustam had asked that he sneak through the back wall. *Sneak into my own house.* He turned into the back street.

Zahir was sitting in the corner, shivering. "They fought bravely. I watched it all. The whole street was full of bodies. They killed so many. You should be proud, boy," he said in his old trembling voice. Hari didn't say anything. "Leave soon. They will come again," Zahir shouted. Hari could see the broken back wall. The street was dark and calm. In the dim light, he saw a dead body lying near the broken wall. He looked closely. It was Chaman Talwar, the family friend and advocate who'd lived two blocks away.

Hari went in through the broken wall. It was dark inside. He found his way to the temple room upstairs, where they always had matchsticks, lamps, and candles. He lit the matchstick. The temple was vandalized. Everything upstairs was ransacked; almost everything had been taken away. The family safe was open and empty. As he came downstairs with a lamp, he noticed his father's shoes and legs, and then his face, as he moved into the drawing-room with the lamp. Jai's clothes were soaked in blood. Hari closed his father's eyes, held his hand, and cried a little. *Someone, just kill me as well.* Then he remembered what Baba-ji had said: *Never give up. Never.* He picked himself up and inspected the dark rooms. Close to Jai was his uncle, Satwant.

Hari walked towards the well on the veranda. His eyes were fixed on the well. *Oh, Mother, I know you died long ago, but I always feel you here.* Tears flowed down his cheeks. He dropped the bucket in the well and pulled up some water. He sprinkled water on his father's face. "Be in peace. You are with her now." Tears dropped from his eyes.

As he turned back, he was startled, and the lamp dropped from his hand. A little boy ran up and pulled his arm. "They killed everyone," the boy whimpered. "We need to hurry up and run away."

"Kishan? What are you doing here?"

"They are all dead. You must run away. Save yourself."

"Yes, I will. Just let me see my family. Please stop," Hari said as the boy ran away into the darkness.

Farther in the yard, he found his cousin Lakhbir. On the floor, he found some money, which apparently had fallen from the loot. *There was lots of money and gold in the house, but apparently, they took it away after killing everyone.*

He pulled his uncles' and baba Jurnail's bodies close to his father and lay them together. He heard someone walking behind him. He cocked the revolver as he hid behind the kitchen wall. It was Rustam. He had followed him after waiting. On seeing him, Hari came out and continued pulling the bodies together. "Help me," he said to Rustam.

"Who was that boy that ran out?" Rustam asked as he helped move the bodies.

"Kishan. He is the son of Uncle Chaman. We should take him with us. He is a little boy and will die out there."

"He ran away. We can't find him now. Let's go."

"We are no good if we don't help him."

"He may be okay. Sometimes they don't kill people that young if they are alone."

Hari looked around, confused, and then sat down on the floor in front of his father. "I can't leave them like this. I can't," he burst into tears.

Rustam pulled him up by his arm. "I promise you; I will cremate them. Please, let's go. It is not safe here. When I was here a few hours back, Chaman-Bhai Jaan's body was not there. They must have killed him recently."

"Promise me you will cremate them," Hari said as he wiped his tears.

"I promise. Let us go now. Pick that money up and put it in your pocket. It may help."

Hari hesitantly picked up the money from the floor.

They briskly walked out of the haveli. Hari listened as Rustam told him about the plan for his escape. "Bazam and I will drop you off past the bridge by Nowshera. Army people told me the Gorkha army is helping with evacuating Hindus and Sikhs. After that, I can't do much. They should be able to help you."

Hari stopped in the middle of the street. "I will go to Preet House before we leave."

"Are you crazy? There has been rioting all day there. You have seen the situation." Hari stepped back. "Balwant and Joga baba — I've got to see them. They may be alive." Rustam tried to touch his arm as he stepped back further. "Where will you find them? The mob will kill you. We must go. You are the only one left in your family. Save yourself."

Hari started walking as he mumbled, "I did not see Uncle Mehar, Uncle Daler…. All in the house are dead. Everyone is dead." He was shaking.

"I am sorry, Hari. That is what it looks like," he said as they walked briskly towards Kabli Gate, where Bazam was waiting in the car for them.

"It was only yesterday that they all were together. How can so much change so quickly?"

Rustam opened the door to put Hari in the back seat. Hari was in shock. To him, it all looked surreal, like a nightmare that soon would be over, and then everyone would be fine, and the clan would be back together. As the car drove on Peshawar's streets, Hari could still see burning houses and shops. There were still rioting mobs. He felt sick. His trembling continued; the shock of what had happened had given him a fever. His eyes had sunk in. He was having a hard time connecting with reality. He continued with mumbling and then cried loudly. Rustam could hear him crying but was unable to help.

The streets of Peshawar felt very strange to Hari. He suddenly said, "Is it real?"

"What, Hari?" Rustam asked.

"That they are all dead? Papa, Baba-ji, Uncle Mehar?"

"You were there at Dil Mahal."

"This is not true. It is just a story? Why am I in this strange place?"

"He seems to be in shock," Bazam said.

"Where are all the familiar faces? Are they all dead? Where are my friends and classmates? *The place I lived in…I have to go back to my place.*" Then he screamed, "Rustam, take me back to my home, to my family."

Bazam kept driving.

\*\*\*

After dropping off his father, Joga, baba Balwant, and his family on the train to Amritsar, Daler drove towards Dil Mahal. It was late at night. Most rioters were already tired. The fires were done burning, and the dead were done dying. The world of so many Hindu Sikhs in Khyber was already destroyed. Daler parked the car across from Mohalla Shah Wali Qattal and walked to the burnt gate of Dil Mahal.

There, he stood looking at Dil Mahal in shock. He sat down at the gate and cried for a moment. Then, as he wiped his face with his turban cloth, he was startled by a boy who appeared in the darkness. As Daler pulled out his gun, he recognized the boy.

"Uncle Daler."

"Kishan? What are you doing here so late?"

"They killed my family."

"Oh, my god, you come with me. You will be fine."

"You have to go in from the back. They broke the wall." Kishan walked ahead.

The boy led Daler to the back of Dil Mahal. Daler walked around the bodies with tears dropping as he gasped, and then he started piling all the furniture, clothes, and anything flammable he could find. He took the cooking ghee in the kitchen; "This should work to start fires," he whispered.

"Are you going to burn them?" Kishan sat there and watched Daler.

"Yes, Kishan. I am going to cremate them here."

"Can you cremate my papa? He is outside. He was trying to escape here when they attacked our house."

"Let's get your father. Then we start the fire. We have to leave before people notice us. Okay?"

After making sure there was enough combustible material, Daler started the cremation of the dead. He chanted a few mantras. As the fire peaked, he ran with Kishan to the car and sped away.

Bazam and Rustam reached the bridge with Hari. Bazam slowed down as they approached the barricades set up by soldiers of the Gorkha regiment. Rustam came out and opened the back door as two soldiers inspected the car. "Sir, he is a Hindu boy. His uncle is a big officer in the British army. Royal family, sir. Please take care of the boy. He is in shock. Everyone was killed, sir. Everyone," Bazam said in broken English.

Soldiers asked the boy to come out of the car. Hari got out and onto the street. Disoriented, he fell on the road. Rustam helped him get up, "Be strong, boy. We have to go back now." Then he returned to the car, and they left.

Hari sat on the roadside, unable to believe what had happened when a short Gorkha officer approached him. "Boy, what is your name?"

As Hari, dazed, looked at him, the officer repeated the question.

"My name is Hari. They killed all my family."

"Are you hurt?" the officer asked Hari, looking at the blood on his clothes.

"No, this is my father's blood on my arm, or my uncle's here. It is all mixed, my family. I am..." He then started crying.

"You have to be brave. Here, you are safe, and if you die, you won't die in vain. I promise you. You are now in my protection." The army officer helped him into a tent. "I am Captain Bhag Singh." The captain pulled Hari by the arm to stand him up. "Sepoy Suba Singh," he directed one of the soldiers, "take the boy, help him wash up, and give him something to eat." Then he turned to the boy. "Boy, you rest now. Gain some strength. Things are not going to be easy from here."

Hari was put in a tent with a few Hindu and Sikh families. As the days passed, he got sicker. In his fever-state, he talked to his father and mother, his cousins, and his friends as he shifted between consciousness and unconsciousness. But mostly, he talked to his mother, asking over and over why there were so many strangers in this story.

Everyone in that camp knew about him. The Gorkha officer took a special interest in the boy. Soldiers in the platoon talked about him, and among them, there was general agreement that the boy would not survive more than a few days.

The next day, the platoon got surrounded by the Baloch regiment of the newly formed Pakistan army. The Gorkha captain was asked to surrender his arms and told that if he complied, he would get guaranteed safe passage for everyone. The captain refused. "I received my arsenal from the Government of India, and that is where I will surrender it." The captain was adamant. He knew well that if he gave up his arms, everyone would be slaughtered without mercy and without regard to any commitment. "None of their promises can be trusted." The captain told his soldiers, "We would leave fully armed."

Days of negotiations to ask him to disarm followed.

Captain Bhag Singh was a tough man. After seeing the butchery of Hindus and Sikhs, he had become very protective of the refugees in his care. Considering his position on the high ground and his control of the bridge on Kabul River, the captain had more weight in negotiations. An agreement was reached, and the Gorkha platoon was allowed to leave with their weapons. The Government of India gave him a train with twenty-five bogies and directions to pick up every refugee he could en route to Amritsar. Captain Bhag Singh positioned heavy machine guns on the first and last carriage of the train. In the middle, he requested boxed bogies where he boarded every civilian under his protection.

As they got ready to leave, his juniors asked him if the boy, along with seven other sick refugees, should be left behind as they were unlikely to survive the journey. The captain replied angrily, "We have enough space for the living and the dead." And the train of two hundred or more soldiers of the Indian army left with more than a thousand or so refugees for Amritsar.

As part of the agreement, before every civilian boarded the train, they were frisked and only allowed what belonged to them. Other than the soldier's weapons, every useful bit was stolen from the refugees. The money, the jewelry, the weapons of civilians were all taken away. Hari was helped by soldiers into the compartment. Before he could board, he had to part with his fifty-three rupees and change. They also took away his revolver.

As the train moved from Peshawar to Rawalpindi, picking up loads of refugees on the way, the Gurkha officer frequently asked about the boy's condition. Sick, injured, smelly, hungry humans were stuffed into compartments as the train stopped at stations en route. Many had gone crazy with what they had seen; their families murdered, their women raped and taken away.

The officer told his soldiers to do as much as they could to take as many refugees as possible. "It is all surreal to me. Worse than I have seen in any war. The hopelessness of this situation is beyond my belief," the captain told his young lieutenant.

"How is the boy?" he asked.

"Unconscious, sir. Sometimes he talks. He keeps asking who the strangers in the story are."

"He is asking a valid question. Strangers are killing people, strangers are saving people, strangers get together on the trains and caravans and are migrating to strange lands together... aren't they?" Captain said.

The train had no space left on top or inside, but the officer kept picking up the refugees. When soldiers requested that the train not be stopped, as there was no space at all, even for moving your arm, the captain replied, "What train will they board? Is there a train coming this way behind us? They will die here if we don't pick them up. Don't expect Gandhi to come here and save them."

As the train reached Rawalpindi, it was attacked from both sides of the track by gunfire. A slow-moving train was an easy target. Heavy gunfire erupted, with soldiers returning fire. For rioters, there was no need to aim. They just shot at the train and would hit someone. Close to a hundred refugees died in that attack.

Once the gunfire ceased, the train stopped. "Sir, can we drop the bodies here?" the soldier asked.

"Separate a carriage. Move all the injured there. We will keep the injured. Remember what I said. Move the dead only. Check for a single sign of life. Can someone check the boy for me?"

The dead bodies were taken from screaming relatives and thrown on the side of tracks. There was no time for bereaving or honoring the dead. Under the pile of dead bodies, a soldier located the boy. "Sir, I have found the boy. He is hit, sir. He is all soaked in blood."

The Gorkha officer rushed to the compartment with a soldier. He ordered the boy to be pulled out of the compartment. Blood dripping from his hair and face, his clothes soaked, he was laid on the ground.

"He is breathing. He is breathing. Get the bucket of water," the captain yelled. His concern for the boy surprised the soldiers. There was pain and anxiety in his voice they had not heard before. "Remove his clothes. All clothes. Wash him." One soldier removed his clothes as the other poured water on the boy.

"Are you good? Are you hit?" The Gorkha kneeled to check on the boy.

There was no response from Hari.

"Sir, he is not hit," a soldier replied as he inspected the boy's hair and head.

"Wash him, give him some clothes, and ask someone for some spare clothes. And put him in one of the soldier's compartments. Give him something to drink and eat," he said, then stopped to think. "Put him in my cabin. Give him part of my ration."

273

The train continued to India, picking up refugees and leaving the dead behind. The boy kept asking about strangers in the story. The captain told the soldiers to check on the boy at every station. "I don't know what will happen to him later, but I would like to deliver him alive in Amritsar." The train continued along the tracks, warding off attacks day and night.

The boy fell asleep after the Gorkha officer gave him some brandy.

Every now and then, gunfire would crack the silence of death. But the train kept moving. It was only a few hours away from Amritsar. The train stopped before the Lahore station. "Keep the dead where they are," the captain yelled to his soldiers, and then he came back inside his carriage. "I hope the dead feel their freedom," the captain said to himself as he looked at the boy who had just woken up from sleep.

"How are you feeling?"

The boy shook his head to indicate he was better.

"Soon, we will be at Amritsar station. I will hand you over to someone at the railway station. There will be lots of kids like you. So, they may have arrangements for kids without families. Remember that there is a purpose for you to be alive. I hope you find it."

Hari looked outside as the train approached Amritsar and saw dead bodies scattered around the tracks.

"Stop looking at the dead. Look at the living. Look to the future." The captain turned Hari's face away from the window and closed it.

# Chapter 10
# [1947] Orphans of Peshawar

In the refugee camps near Amritsar, a sea of people converged as refugee trains, and caravans continued to arrive. People had horrific stories to tell of things that had happened to them. Many had seen family and friends mercilessly butchered. Women were raped, their bodies dismembered. Children were murdered. Refugees searched for their missing wards in the camps. By 1948, about ten million people lived in refugee camps on both sides of the border in deplorable conditions, and people were dying of diseases.

In the corner of a camp in the border city of Amritsar, a few young boys stood in despair, hungry but calm. An old man from Peshawar's Qissa Khwani Bazaar met a sick young boy while searching for his son and his grandchildren. He recognized the boy from his association with his father. The old man started caring for the boy, who was still in shock. In a few days, as the boy gathered his senses, the old man asked, "You are Jai Dil's son, right?"

The boy nodded.

"What is your name?"

"Hari."

"What happened with your family?"

"They killed them." Then the boy gathered the energy to sit down. "My uncles and cousins may have survived."

"I will help you, and you help me. Together, we will look for our loved ones."

The old man's grief for his family became lighter by caring for the boy. Over the days, together, they made a small family of their own in the camp. Every day, they walked around the camp, seeing the misery that the partition had brought on people. "This is their doing. Gandhi and Nehru left nothing for peaceful people, gave half of India to Muslims, and took away another half from Hindus," the old man lamented as tears rolled from his eyes. "Then these people have the audacity to claim they have sacrificed. What have they sacrificed? Come here, Gandhi. We will show you the sacrifice. Here, look at these orphans. They are a sacrifice that you gave on the altar of your schemes." Then the old man walked behind a tent where a few boys were sitting on the ground. "Those are the orphans of Peshawar. Let's ask them if they know of any new arrivals."

The two boys walked over to Hari and started conversing in Hindko.

"My name is Madan, and he is Dayal."

"I am Hari."

"Where are you from?"

"Peshawar," Hari said.

"Where in Peshawar?"

"We had havelis in both Qissa Khwani and Sadar."

"Did they kill your parents?" Dayal asked.

"Yes. I am looking for anyone who could have survived. My cousins, Jigar and Raji, are a few years younger than me. My uncles, Mehar, Daler, and my elders...." Hari started sobbing.

"Almost everyone from Peshawar who had elders in the family has moved on to Delhi. Only orphans are left here."

Every day, the old man and Hari walked around camp looking for information on their relatives. As time passed and diseases started spreading in the camp, one day, the old man fell sick. "Son, you must leave this camp. If you stay here, you will die. Go and create a place for yourself in the world. Leave this camp."

"What about you?" Hari asked.

"My time is done. There is no point in you staying here to watch me die. You can get sick here." The old man could barely talk but continued, "Your father had strong business contacts in Amritsar. He used to visit a grain merchant named Darshan Singh. He lives somewhere around the Golden Temple. Go find him. He should help you."

Hari refused to leave the old man. Within a few days, the old man died. After his body was taken away, Hari left the camp looking for Darshan Singh. Asking grain merchants, it was easy to find his place. But it was difficult to get his attention. He was a rich man who had been actively helping refugees. His own house was full of refugees; many families from his relations who had escaped from Pakistan were staying with him. Hari waited outside his house for hours for him to arrive. Later in the evening, when Darshan Singh arrived, Hari had a brief conversation with him.

"So, you are Jai Dil's son?"

Hari nodded.

"You are saying Jai and others in your family died there?"

Hari again nodded. Darshan shook his head in disbelief, then, looking back at Hari, said, "What can I do for you?"

"I want to work," Hari said. "I can read, write, and speak in English."

"I know you can read and write. You are a Dil's child," Darshan said. Then after looking around for a moment, he said, "I will find you work. But that is just to get you started. Don't aim for something small in life. I am sure your father had high hopes."

Hari nodded his head.

Darshan gave him work in his warehouse, where Hari counted the inventory of bags of grain. He asked his assistants to help find a place for Hari to stay. They put Hari in a *dhaba* restaurant near Darshan's warehouse, where Hari stayed at night with an old man who owned the place. At the end of his work each day, Hari visited the camp to check if anyone in his clan had turned up. Each evening, he hung out with the orphans of Peshawar. Orphans were connected through their pain and desire to take revenge.

"You can stay here with us. We sleep here," Dev, one of the orphans, said, pointing to a small ragtag behind a tent.

"You can't stay here too long, though. You will die of the disease. I stay outside the camp," Hari said.

"You stay outside alone?" Madan asked.

"Yes. I have a place to sleep, in a dhaba. I help there. They give me food, and I get some money by working at a warehouse."

"We wait for food. It is more like begging for it. Sometimes, we get something. Other times, people come to give us some food. But mostly, we are starving here."

"I break coal at a *dhaba* restaurant to pay for sleeping there and count bags at the warehouse for some money. You guys should find work as well. This is not a good place to live."

"You stay alone? Don't you get scared? I get nightmares of them killing my parents," Dayal said.

"I didn't watch them kill my family. I don't get too many nightmares. Sometimes, I see nightmares of strangers surrounding me," Hari replied.

"Everyone is a stranger here. We are surrounded by strangers," Dayal said.

"It is different. I am looking for my family in my dreams in a sea of strangers. I wake up with deep anxiety. But it is ok. We have lost everything, so it is natural."

One of the few men who was listening to their conversation said, "There are a lot of Muslim villages here. They live peacefully, protected by Gandhi, while your lives are destroyed. Every evening, a group of men who have lost everything go and try to find something in these villages and distribute in the camps whatever they get. You all from Peshawar suffered a lot. If you know how to shoot, you can come with us. You can take a little bit to build your life."

"They are too young for this, Waheguru, what you have put us through," an older man standing near-by said.

The men in the group were not amused at the comment. One said, "These children have lost all, witnessed the murders of their families and friends, lost their homes and everything, and these people come here and tell them not to fight back. They have nothing more to offer them except an empty Gandhian philosophy that only protects Muslims."

"Do you know how to shoot?" the man asked Hari.

"I can shoot a flying sparrow," Hari whispered.

"Did you see your parents getting killed?" the man asked Dev.

"They beheaded my father in front of me, and then they dragged my mother as she screamed, "Run, Dev, run. For God's sake, run.

"And I ran towards her, and this man lunged at me with a sword, and my mother pulled him back by his arm. His sword hit me hear. See," he said, showing a long cut on his forehead. "And then she screamed at me to go find my grandma.

"As I ran away to look for her, I heard my mother scream. I ran back to the house, and there she was with her head cut off. I found my grandma dead on the street outside. Then I heard a Muslim man I called Chacha say, 'Run, or they will kill you.' I ran to the railway station."

Madan told how his sisters were raped and taken away after his father and mother were murdered and how he ran away.

At dusk, young men gathered in the camp. A Muslim village was selected for attack. About forty young men with rifles headed towards the village on horses and on foot. Among them was Hari, who, after a lot of soul searching, had convinced himself that if villagers have butchered their Hindu neighbors, they should be prosecuted. These orphans from Peshawar, having seen their houses burnt down, families murdered, and women raped, were full of hate and bitterness. More than looting, they were in it for revenge.

Gunfire rocked the village before dawn. As Muslim men fled, they were shot. Young Hari was in a group led by a man named Himmat Singh. He asked Hari to search a nearby shed for anyone hiding there. Hari opened the shed door with his gun drawn. He had a feeling there was someone inside. The shed was full of grain and hay. Behind the stacks of hay, he could tell there was someone hiding. With his gun cocked, he walked towards the sacks.

"Bhai Jaan, please." A young Muslim girl stood up, shivering.

Hari stood there, frozen, looking at the terrified face of the girl. She was of the same age as his cousin Raji.

"Hide," he whispered as the surprised girl looked around. "Hide," he said louder.

She sneaked further behind the sacks. He walked out of the shed.

"Anyone inside," asked Himmat.

"No one," Hari replied.

"What is inside?"

"Hay. Only hay."

"Okay, check that house."

"I am leaving. I can't do this," he told the man.

"What? Say it louder," the man on the horse yelled.

"I want to return to the camp."

"Don't you remember how they killed your family," the rider yelled.

"Yes, but I am not ready to live with the guilt of killing innocents. It is about me. All I have learned and read in life is to fight injustice."

"You are a coward," He pointed the gun at Hari.

"I will shoot anyone who is wrong, guilty, or in battle, but I won't hurt innocent people." Hari looked at the man who was still aiming the gun at him. "You don't have to agree with me. You do what you choose. I choose my path." Hari looked into the eyes of the rider.

"Let him go," an older Sikh man shouted. "The same useless philosophy is in his head that has gotten us to this point. This philosophy is fine for any community but not for Muslims. They will slit your throat at the first opportunity," the old man told Hari.

"I hope they showed mercy to your family," Himmat said.

"My family didn't need mercy. They died fighting," Hari said.

"Leave before I shoot you," Himmat said.

"Listen, boy! Only the very brave and wise have the courage to stand apart from the crowd. I respect your upbringing. But to rise beyond the fear of right and wrong and do what is needed requires more courage than standing apart alone. It requires leadership. While you walk away today, I suggest you think about it," the old man said as he trotted into the raging village.

Amid the sound of intermittent gunfire, Hari walked away from the village with a gun on his shoulder, consumed by the thought of his little cousin, Raji. *I hope someone showed her mercy. I hope God showed her mercy.* He looked back at the village, wondering about the fate of the children in his clan.

\*\*\*

Hari wanted to go away from the ever-growing crowds of refugees. Their miserable situation made him sad and hopeless. The anger and bitterness in their hearts, which he completely shared, provoked him to be part of the crowd. "I am not the crowd. I am Hari," he murmured at night.

"What is bothering you?" the old restaurant owner asked him.

"Someone at the camp told me I have a relative in Jalandhar. I want to go there," he lied so as not to offend the people helping him.

"You are in a better situation here. Don't put yourself at risk. Are you sure there is someone there who can take care of you?" the old man asked.

"I have to try," Hari said.

That night, Hari could not sleep. In the morning, he packed his few belongings, a bedsheet, and a mat that he had bought with the money he had earned, thanked the old man, and left Amritsar for Jalandhar, a town away from the border that had fewer refugees.

When he got down to the Jalandhar railway station, he was approached by a Sikh couple looking for labor for their foundry. Scores of refugees were arriving without any livelihood after losing their homes and valuables. They needed work. The couple wanted to find some young, healthy men to work in their foundry. Hari had no idea about the foundry's working conditions. When the couple approached him, they were nice to him. They first offered him food and a place to stay. They also told him he had a choice to work in their foundry or find other work and that they only meant to help him.

The day after arriving in Jalandhar, Hari started working in the foundry, pouring molten iron into casts. The working conditions were terrible. The high temperatures made it very difficult to work. His body hair started disappearing. He covered his head, but his eyebrows were starting to thin. The money from work helped him pay for new clothes and shoes that he badly needed. He rented a small space to sleep. Three months passed, and Hari's skin showed considerable heat damage. An older Sikh man named Jivan Singh tried to help him. When Hari was exhausted, Jivan gave him water to drink. And told him to take breaks as he covered for him. Jivan had migrated from the city of Lahore. He had lost most of his family, including the eldest son and brothers in the riots, but his two younger sons and wife had made it out alive. He was very religious and prayed most of the time. He happily shared his food with Hari and insisted Hari take it.

"*Sardar*-ji, you work so hard here, and then you share your food with me. I would like to pay you for food, and then you can bring me food all working days."

"No. then it will not be sharing. It will be selling," Jivan Singh smiled. "Does that old lady outside in the street that you so often give food pays you back?"

"But I am not old and helpless like her," Hari smiled.

Hari realized that Jivan was an upper-caste Sikh, and he was nice to him and only ate with him. Hari thought highly of him, and they usually discussed all kinds of topics. One day, Hari decided to ask him, "Why do you not eat with others here?"

"They have their own interests, and I have my own." Then after a pause, Jivan asked, "Why don't you eat with them?"

"I don't think they like me," Hari replied. "Besides, they are always together. I don't trust any groups anymore."

Except for Hari, all workers at the foundry were Sikhs and spoke the same dialect. Hari stood out both from his accent and appearance. Although they were not hostile, they by no means were friendly to Hari. Jivan's presence to Hari was both comforting and necessary.

"Many of them here, they think we hang out together because we are both from an upper caste," Hari said.

"Few times they came and asked me why I hang out with you. They complained that you go to *Arya Samaj*," Jivan said.

"I also go to Sikh Gurudwara," Hari said, "did they tell you that? They have seen me there."

"No. They rather have people like you not come to Gurudwara. I don't know who is feeding poison in their minds. If we are going to behave like Islamists, why come to India, just stay on the Pakistan side. That is where the majority of us lived anyway," Jivan said as his face became grim, "We came to this side because we were butchered there. Now here, we have started behaving the same as Islamists."

"Glad that you have no problem with me understanding other beliefs," Hari said. Then after a pause, he said, "I do read *Japji Sahib*."

"I only respect people who seek knowledge and truth. No amount of symbolism will help if we don't understand what our religious books say and then use our minds to accept and reject ideas. Unable to think for themselves, people blindly follow whatever their religious leaders and books say," Jivan said as he finished eating.

"I like that you gather knowledge and make your choices using your own mind. I like that you have the courage to stand apart," Jiva said as he looked at Hari.

"I don't believe anything is God's word. All ideas get outdated. Even the ones that seem reasonable today may get outdated in the future," Hari said.

"India was a country of debates and discourses. About influencing each other by the strength of the argument. Our land created scores of belief systems and philosophies. But now, no more, because we have to follow a book or pretend to follow it. If you disagree, stay quiet, else the believers will come after your neck," Jivan said.

Jivan wrapped up his leftover food in his kitchen towel. "You know why do I like to have my lunch with you? When I saw you the first time and learned that you are a partition orphan, I felt like protecting you. So, I kept a watch on you. I saw you reading scriptures in your free time. I found that you are kind and truthful. Kindness is the basis of dharma. Seeking truth is the basis of dharma. You seek knowledge. Talking to you makes me happy."

Despite their age difference, Hari and Jivan became good friends. Jivan invited Hari to live with his family, but Hari politely declined. Though, he frequently visited Jivan's family. Over time, Hari learned that Jivan was a follower of some sect of Sikhism, and he was a former member of a militant organization against British rule.

\*\*\*

On the morning of January 31, when Hari was getting ready for work at the foundry, he learned that Gandhi had been assassinated. The foundry was closed that day. Jivan Singh asked Hari to join him for lunch at his home. There, his family seemed in an unusually good mood.

"You look sad. You really liked Gandhi?" Jivan asked Hari.

"Not really. I just wanted to ask him why he didn't do *satyagraha* against the decision to partition India?" Hari said.

"Are you kidding?" Jivan looked at Hari's face with a smile.

"No. I really wanted to ask him how he let all this happen. Why didn't he visit Pakistan, where Hindus and Sikhs were butchered? Why didn't he try to save them and their temples?"

"Gandhi was a man with selective non-violence and selective silence. Millions of Sikhs and Hindus suffered terribly in partition violence. He had no care for whether they lived or died. Only for Muslims and Mosques did he stand up with a strong voice for non-violence. He didn't care when Indian men and women died through British atrocities. Only when we fought against the British did he have the problem," Jivan said as the smile on his face disappeared.

"Sorry that you didn't get to meet him. I despise that man. In the middle of an attack from Pakistan on Kashmir, while Pashtun tribesmen were raping our women and butchering Hindus and Sikhs in Kashmir, this mahatma forced the government of India, headed by his own favorite, Nehru, to release the money to Pakistan. We funded the enemy because Gandhi forced us. Maybe they could kill more of us and rape more of our women. Believe me, this is treason of the highest order. Jinnah would have been better for India than this mahatma. Instead of mahatma, he should be called the God of Deceit and Chaos." Jivan's face turned red with anger. "Mark my word, these Muslims that he is protecting to keep here are going to come after our throats. They can't help it. Jinnah's ancestors were Hindus who converted to Islam. These converts are faster than originals."

"We lived with some loyal Muslim friends back home," Hari said as he hesitantly looked into Jivan's eyes.

"Then how come you are an orphan? Why didn't those loyal friends help? When you pay for loyalties, they don't last. Your servants and fair-weather friends will soon come after your neck when they find the opportunity."

"Hate is hurtful. I choose to live with hope," Hari said with an expression of pain on his face.

"Lots of people with unrealistic hope died and lost half of their country. If hate helps me destroy evil and save my world, so be it," Jivan said as he turned restless. "Look, boy, I didn't invite you to discuss this. I see you working at a foundry under these terrible conditions, and my heart breaks. I will not let my son work there. I thought I would give you a suggestion. I know you need this work. Do you want to hear it?"

"Yes, Sardar-ji."

"You should not work in these conditions. It will damage your health. My health is getting ruined here. But you are a kid. The owners should know better. You can work here till you find a better job, but don't work here too long." Then after a pause, he said, "Don't tell the owner because I will lose my job. I have a family to feed."

"You sound like a person with an education. Why do you work here?" Hari asked.

"I need this job to feed my family. They burnt my shop and killed my boy and brothers in Lahore. We escaped with no material possessions. My two boys are also looking for work. But for the time being, I need to work," he said, then looked away, apparently to compose his emotions. "I'm not sure what educated means to you. I am a Sikh. I should always seek the truth, not just follow what is written in books.

"I went to school till eighth grade. Then I decided I didn't want to learn what the system was teaching me. Once I learned to read and write, I educated myself on a lot of things. Someone once told me that you become the books you read. I don't want to be 'taught' fake history, biased theories, and a system that glorifies the same people that exploited and traumatized us. I left school for that reason."

"But now we are free. I am totally free. No family. No material possessions. Not much food to eat," Hari said and laughed.

"Now we are free from British. We will be taught what Congress wants us to learn. Freedom is not just of the body. We also need to have freedom of thought and mind. An enslaved body can be freed, but an enslaved mind is very difficult to free. These so-called intellectuals went to these British schools, and they came out brainwashed. They are no different than fanatic followers of religion who can't think freely."

"I have found more smart and helpful people among the uneducated. I really appreciate your advice."

"I take offense to you calling me uneducated."

"I meant formal education." Hari smiled.

"The most useless and selfish found in this world are among so-called educated intellectuals. They don't do any good to anyone. They create chaos like partition, large-scale agitations, raise one issue after another, unable to think for themselves, they can be recruited into all kinds of things and ideas. And at best, they get a job and selfishly pay for their needs and pleasures. It is better than begging and stealing, but no more than that."

"So maybe I should drop the idea of night school." Hari smiled.

"Should you? Will you follow what I say without even understanding it? Go to school and learn a skill. But if you are going there to learn history, philosophy, or religion, keep in mind that your teachers and books will have biases. Many teachers not only have biases but also an agenda — a political or social agenda. Be careful because they will steer you on paths where you will become a slave of the ideology they follow. Sadly, many times, it is not even their ideology. It is something they were recruited into as a student by their teachers. You will forget free thinking. Then, you will raise children who will by birth be enrolled in some nonsense."

"Don't worry. I want to go to school to learn mechanical engineering, and even if I am in humanities, I will keep my free-thinking," Hari said, smiling.

"Find a better job first," Jivan said.

When Hari left Jivan's place that evening, he had decided he needed to find a better job. As he walked around the town, he saw a General Motors car dealership and thought of trying his luck there.

\*\*\*

The next day, he wore new shorts, shirt, and shoes and walked into the car dealership to seek work. He looked like a rich boy from a good family.

"I would like to meet the manager."

They pointed him to a white man who had come out of his office and was keenly noticing the arrival of a boy.

"Sir, I am an orphan of partition from Peshawar. I need work. I can speak English very well, sir."

"Come to my office."

Hari followed the white man into his office. The man asked him to sit down.

"What is your name?"

"My name is Hari. Most of my family was killed in Peshawar. I don't know of anyone who is alive."

"What work can you do here?"

"I can clean cars. I can start cars."

"Start cars?" The man laughed.

"My family owned two cars, sir. A Packard and a Cadillac."

"I see. I am sorry about your family." Then after a pause, the manager said, "I will give you work. When a customer arrives with their car for service, you open their car door, and you take the keys and bring them to the service clerk. Can you do that?"

"Can I also learn here, sir?"

"Sure, you can read all you want when you are not attending customers."

"Can I learn how to work on cars?" Hari asked.

"Yes. You can watch and learn. But I also need a little help from you, and for that, I will pay you extra," the manager continued. "See, my daughter has no company here. You know English well. It will be nice if you can join us on Sunday afternoons to give her company. You can tell her about your culture and family. Would you be willing to do that?"

"How much money will I get from my job?"

"Thirty rupees a month, and one rupee for every Sunday you visit my house for a few hours, and lunch is free on Sunday."

The manager waited for Hari's response. "Do you wish to join?" he asked.

Hari thought a little. The money was ten rupees less than at the foundry, but Hari saw his future as a car mechanic, so he gladly accepted it.

"Very well. My name is Paul McDermott. My wife's name is Mary. Our daughter is about your age. Her name is Nancy."

"How old did you say you are?"

"I am twelve, sir. Actually, I just turned thirteen."

The following day, when Hari told Jivan that he'd found a new job, Jivan became sad. "You wanted me to find a better job. Right?" Hari said.

"Yes. Don't get me wrong. Every morning, I looked forward to coming to this place just so that I could talk to you. You are an amazing boy. Kind, wise... I hope you will continue to come to see us once in a while."

"I will come to your place every week."

"Very well. Best wishes for your new job."

"I am lucky to find people like you, Sardar-ji."

"Wherever you go, you will continue to find people like me because of who you are."

\*\*\*

Hari worked there at the dealership for ten to twelve hours a day. When he had free time, he read car manuals and books. He watched mechanics repair cars and even asked them questions. When he was not at the dealership, Hari searched for anyone in his clan. He bought a radio to listen to announcements of missing relatives. He gave radio announcements for Mehar, Daler, Joga, and Baba Balwant but never received any information. Over weekends, he visited Jivan's place and shared a meal with his family.

On Sundays, he met the McDermott family. He realized that the McDermott's were different than the British families he knew from Rawalpindi. They were easy-going, fun, and informal. For a few weeks, Hari told Nancy stories of his family, about the city of Peshawar, and about his religion and culture. Then Nancy got bored, and Hari only visited every other week. And then the visits became invitation-only.

Once a month, Hari visited the Amritsar camp to check with anyone from Peshawar that could tell him about his clan. On one such visit, he was introduced to an orphan girl from Peshawar. He was told that she belonged to his clan. She did not resemble Raji, but when asked if her name was Raji, she said yes. She called him brother and told him the names of Joga and Daler. But Raji's father was Satwant, and she could not tell him his name. Hari adopted her as his sister anyway. Together, they were a little family.

Sometimes, Hari doubted she was really his responsibility, but then he wondered where she would go and who else she would trust. He was convinced she was not his cousin Raji, but he also knew she was related to some Dil clansmen. When Hari told Jivan, he encouraged him to take care of the girl.

"So, the girl is from Peshawar. She is related to someone in your family?" Jivan asked.

"Not necessarily to *my* family, but to someone in the clan. They could be a farmworker, militia…."

"Everyone in your family is dead. So, you are the leader of the clan. And you brought her home as your sister. Now she is your responsibility," Jivan said with a smile.

"I understand that. Just that I feel she is taking Raji's place. The last time I saw Raji was in 1941. She was seven. I don't remember well what she looked like. My family fought over my custody, partition happened, the situation had been hard, and you know people look different when they are seven and when they are fourteen."

"Well, don't worry too much. It is the right thing you are doing. Even if she is becoming your burden, she needs a place and protection," Jivan said. Then he remembered something that had been on his mind for some time, "Regarding your family elders. Did you complete their last rights?"

"No. I have not," Hari replied.

"Well. I think you should talk to some priest."

"We have a family purohit in Haridwar. I will visit him sometime in the near future," Hari said.

Hari enrolled Raji in school. During the time he worked at the dealership, the school was the safest place for her. Within six months, Hari had learned how to change engine oil and brake fluid. He had a really good idea about how to change brakes. Because of his extensive reading of books, he understood pistons and other parts of the engine better than anyone else. He knew what sounds pistons could make and why.

\*\*\*

After a few months, Hari decided to visit Haridwar to see priest Daya Shankar.

"I had a feeling you would come," Daya Shankar smiled as he saw him.

Hari touched his feet to pay respects, "I am here to do their last rights."

"I assume they died in partition riots."

"Yes. They died fighting," Hari said.

"That is understood. Jurnail and Jai and their brave clansmen...I knew they wouldn't come back alive unless they left before the partition. To fight injustice was part of their nature," Daya smiled as he nodded his head. Then he said, "They don't need their last rights done. They were very wise. Completely in peace with their mortality. But you need it, so we will do it for your peace of mind," Daya laughed.

After the ceremonies, Hari sat with Daya to note their deaths in the genealogy register.

"Tell me what you want to write here," Daya said.

"Write that On September 17, 1948, Hari Dil visited Haridwar to complete last ceremonies of his father Jai Dil, his uncle Baba Jurnail Singh Dil, and Baba Balwant Trehan who died fighting against oppression."

"Only Dils go in this register," Daya interrupted. "We can add Trehans in their register later."

Once entries were completed, Daya asked Hari if he intended to stay.

"No. I will head back. I have a little sister back in Jalandhar. A cousin."

"Anything you wish to ask me?" Daya said looking at Hari.

"Is anyone in the clan alive? Anyone came here before me?"

"No. I am afraid no one except you," Daya said as his expressions became grim. He looked at sadness on Hari's face and said, "Don't worry too much about those who are dead. They knew what they wanted. They had little desire to leave Khyber. Even your father's efforts to move east were just because of his responsibility to protect the clan as its leader. Personally, he wanted to stay there."

"So many people died. Innocent people, men, women, and children, in the most violent and brutal manner. Why did God not intervene? why he did not help us?" Hari asked.

Daya smiled with his eyes closed. Then he said, "I think God does nothing. God is consciousness. Ultimate and Supreme consciousness. But consciousness itself cannot do anything. God must incarnate to act in the material world. But one shouldn't wait for the incarnation to destroy evil. Your ancestor knew that very well. They acted listening to their Atman and fought bravely for generations. When it comes to evil, consider yourself an incarnation."

"Then why do we need God?" Hari asked with pain in his eyes.

"God is cosmic consciousness. It is there. You need it or not. It is not dependent on your respect or prayer. What are you trying to ask?"

"If God does not help, why so many people are praying for help?"

"Many people actually pray for help because of lack of consciousness. All humans, except the enlightened few, lack higher consciousness. That affects senses and perception. You experience fear, loss, sadness, greed, and many other emotions. When you don't know how to separate your actions from how you feel, your feelings run your life. You are afraid, you need assurance, and you look for God in some way."

Daya paused and looked at Hari, then said, "But then there are people who drive inspirations from incarnations of God, their life, values, and teachings. These incarnations are not the pie-in-the-sky type of God. They were real people, such as Rama, Krishna, Buddha, Jesus, and many more. I suggest you live a life full of inspiration, be an example to others."

After a pause, Daya said, "Your clan, whatever their beliefs were, lived as if they had Bhagavad Gita flowing in their blood. When I see you, I see your father and grandfather."

Hari sat there, looking down. Just a year back, he was there with his father. He remembered when Daya had initiated him as a warrior sitting in the same place. He felt broken, as if someone had taken away a big part of his soul.

"I know you are hurting. Read Bhagavad Gita. It will help," Daya said. "It does not take much time to read it. It is a short book."

Then after a long pause, Daya asked, "Did you kill any innocent Muslims?"

"No," Hari replied. He was a little surprised by the question.

"Did you kill any evil men?"

"No," Hari said.

"Never kill an innocent man. But also remember, if good men don't check on evil, this earth will be run by evil. Remember, it is our duty. That was the whole idea of the Dil clan. Your Baba Jurnail used to say - the idea is more important than people. The idea should live on, even if your people are gone."

Daya Shankar closed the register and tied it with thread and put it in his trunk.

"And all these people who were running around murdering innocents are just the tools. They are tools in the hands of those who are seeking power. These schemers…don't be fooled by their disguises. They pretend to be *mahatmas* and *pandits* but look carefully and see for what they are. They are the same breed as Jinnah," Daya said. Then he looked at the shadows and clock. "Well. If you are going to head back today. It is getting late. Come again when you have more free time and plan on staying here for a few days."

***

One year had passed like this. Hari asked Paul to give him mechanic work, but Paul declined, saying Hari was too young. Instead, Paul asked him to get certified from City and Guilds, a British distant-learning institute. So, Hari started preparing for exams. One evening, as Paul was ready to leave the office, as usual, Hari was waiting for him to leave when a customer arrived. A senior government official called Mr. Banerjee drove into the dealership. Mr. Banerjee complained of noise under the hood of his car and wanted it checked immediately so he could be on his way for his important meeting in Jammu the next day.

Paul told Mr. Banerjee that there were no mechanics available. When Paul stepped away, Hari offered to check the car if Mr. Banerjee could convince the manager to allow him to. Although surprised at the boy's request, Mr. Banerjee obliged.

When Paul returned, Hari asked him, "Can I check Mr. Banerjee's car, sir? I won't fix it. I will just check."

"No, Hari," Paul replied.

"Well, I see no harm in him checking the car," said Mr. Banerjee.

"Yes, sir. If you start the car, I would like to just listen to the sound under the hood," Hari said.

As Mr. Banerjee started the car, Hari carefully listened and then announced, "Sir, your piston rings are not aligned."

"That was quick." Mr. Banerjee laughed.

"Sir, it is the noise of pistons."

"So, how do we fix it?" Mr. Banerjee asked.

"They may need to be replaced. I can do a temporary fix that may allow you to drive for a few days."

"Are you so sure?" Paul asked.

"If I fix it, and the noise goes away, and the car runs smoothly, then we know the problem is fixed."

"Sounds like a plan to me," Mr. Banerjee replied.

Hari drove the car and parked it on the service jack, and the car was back in an hour.

"See, sir. No sound anymore."

"Wonderful. What is your age, boy?" Mr. Banerjee looked surprised at the boy's skills.

"Fourteen, sir."

"Amazing. So, how long can I drive before the car starts making noise again?"

"At least seven days, sir. It could be a few months as well. Just go easy on the speed."

"You deserve an award. Here is something from me, and your boss should give you an award as well," Mr. Banerjee said as he looked at Paul.

"Of course," Paul said and smiled.

So, Paul hired Hari as a mechanic for a salary of fifty rupees per month.

As time passed, Hari forgot to ask who this Raji was. *It does not matter anymore*, he thought.

But there were days when he wanted to know more about Raji and asked her questions that she didn't have the answers for.

"You really don't think I am your cousin?" she said one day.

"No, I am just trying to figure out what happened to the others."

Four years passed with Hari working at the dealership. Raji was sixteen and decided she would join the military nursing service. Hari was against it, but Raji insisted.

"The military is for men," Hari said.

"I will be a nurse."

"You will have no home. You will travel place to place," Hari objected.

"Yes, and I will love it," Raji argued.

"You are still too young to be out."

Raji was upset that Hari did not support her. She met a young military officer who told her that if she was an orphan, she would not require an adult's permission. So, with the help of the officer, Raji enrolled in the military nursing school without informing Hari. One day, when Hari returned from work, she had already left to join her school. She left him a letter, thanking him for his help, and asked that he not look for her.

After Raji left for her training, Hari visited Jivan, who told him it was good that Raji had left to chase her dreams.

"She did great. What would you want? She was sitting here as a burden to you."

"She was the only family I had."

"You can't have it both ways. You felt she was someone you should not be responsible for, and now you are upset she left."

"I did so much for her. I wish she had listened to me."

"Don't control people. Let them go."

After a few months, Hari found a good job in Bombay that paid him two hundred rupees a month working on heavy machinery. He decided to move there. Jivan and his family came to see him off at the railway station.

"Just seek the truth. Ask your heart, and it will tell you what the truth is to seek, and just go for it, like your sister, Raji."

"If she comes back to see you, take her address. Tell her I am happy she went after her dreams."

# Chapter 11
# [1951] Boy with Hazel Eyes

As a train full of workers from the under-construction dam approached the town, the sound of its whistle could be heard in the main bazaar. The train took workers from the Rampur colony to the site where one of the highest gravity dams in the world was being constructed. Thousands of workers toiled day and night to build this dam. There was no shortage of labor. Millions of people displaced after the partition had lost their homes and livelihood and needed work. When they returned from their shifts, they bought goods for their daily needs, and for business owners like Bakshi, that meant rush time.

The sound from the train's horn gave him enough notice to get ready. He had trained himself to pick out the sound of a train from thin air when it was a few miles or so away. He could tell where the train was by the horn. The first horn sound came before crossing the river bridge; the second, before crossing the main street; the third, before entering the railway station. By that time, he could hear the squeaking of the wheels on the track. After the train stopped, many workers came out with their empty *tiffin* boxes, which had been packed by their wives or mothers for their shift. As these men came out of the station, they lined up outside the two main grocery stores in the bazaar.

Bakshi and Sons was one of the two main grocery stores in town. The other was Madan Lal and Sons. Bakshi had the advantage during weekdays, as his shop was first from the railway station on the south side of the town. Madan Lal and Sons had the advantage during weekends, as their shop was on the northern end of the town where most of the workers lived. Bakshi was also known for quality food, in part because he loved good food and in part because he never stopped bragging about it. He looked at food as a blessing from God and would boast about the quality of his products to justify his higher prices. Madan Lal and Sons called his explanation of higher prices nonsense and told their customers there was no difference except the price.

On a hot summer day, tired and dirty from a hard day's work, the regular shift workers had just arrived. Store boys at Bakshi and Sons were filling the orders fast. The business was busy, with a long line of waiting customers. Bakshi's wife, Svitri, was helping direct the store boys to speed up the service while he collected the payments at the cash counter. A young man who looked more like a boy stood in line with his tiffin lunch box. The earring in his ear caught Bakshi's attention as he counted the money from a customer, causing him to lose count.

"Look at the boy with hazel eyes and an earring," he whispered to Svitri, who didn't respond.

"I knew someone of his age who looked like him in Peshawar," he continued.

After taking the payment, Bakshi made a receipt with the name of the customer and all the items that were bought. Bakshi usually asked about the name of the father of adult customers. He did this to know his customers personally and, in some cases, to differentiate customers with the same names. He liberally gave groceries on credit, and customers paid him on their payday. His eyes were on the boy, who, for some reason, had raised his curiosity.

It was the boy's turn. Svitri read his order: one kilo of almonds, one kilo of raisins, one kilo of cashews, one kilo of desi ghee, five kilos of Atta, one kilo of dal. As the order was packed, Bakshi read it back. This was done to correct any mistakes, and then he would calculate and announce the payment. If the customer forgot certain items and those were on his receipt, he would trust the customer and pack them again for free the next day.

"That will be two rupees and seventy-five paisa. Your name?"

"Hari Dil," the boy said.

Bakshi stopped writing the receipt and asked, "Come again, please?"

"Hari Dil."

"Where are you from, son?"

"I am originally from Peshawar," the boy said.

"One kilo of lentils, one kilo of rice...." Bakshi's wife read the next order.

"Hold on..." Bakshi looked up over the top of his glasses, "What is your father's name?"

"I pay cash. It is not credit."

"Just for our records, son."

"Jai Dil."

"Come on, there are so many customers. Can you pick up the conversation later?" Bakshi's wife yelled.

"How many times have I told you never to interrupt me when I am talking to a customer. You give the groceries to the boy and take over the counter here." Bakshi got up from his seat. "Inder, you take the orders." Inder, the short middle-aged helper, started taking orders from customers.

"You are crazy. Can't this wait?" Svitri angrily muttered as she took the payment from the young man.

"No. You pay tomorrow. Or next week," Bakshi returned the cash to the man.

"But I am paying now."

"No, I can't break that big a bill. It is okay. I have no change now. Pay tomorrow. Please go. We are very busy today. Next customer."

As the boy looked at Bakshi with surprise, he said, smiling, "It is okay, son. I've got your name, your father's name. I have noted the amount in the book. I am in a hurry. I have to go out of town. You come back in a couple of days, and we can settle this."

As Hari was confused, as waiting customers moved ahead of him, he stood behind them all trying to make sense out of it. He had only arrived in town three days back after accepting a new job at the dam and was just getting familiar with the town.

"Have you gone mad? Why did you not take his payment?" Svitri was confused.

"Because I want him to come back. Don't talk back, and don't interfere. Just do your work," Bakshi looked angrily at his wife. Then he turned back, "And listen, I am leaving for a few days. This is very important. If he comes back, don't take his payment. Tell him to pay me. Make sure nobody takes money from the boy. Do you get that? Or else you will make me angry."

"You always have these crazy bouts. It must be someone from Peshawar. Everyone from Peshawar has to get stuff for free from this shop," Svitri contin- ued her angry mumbling.

"Cut it out. He will never take anything free. I know that. I am leaving for some work for a few days. You take care of the shop. I will be back in a few days."

"What has gotten into you? Who is this boy?"

"Someone very special. I will tell you when I get back. Just do as I told you. Don't take money from him," Bakshi said as he left the shop from the back door that opened into his residence while mumbling, "Oh, my god. The boy is alive. The boy is alive. Everyone said they all died." Inside his room, he packed some clothes into the bag and took some mon- ey, a photo, and a diary, and left from the front en- trance of his house to the bus stop across the street. He reached the town bus, stood in a hurry, and said, "Ticket to Haridwar," as he handed over the bills to a clerk at the window.

"When does the bus depart?" he asked ner- vously.

"Five p.m."

Bakshi looked at his watch. It was still one hour away.

After leaving Peshawar several years back, Bakshi had found Kedar in Haridwar living in a cottage on a small farm. There on the farm, Kedar lived as a sadhu and prayed for penance for his 'sins.' When Bakshi arrived in Haridwar late that night, he found him sleeping in his cottage.

When Kedar opened the gate of his cottage, Bakshi hugged him in excitement and shouted, "The Boy. The boy. I found him. I found Hari."

"You found Hari? He is alive! He is alive!" Kedar prayed as he made circles with folded hands. "That is such great news. Come here and give me a hug!" Kedar said as he hugged Bakshi.

"Kedar, I have been asking you for years. Now there is a solid reason for you to move to Rampur. Let us go back by bus tomorrow morning."

"But when he finds out who I am, he will hate me."

"Don't you want to see him? Let's go and first meet him, and we will sort out other things later."

"Yes. Yes, I want to meet him. But not tomorrow. You stay here. Let's think it through," Kedar said as he scratched his head and paced around the room.

"I can't stay too long. I came here leaving my shop open."

"Just give me one more day to think."

So Bakshi stayed there one more day as he tried to convince Kedar to travel with him to Rampur.

\*\*\*

The next day, at Bakshi and Sons, Svitri was busy with customers. Jamuna, the spice-making lady, was already at work. She lived in the mountains and came down every day to grind fresh spices and help Svitri with small jobs. Fresh spices sold for a premium and were a specialty of Bakshi and Sons. Many customers visited their shop just for the fresh spices. Jamuna was a hard-working woman. She and Svitri both got along well. As both women were chitchatting about their day, the young man came back to pay the bill.

"Bakshi sahib is not here, so please come back in a couple of days," Svitri said loudly on seeing the young man.

"I just want to pay for stuff. Why can't you take my payment?" Hari was upset over what he thought was strange behavior.

"Because I don't know how much it is."

"Here is the bill." Hari pulled it from his pocket and placed it on the counter.

"Please, sit down. Inder, bring the chair for sahib and a cup of tea."

"No, thanks. I don't want tea. I came to make a payment, and I have to go."

"Please, sit down. Have a cup of tea. Unfortunately, I won't accept any money."

"What is going on here? I won't visit your shop again."

"Well, I understand you are frustrated. So am I. After Bakshi talked to you, he left home. I have not seen him. Help me understand what happened."

"Okay, here is the money. Thank you. Namaste." The young man grabbed his bicycle and left.

Svitri was all smiles. "There goes Bakshi's boy. Stupid ass. *'Don't accept payment.'* Hey, Inder, go after the boy and see where he lives. Otherwise, Bakshi will lose his mind when he returns, and I will lose mine. Take the bicycle."

It was evening, and more than a day since Bakshi had left for an unknown place. Svitri was worried and angry. "Who does business like this man? Left the shop and family for some boy."

Bakshi had not returned, even the following day. Svitri was upset when she got up and had to do all the chores to open the shop. She talked angrily with everyone. In the afternoon, she sat in the sun outside the shop to dry her hair, which she had washed with herbs. Inder brought her some chai tea. With her hair open, she sipped the tea in full view of the bazaar. Bakshi would not have approved. Not that she needed his approval. She would normally back down on a public argument, but this was her time to enjoy it without worrying since Bakshi was away. But then her eyes caught sight of a rickshaw about a hundred yards away with two men in it. One of them looked like Bakshi.

"Who else is there with Bakshi? Inder, Lala-ji is here with someone. Take this chair inside."

The rickshaw stopped outside the shop. A thin-framed man alighted after Bakshi.

"This is my shop, Kedar, and this is my wife, Svitri."

"Namaste, *Bhabhi*-ji. Very happy to see you," Kedar said and smiled as he stood behind Bakshi.

"Oh, Kedar, I heard a lot about you from Bakshi. Pleased to meet you."

"Let's go inside. Inder, two cups of strong tea." Bakshi walked in with his bag, and Kedar followed him.

"When is the boy coming?" Kedar asked.

"I am guessing it is the same boy. He came two days back, dropped the money, and left," Svitri replied as Bakshi looked upset.

"Didn't I ask you not to take the money from him?" Bakshi said angrily.

"Calm down. He dropped the money on the table and left."

"Hell, where will we find him?" Bakshi paced restlessly.

"I sent Inder after him. He knows where he lives," Svitri replied calmly.

"Very smart. You are the best," Bakshi said with a smile.

"So, the boy is the lost prince or something like that?" Svitri asked.

"He is Hari. The Dil clan's only heir. A family that had done many favors on Kedar and me."

"How will you see him again? Your idea of holding him on ransom on our own payment was pretty lame."

"We will go knock at his door," Kedar said.

"For what?" Svitri asked.

"Leave it to me. Just show me where he lives. Let's go there after tea."

"Aren't you tired? Rest a little," Bakshi was himself tired after three days of travel.

"Are you kidding? Tired? I can't wait to see him. Thanks for doing this, Bakshi. You have been a true friend," Kedar said.

Bakshi smiled as he put his arm around Kedar's shoulder, "I am selfish. I want my friend back and want to help the boy."

Inder brought the tea, and each took their cup from the tray.

"You want to freshen up? Take a bath or something? The boy came in on the regular-shift train. Still, there is plenty of time," Bakshi said.

"No, this shabbiness will come in handy." Then, looking at Inder and his dirty jacket, Kedar asked if he could borrow his jacket.

Inder reluctantly chuckled, and Bakshi asked him to hand over the jacket.

"Come on, Inder, he is my friend, brother, means a lot to me, I can buy you a new jacket."

"If you have one dirtier than this, even better, I want to go there as a hermit," Kedar said.

Inder brought a torn, dirty, and smelly jacket from his sleeping quarters. Then Kedar opened his turban and laid it on the bed. "Give me something to pack in it. Anything... potatoes, onions. Something edible."

Svitri gave him onions and potatoes to pack.

"I should look like a beggar. I will go to his house and beg for food."

Bakshi laughed at him, "I did not know you got this acting skill as well."

"It is a necessity. I desperately want to meet him, and I desperately don't want him to recognize me. I have to do it this way."

He looked in the mirror on the wall. His face had stubble from not shaving for two days. His hair was a mix of gray and black. Inder's jacket on him made him look older than what he looked before. He removed his shoes and wore a broken sandal, which Bakshi had picked up from storage at the back of the room. Bakshi was excited and now was giving all kinds of ideas to disguise Kedar.

The regular shift train whistled close to the bridge.

"Train will be here in a few mins."

"I think we are good, now we can go," he picked up the bundle behind his shoulder and was ready to go.

"Limp a little when you walk," Bakshi said.

"Bakshi, let us go now. We don't want to be late," Kedar was getting restless.

"Inder, let us go. Show us where he lives."

The three of them left on a rickshaw to the south of the town. On the way, they crossed Madan Lal and Sons. Bakshi looked at the shop with a lot of attention till it was out of his view. He observed the layout of the shop, the number of customers, Madam Lal on the cash counter, his sons helping inside the shop. He wondered when his sons would be old and wise enough to help him. His three boys were seven, nine, and eleven. They were all in school and rarely helped in the shop.

"How does the boy look like?" Kedar asked.

"Hmm. He looked like Jai's son. Well-built, medium height, little shorter than his father, talks very softly, hazel eyes."

"Yes, he had hazel eyes of his grandma," Kedar said with a smile on his face.

"How far do we have to go?" Bakshi asked Inder.

"Not far, Lala-ji. Into that street. That is where he lives."

"You stop there. Tell me the number of his house," Kedar said.

"I don't know the number. That row. His quarters have a tall jamun tree. That third house."

"What? You should have noted the number," Bakshi reprimanded Inder.

"That is okay. The third house and his name. I will find out," Kedar got down the rickshaw and started walking towards the house.

Bakshi looked at Kedar. He could see the pain and optimism in his eyes. "We will wait here."

"No, no, you guys go back. I will meet you at the shop. I will catch a rickshaw or walk. This will take time," Kedar said as he looked visibly tense.

"Are you sure? You don't know when he will arrive. He may have a different shift," Bakshi said.

"Please, go. Go," Kedar looked anxious and scared. He waved them away. Bakshi understood the emotions Kedar was going through.

"Wait." Kedar turned back and came close to Bakshi, "You will never tell the boy anything. If you ever tell anything to the boy about me, you will not ever see me again."

"What?" Bakshi was surprised by Kedar's demand.

Kedar waved his finger, "The boy should never know my name or my relationship with him." His eyes were wide, his face twitching with emotions.

Bakshi nodded in agreement, "Fine. I understand. Don't make these creepy faces. You will scare the boy."

"Please tell Svitri as well. No one tells the boy anything," Kedar said.

"No one else knows anything. Svitri does not know anything."

"Thanks. Please leave now. I will see you at the shop," Kedar walked away towards the street.

Now he could see a house with a jamun tree. There was a small *shahtoot* tree outside the house, which Kedar sat under. It was already late in the afternoon. Kedar had tears in his eyes. He smiled and thought, *You never know what time has in store for you. Never believed I would ever see him. Now I don't know how I will face him.*

A few men entered the block with lunch boxes. Kedar's senses became alert. He eyed their body language, walking posture, features, age — anything that would indicate if Hari was one of them. As they came closer, Kedar noticed they were all middle-aged men. Then he saw a young man with a broad chest walking along with straight posture and swift like a soldier, coming directly towards him. Kedar's eyes fixed on him. The young man came to the door of the house with the jamun tree, entered the house, and closed the door. Kedar waited under the tree, restless, not able to make up his mind as to what he should do. Then he got up and knocked on the door. After a wait, he knocked again.

"Wait. I am coming," the boy opened the door.

"Yes, baba, what do you want?"

Kedar kept looking at his face.

"Baba? Why did you knock on the door?"

"Can I get some water? I will sit right here outside, son."

"Sure, I will get some water."

The boy came back with water and handed it over to Kedar, who drank it and handed back the tumbler.

"What is your name, son?"

"Hari."

"Son, I know you are alone. I was alone once in this world. But now I am not," Kedar said in a tone that was a mix of a sermon and street performer trying to grab attention.

Hari stopped at the door and listened.

"Son, if a seed has to turn into a giant tree, even it will travel through a bird's stomach, and even if the bird droppings fall on a wall, it grows on the wall. It will if that is its destiny. It is true for the mightiest of trees, like *banyan* and *peepal*. You will also flourish here because that is your destiny."

Hari was captivated by what Kedar said. It connected with his heart and mind.

But he was also wary of strangers' intentions. Hari pulled someone's money from their pocket and said, "Baba, here is some money. Please go. I am tired."

"No, son, baba is not here for money. Baba is here for destiny. Baba is a traveler from Haridwar, and baba is Hari *bhakta*," Bakshi said smiling. The happiness on his face was captivating.

"Baba, wait. Let me get something for you to eat. I have bananas, apples, or do you want some lentils and flour?"

"No, I can have chai at your door if you don't mind," Kedar said.

"Okay. I was about to make chai for myself. I will make some for you as well. Sit here."

"God bless you."

Hari came back with chai in a ceramic cup and some cookies and gave them to Kedar. As Hari was about to go inside, Kedar said, "Won't you drink chai with me?"

Hari laughed. "Sure. I will bring my cup of tea and drink it here. Hope you don't ask to move in."

"No, not even if you invite me. I won't be able to stay."

There Kedar sat for another half an hour talking about all kinds of things, staring at Hari's face. He felt like touching his face, hugging him, crying with him, laughing with him. But he could not. *What would I tell him? I am the one who destroyed his childhood. It was my actions that caused your mother to kill herself. No, he should never know.*

"Where are you from, boy?"

"From Peshawar."

"Where is your family, your father?"

"He died in partition riots. You are not looking to discuss a marriage proposal, are you?" Hari laughed.

"No, you are too young for marriage, but maybe another day. Sad to hear about your father. What was his name?"

"Jai Dil."

Kedar, after finishing the chai and handing back the cup to the boy, said, "You are an amazing kid. As good as they come. God bless you." Then he looked at Hari's face one more time and walked away.

"Baba, you left your stuff."

"No, that is for you. You gave me tea. This is my gift. Please use these," he said as he walked away. "Take your sheet, baba." Hari handed over the turban cloth to Kedar.

Hari kept looking at him as Kedar walked away while tying the turban. Hari felt strange about the sadhu, and as Kedar turned on a street corner, Hari went after him to check where he was going. He stood at the corner watching Kedar go towards the bazaar, and then he came back a little confused. He felt, for a stranger, the man knew more about him. He came back and picked up the onions and potatoes. He had never looked at those with that much interest and attention in his entire life. The next few days, they reminded Hari of the sadhu.

# Chapter 12
# [1951] From Ganga to Jamuna

Kedar had left Hari's quarters a little shocked after meeting him. He walked all the way to Bakshi's shop in a sad state of mind. Images of his sister and her little boy flashed in front of his eyes. He walked towards the bazaar, reliving the horrors of his crimes. The storm of guilt had crept in and engulfed his heart. He felt a little breathlessness and stopped as he entered the bazaar. It was dark, and most shops had closed. He sat down on a bench outside a closed tailor shop. A man standing across the shop asked if he needed help.

"Baba, are you ok?"

"Just catching my breath. Can you tell me where Bakshi and Sons' shop is?"

As Kedar walked back to the shop, Bakshi was sitting outside on the chair waiting for him. Upon seeing Kedar, he got up, "What took you so long? Did you meet him? What did he say?"

"Let me sit down, please. Get me some water," Kedar dropped into the chair.

"Inder, get some water. Hurry up," Bakshi said as he pulled his chair near Kedar. Inder ran back with the water and handed it to Kedar, who gulped it down, spilling some on his shirt. Wiping the water off his face with his turban cloth, he said, "Why did you have to come to get me? I was living peacefully. Now my mind is going crazy."

"Okay, you can go back by tomorrow's bus, but first, tell me, did you meet him?"

"He is such a sweet young man. His features resemble his mother's so much. But I could not hug him. I could not tell him."

"Great. So, you two met. Now go take a bath, and we will eat and talk later. I am so hungry." Bakshi heaved a sigh of relief.

As Kedar and Bakshi sat down to eat, Svitri wisely stayed away from the dinner, letting friends catch up for a long time. After dinner, Bakshi asked for two cots to be laid together on the roof. The cots were laid out with a side table in the middle. On the table, there were a jug of water, two glasses, and a bottle of whiskey. Bakshi made himself a drink and poured some into the second glass.

"You should know, a sanyasi doesn't drink," Kedar said.

"For old times? No?" Bakshi asked as he poured his drink.

"Old times bring terrible memories. Let us not go there," Kedar sighed. "How were they killed? Jai and the family?"

"They were all killed. Why does it matter? Let us not talk about it. It fills me with rage, those Muslims," Bakshi bottomed up his drink.

"They don't fill me with rage at all. I killed mine. All of them. And the pain I carry, the hate for myself, is far more than I can hate anyone else."

"Please don't talk about it. I feel terrible about that day. I wish I had not driven you to the party that night. I wish I had asked you to stop gambling. I wish I had gone with you when you left. In the middle of the night, sometimes I wake up, and these memories haunt me," Bakshi said as he bottomed up his drink.

"You just feel guilty because you don't want to blame me. Just like other people who loved me, like Lakshmi, my wonderful sister." Tears rolled down Kedar's face. "She killed herself because she could not bear seeing me in that much pain, because she felt she could have or should have done something to stop this, just like you." He paused and looked at the sky with tears in his eyes. "And you know who my biggest victim was? Hari." The last word made him go into loud crying, which he silenced with his face in his hands.

"You must forgive yourself. Now it is time for redemption. You have the opportunity to do something good for the boy."

"He is fine. I ruin all things I touch. Leave me out of this one."

"He is alone. I suggest you move back here. He has no one of his own." Bakshi paused to light his *beedi* cigarette.

"No, no. That is too dangerous. What if he finds out who I am?"

"Then what? He was four or five. He won't remember anything. Here, take a smoke."

"He was eight when I came out of jail. I remember standing outside Dil Mahal, waiting for a whole day for him to come out. You have to swear on Bhagavad Gita. You will never tell him about me."

"If you move here, I swear I will not tell him," Bakshi got up and walked away to the boundary wall of the roof.

"What about your wife? She will tell him. I know you have told her everything about me."

"She does not know who this boy is," Bakshi turned his back.

"What will I do here? I am a sadhu," Kedar said.

"You should come back to the world. You are like, what? In your thirties? Come back, get married, and have a family. Your ancestors will forgive you. They will be happy there is someone after you to carry their name."

There was silence. Kedar thought if all this was even possible. "It is too late. I have gone too far on this path, and thanks for fudging the numbers on my age. You and I know the reality of our age."

"Okay, fine, don't get married, but come back and settle here."

"What would I do here? I live in solitude in the mountains near Rishikesh on the banks of the Ganges, and I don't like to be around a lot of people."

"That is not even a problem. There are a lot of mountains here, and you can buy some land in any of the villages in the mountains you see from here. Look there," Bakshi pointed to the lights far north after the train tracks. "That is the Goddess Temple. Behind that mountain, there is a village. Very few people live there. You can buy land there and live there. You can come to town here to meet me when you want, and you get to see the boy as well. That village has a river close by, and a creek runs through it. There are no lights and no roads to that place, so you will have all the solitude you want and more."

Kedar looked where Bakshi pointed. In the dark of the night, he could tell there were mountains, but he could not see anything more.

"Come on, I get my friend back, you get your nephew, and the boy gets two uncles. In disguise, of course. Assuming if I can count myself as an uncle."

"Of course, you are an uncle."

"So, what do you say?" Bakshi looked at Kedar in anticipation.

"Okay, let me think." As Kedar said this, Bakshi gave a big, long hug that suffocated Kedar. "Awesome. This is so great. This is so great." He ran down the stairs, saying, "Hey, Svitri. Hey, Svitri…" He ran to the kitchen where she was cleaning dishes. "Kedar will move here."

She stopped washing, "Okay, where will he live? Here?"

"No, he will live in Jamuna's village."

"Great. Why don't you marry them as well, so he can live in her house?" she taunted him as she resumed cleaning the dishes.

"You know what? That is not a bad idea." He became quiet as he pondered the new creation in his mind.

"You are crazy. Let him go back to his hermitage and live his life," Svitri said as she scrubbed the pots harder to indicate her displeasure. As Bakshi was about to leave the kitchen, she stopped scrubbing. "Wait. Is this the boy that you two are after, the same boy?"

"Same as what?" Bakshi walked out of the kitchen.

"The boy of his sister."

"Are you crazy? They all died there. What has gotten into your mind?" Shaking his head, Bakshi took the stairs to the roof and, upon seeing Kedar, he again started dancing. Bakshi and Kedar talked about their days in Peshawar late into the night. They were excited about living in the same town and being able to meet each other, and all the time they could spend together.

\*\*\*

In his quarters, Hari had retired to bed after finishing his dinner. The onions and potatoes in the kitchen reminded him of the sadhu. The thought that some stranger knew him that well disturbed his mind. He turned on his night lamp and sat down in bed. Suddenly, he jumped out of bed, put on his kurta, took out his bicycle, and rode to the bazaar. In the empty market, there were few men. The quietness was broken by the barks of stray dogs. There was a drunk man yelling in the middle of the road. Hari took a left turn towards the railway station. After he reached Bakshi and Sons, he stopped in front of the closed shop. He rode the bicycle to the back of the shop, to the entrance of Bakshi's house. He stood there, looking at the door for a few minutes, and then he got down from the bicycle, put it on the stand, and knocked on the door. Svitri opened the door.

"Namaste, can I see Mister Bakshi?"

She was surprised but happy to see him. "Come inside," she said.

"Wait here on a chair. I will call him," She went upstairs and told Bakshi he had a visitor, deliberately hiding his identity.

When Bakshi saw him, he was a little shocked, "What can I do for you?"

"I wanted to ask if you know of anyone from Peshawar here."

"I am from Peshawar. And I know your father. Sorry to bother you over the payments. It won't happen again."

"Do you know anyone else?"

"Anyone else from Peshawar? No? Why do you ask?"

"I had a strange visitor today." He was not sure why his mind brought him to Bakshi and Sons. "I am sorry to disturb you."

As Hari left, Bakshi stopped him. "Wait. I was close to your father. Whether you pay me for groceries or not, if you go anyplace else to shop for them, my feelings will be hurt. Next time you come, let's talk about your family."

A little disturbed, Hari nodded in agreement, folded his hands for respect, and left.

Bakshi bolted the door from inside. "Why did you let him in?" he asked Svitri angrily.

"What should I have done? First, you want him not to pay so he can come back. Now, you are upset because he is back. Do you know what you want?"

"Time. Think what time it is." Bakshi showed her his watch. She shrugged.

When Bakshi got back upstairs, his mood was not jovial.

"When you are back, we will give you a new name. Something like that of a countryman, like from Kedar to Kadu Nath. Well, no. Kadu Nath does not rhyme that well. Kadu Das or Kadu Ram may be better," he said in a serious tone, then added, "You have to get rid of this sadhu look and change it to a villager look. Like, get rid of the big beard and maybe just keep a mustache and stubble. Always tie a turban, wear a dhoti instead of this chola gown, and get rid of your mala. That one must go."

"Yes. Do you think he may get suspicious that I was the sadhu who visited him? Do you think he may remember me?" Kedar looked at Bakshi with concern.

"I don't think so. But going to the boy's quarters and telling your eternal knowledge was not a very wise idea. You should leave tomorrow morning. Pack your stuff now. I will drop you off at the bus stand." Bakshi's hurried talk made Kedar a little concerned.

"Who was it at the door? Did he come here? Was it him?" Kedar looked concerned and agitated.

"No, no. Calm down. It was our neighbor asking to borrow milk. Now let's pack."

"What is the matter? Is Svitri upset that I am here? You know I have almost nothing to pack?"

"No, she is not upset, but she keeps asking about the boy and you. We have a plan. You come back in a week. I will have a place for you to live," he said as they walked downstairs.

Kedar picked up his bag from the living room. Bakshi showed him his bedroom. Kedar could not sleep that night. Bakshi needed two more drinks before he could fall asleep. Early in the morning, Bakshi dropped Kedar off at the bus stand. There, they had tea and promised to meet again in a week. Upon his return from the bus stand, Bakshi asked Svitri to talk to Jamuna about the possibility of Kedar settling in her village.

"Let me tell you the possibility," Svitri responded angrily, "None."

***

Svitri and Jamuna were childhood friends. Jamuna was married at an early age to Des Raj Rana. They had a boy together named Nika. Jamuna's husband, Rana, as he was known, was the owner of a rental business that rented party equipment and supplies. He also owned a truck and did deliveries across states. In reality, under the guise of his businesses, Rana was smuggling drugs. One day, he got into an argument with some people at a wedding where he had rented out some equipment. It escalated into a fight, and Rana stabbed and killed a drunk young man. He was arrested and released on bail. During the investigation, police found out that the murder was related to drug money. But Rana jumped bail and was never seen in the area.

Although Rana was a bad husband and routinely abused Jamuna, his disappearance put Jamuna and her little boy in great hardship. Svitri knew Jamuna had great recipes for spices, so she hired her to make those spices for her shop. And since then, Jamuna had been working at Bakshi and Sons, grinding spices day after day. She had been working hard to make ends meet. She had some help from her father, Sant Das. He had given her some land and built her a small cottage to live in the village. Many times, Sant Das suggested she get remarried, but Jamuna refused.

"I already have too much going on in my life. I need to raise the boy, and I don't want to worry about another husband and more kids," she had told Svitri.

"I feel sorry for you, girl. You are young and beautiful. This is tough, but you are brave. I must say that living in this world as a young, single mother is hard." Svitri and Jamuna were close and often chitchatted as Jamuna worked on spices.

"Long live my father. If days can pass like this, I will be content with my life, but one thing worries me." She paused to think. "The boy is growing up, and I don't know how I will raise him to be a good man. I hope he does not turn out like his father."

"They need a man to keep them in control," Svitri said as she organized the bags of lentils. Then Svitri talked to Jamuna about Kedar. "Jamuna, a very close friend of Bakshi is moving to town. Bakshi was wondering if he could settle in your village."

Jamuna wanted answers to the questions her father, Sant Das, would ask. "Who is he, Svitri? Does he have a family?"

"He is like a brother to Bakshi. He does not have a family. He is a single but very religious man."

"How old is he? You know villagers won't allow strange young men to settle there."

"That is where we need your help, Jamuna. Ask your father. He is the village head."

"I will, but it won't matter much. Village panchayat, the council of elders, will not allow a strange man to settle in the village."

When Jamuna asked her father, he refused to allow a single stranger to settle in his village. But after meeting Kedar, he liked him. He asked for more information about his family background from Bakshi. Bakshi told him that Kadu belonged to a renowned Punjabi family from Peshawar and that he had "enough money to live a comfortable life." Although Kedar had donated all his money, Bakshi believed he owed Kadu his share of the emporium that Jai generously had gifted him. Sant Das told Bakshi that although he would not allow a single stranger to settle, it wouldn't be a problem if Kadu was to marry Jamuna. "Only if she approves the marriage."

Bakshi was thrilled at the proposal. He told Sant Das that it was a terrific idea. However, when Bakshi told Svitri, she vehemently opposed it. "Why would she marry a crazy maniac who killed his family?" They had a big argument over it.

"You know nothing about the man. You met him. Does he look like he is crazy to you?"

"I am not going to be part of this. Keep me out of it, like the poor lady has not suffered enough in her life," Svitri said.

Bakshi said Jamuna should meet Kadu and make the decision herself. This would also absolve Svitri of any guilt for being party to getting Jamuna married to Kedar. Thus, Kadu Ram started working at Bakshi's shop as manager. As usual, Svitri and Bakshi had frequent arguments at the shop. Sometimes they argued over such trivial matters that Jamuna would say Kadu was the only sane person at the shop.

"You've known him for less than a month, so you better be careful. He may have killed twenty people before coming over here," Svitri said.

Bakshi quickly interrupted, "All men displaced from partition have seen too much violence."

Jamuna had developed a liking for Kadu. While this bond between the two was making Bakshi and Sant Das happy, Svitri could not stand it. "She talks to him more than she talks to me now."

"Women, women..." Bakshi conveyed his perceptions of women being jealous.

Hari visited the shop a few times a week to buy groceries and talk to Bakshi about his family and

Peshawar. Kadu listened to them talk but kept quiet. He always filled Hari's order. He neatly placed everything in an empty box, reviewed it with Hari, and loaded it onto his bike. Hari liked Kadu and told Bakshi that Kadu was his best worker.

One day, Jamuna did not show up for work. She was not well and had a fever. She stayed in bed late that day. Although it was nothing serious, Sant Das took the opportunity to ask her, "Jamuna, you are the best mother I know. You work hard for your family. Have you ever thought about what will happen to your son if something happens to you?"

"Why? Won't you take care of him?"

"I am old, Jamuna. And your brother, Mani Das, will get married soon. We don't know how his wife will turn out. I am worried about you and your boy's future. Bakshi wants Kadu Ram to settle in the village. I think it will make perfect sense if you two are married, but it is your decision."

At Bakshi and Sons, Svitri missed Jamuna. No spices were grounded in her absence. No conversations happened about life. Suddenly, it hit Svitri that this may be the future. She pulled Bakshi to the side. "So, Jamuna marries your friend, and she will never be seen here again?"

Bakshi, who had been in such a juvenile mood since Kadu's arrival, jumped at the opportunity. "Let's ask him," he said, then turned to Kadu. "Hey, Kadu, if Jamuna marries you, will she still work at our shop?" It was a trick question, and Kadu fell for it.

"It is up to her. I won't have a problem with it."

"Awesome! Svitri, if Kadu gets married to Jamuna, she will still work here." Bakshi was thrilled. "I am going to leave to talk to Sant Das. We will get it over with. Enough of Kadu camping around here." And while Kadu was explaining and Svitri was still complaining, Bakshi grabbed his jacket and left the shop to see Sant Das at his fruit stall.

Jamuna liked Kadu but getting married again was not a decision she was ready to make. Sant Das and Bakshi had a detailed conversation, and it was agreed that Jamuna needed a little convincing but that ultimately, she knew Kadu and understood it was in her interest to get married and settle down. It was decided that Kadu would buy some land in Sant Das' village so he could be projected as a respectable farmer.

"After Jamuna has given her approval, I will call the meeting of panchayat and inform all in the village of the decision," Sant Das said.

After some thinking, Jamuna agreed to the marriage. She felt Kadu was the right person and that living life as a single mother would ultimately be bad for her and Nika. Sant Das called the meeting of the village panchayat, and there he announced that he was selling part of his land to Bakshi's friend, Kadu Ram. "Kadu Ram will marry Jamuna very soon, and they will live in the village." In the village of thirty-seven people, the only question on everyone's mind was, *who is this Kadu Ram?*

Bakshi announced, "Kadu Ram will have a puja before building his new hut. After the prayers, everyone will be served food. Everyone in the village is invited. They can meet Kadu Ram and ask him any question."

When Bakshi told Kadu about his conversation with Sant Das, he was concerned. "Look, Bakshi, if you tell her my past, she will never agree to marry me, and if you don't, that would be wrong. I have a dark past."

"You will tell her before marriage only if she wants to know. You are wiser now. Don't ruin what is possible and good for everyone. That is all I will say."

The following day, when Jamuna came to the shop to work, Bakshi asked Kadu to talk to her.

"Jamuna, I want to thank you for agreeing to marry me. I certainly don't deserve a woman as elegant and beautiful as you are."

"You don't need to say this." Jamuna smiled.

"I want to tell you I have a past, and you have the right to know about it."

"Does your past affect how you will treat my son and me or fulfill your commitments towards my father and village?"

"No, but nevertheless, it is my past, and it is not very pleasant."

"I trust Bakshi. I am sure he knows what he is getting us into."

Soon after that, Sant Das and Bakshi met to fix the wedding date. They both wanted the marriage to materialize as soon as possible.

A few weeks before the wedding, Bakshi asked Hari if there was a job in his office for Kadu Ram.

"I have a lot of daily wage jobs at my office. He can work as a helper on machines or as an office boy."

"Something that does not require him to dirty his clothes and work too hard."

"He can be an office boy."

"Any job where he can work with you, so you can give him a little more accommodation," Bakshi said.

"He can join as my office peon," Hari said.

"That is the perfect job for him," Bakshi said

"Send him to my office. I have moved to the workshop here in the town. Ask him to send me a message when he arrives at the gate. I will take care of everything."

"That is so amazing! Thank you. God bless you."

When Bakshi told Kadu, he happily accepted the job at Hari's office.

Within a few weeks, a simple wedding was performed in the village by the priest of the Goddess Temple. After the wedding, Kadu Ram moved to the village into Jamuna's cottage.

# Chapter 13
# [1956] Stationmaster's Daughter

Over the years, Hari had spent his holidays and vacations traveling around cities with camps of partition migrants. He was looking for anyone from Peshawar that could tell him anything about the fate of the remnants of his family. He once spent two weeks in Kingsway camp after someone told him one of his uncles might be there. He did not find his uncle but met an old classmate and a childhood friend. He paid many visits to the Kurukshetra camp. There, he met men who knew his family well, an old man who was the only survivor in his family. He'd survived because he was traveling when the rioting and violence started. Before he could die peacefully, the old man hoped to see any of his four grandchildren who might have survived the riots, "because who would kill little innocent children?" Although he knew countless children had been killed.

Another man told Hari how aristocratic the Dil family was, and he sympathized with him for what had happened. In one such visit to the city of Ludhiana, he had met an old man who claimed he'd been a rich merchant in Peshawar and known his father well.

The man told him stories about Peshawar and his family. It was all vague and normal since the Dil family was so well known that anyone in Peshawar could have said the same things. But then, the man started talking about Daler and how "he was devastated after witnessing the carnage, having lost his family and Jai and you." He told Hari that he'd met Daler in Ludhiana and that "Daler told me he lives in Sirhind," a small town nearby.

Upon hearing this, Hari became anxious to visit Sirhind to meet Daler. He looked at his watch. It was around noon. There was still time to catch the train to get to Sirhind. He wished the old man good luck and, instead of returning home, left for Sirhind on the train to find Daler. He reached Sirhind after two pm. The station was small; there was a tea vendor and a small office. He talked to the tea vendor, who claimed he made the best chai on the track from Rampur to Ambala.

"How big is the town?" Hari asked as he sipped on the less than ordinary tea.

"Compared to Ambala, very small, sahib."

"I am looking for someone named Daler Singh," Hari said, in case the tea vendor had known him.

"Let me introduce you to the stationmaster, sahib. He should know."

The stationmaster was not in the office. He had gone for a lunch break after receiving the last train.

"You just missed him," his peon said. "He will be back to receive the four-twenty train."

Hari decided to check out the town till the stationmaster was back. He inquired about Daler from merchants, asking about "a tall Sikh man from Peshawar." No one had heard of any such man. Tired and hungry, he returned to the railway station and sat on the bench near the tea stall. The vendor waived, and a middle-aged man in a white kurta and pajamas approached the bench.

"Stationmaster, sahib." The vendor pointed the stationmaster toward Hari. After greetings and learning the purpose of Hari's visit, the stationmaster invited Hari into his office. As always, Hari was dressed neatly and looked like a handsome young man. He was cleanly shaved, and his hair well combed. His way of talking reflected his good upbringing. On the stationmaster's desk, Hari noticed his nameplate engraved, *Mohan Das Mehta* and *Stationmaster*.

"I arrived here this morning. I am looking for someone named Daler that got separated during the partition. I am from Peshawar."

"Did you eat anything?" the stationmaster asked him.

"Is there a place to eat around here?" Hari asked.

"Not many. This is a small town, but we will share our simple food if you don't mind eating it," he said, then stepped outside the door and yelled, "Moji," to the office boy, who responded quickly.

"Get some good vegetarian food for sahib," he said, then turned to Hari. "Vegetarian is fine?"

"Yes. Here. Take some money," Hari pulled out his wallet.

"No, no. You are our guest here. So, Daler is his name?" the stationmaster asked after a pause.

"Yes, a Sikh man from Peshawar."

"I know him," the stationmaster said as he chewed some condiments in his mouth. "He does not live here in the town. He has a farm on the outskirts, in Khera village, and I advise against pursuing him today because it will be a long walk to his village, and it is a dirt road." The stationmaster sat down on his office chair. "I can try to send him a message through the village dispensary. They have a phone there. It would be easier if he comes here while you wait.

"Does that sound like a good plan to you?" the stationmaster asked as he picked up his office phone.

"Yes. That would be great."

"Lunch is here. You eat lunch while I call him. How do you know him?"

"He is family, sir."

The tea vendor came and left a kettle with tea and cups. The stationmaster poured tea for himself and Hari. "What you do for a living, Hari?"

"I am a supervisor in a machine shop."

"So, you are a Punjabi from Peshawar." The stationmaster pulled the cigarette from the pack and then put it back. "Sikh?"

"I don't subscribe to any categorization," Hari said as he smiled.

"How do you pray?"

"I pray where and whenever I want."

"Excellent, but you must have a belief or philosophy."

"I believe there is one God, all-pervasive, in everything."

"And what do you call him?"

"Why does it matter, sir? You can call it whatever. Supreme Soul, the existential power, the nature that moves and governs everything."

"Okay, let me make it simple. Do you consider yourself a Sikh, a *Buddhist*, a Jain or *Nirankari*, or *Namdhari*, *Arya Samaji*, *Sanatan Dharmi*, or anything else?" the stationmaster asked with a smile.

"Oh, I am my own variety, sir. My family was a mix of Hindus and Sikhs who held onto philosophies that had worked and really had our loyalties to the land and its people."

"Loyalties to the land and its people? Sounds interesting," the stationmaster said and took a puff from his cigarette. "Who else is in your family?"

"No one. I am alone. They all died in partition," Hari said.

"Sorry to hear that, young man. My heart aches every time I meet someone like you."

By now, it was already getting dark outside. At night, the train station looked deserted. The next train was not passing through the station until late at night.

"You can wait here or come to my house and wait there."

"I will wait here, sir."

"Okay, then we will have dinner together in my office."

"Thank you, sir. I hate to be a bother. You have been very generous. Allow me to pay for dinner."

"It is free. Comes from my home." The stationmaster finished his tea. "Listen, make yourself comfortable here. It will be at least two hours after the message is delivered for him to reach here, and that's only if the message is delivered and if he is willing to see you." He smiled.

"Moji, make a bed in my office for sahib to rest."

Hari was tired and soon fell asleep.

A young lady walked into the station confidently and headed straight to the stationmaster's office and then to his private room. There, she was surprised to see a young man sleeping on the cot. He looked handsome, but it was a thought she didn't wish to entertain in her mind. She came out of the office and saw the office boy. "Where is my father?"

"He should be in the office, no?" Moji replied.

"Where?" The lady came out and looked around the station, and then she sniffed the air.

"He is smoking, isn't he?" Then she walked behind the office. "Here you are. Bad habit, Papa."

"Oh, my dear, Maya, what are you doing here?"

"I should ask you where you have been, and who is in there?"

"Well, a guest. Tell your mother I will be home late."

"She is already upset and sent me to look for you."

"Just handle it, and also, can you send some dinner here? I will eat here with the guest."

"I will send it with Moji," she said as she left.

"Wait. I need to give you something. Take it home." Mohan Das went inside his private room and turned the light on. He pulled cabinets open as if looking for something in a hurry and slammed the doors back shut. He did this a few times till he woke up the young man. Then he picked up a bundle of papers and slammed them on the table in front of the young man. "These. Please take these home."

"Namaste," the young lady said to the young man and picked the papers.

"Namaste," Hari replied as he tried to get up.

"Wait, Maya. This is Hari Dil. Hari and I will have dinner together here."

"You already mentioned that," Maya left with the bundle of papers, shaking her head and smiling.

"Sorry, young man. You can go back to sleep." The stationmaster left the room with satisfaction and lit another cigarette outside.

Hari woke up after a couple of hours to the whistle of the engine.

He looked outside the window and saw the train said *Frontier Mail*. Then he walked out towards the train and stopped. He gathered his senses. Unconsciously, he had wanted to catch the train. He remembered the journey on the train with his father. His eyes teared up, and he turned his back on the train.

"You must know this train. It used to go to Peshawar. Now it stops in Amritsar. Just waiting here for signal."

"Yes. I have traveled many times with my father on it," Hari said as the flood of memories caused tears to flow down his cheeks freely. Unable to control his emotions, he walked away towards the far end of the platform. After some time, he came back to ask the stationmaster, "Any message from Daler-ji?"

"They could not reach him directly but gave a message to someone on his farm."

"You must be hungry. Dinner should be here soon," the stationmaster added

Soon, the dinner arrived and was laid out on the table. The stationmaster and his young guest washed their face and hands for dinner.

The young man prayed before the dinner until the stationmaster broke the silence.

"You drink any liquor? I can send someone to get some."

"No, I don't drink," the young man said and smiled.

"Excellent. Do you smoke?"

The young man said no, and the stationmaster expressed guilt for the habit that he had been trying to shake. They were still working on dinner when a tall, turbaned man with a long, wide gray beard appeared from the darkness. A young boy followed him with a handbag.

Hari stood up and walked towards the man, inspecting his face, and then he folded his hand to greet him.

"Hari Dil, son of Jai Dil."

The man burst into tears that echoed into the train station. "Hari, my boy" The man hugged him strongly. Tears fell from Hari's eyes.

"This is Kishan. Remember, Chaman Talwar's boy? Now he is my boy," Daler smiled as he put his arm around the tall young boy.

"How is Baba Joga? Your children?"

"Never found them," Tears flowed down Daler's cheeks.

The stationmaster left them alone and went behind the office and lit another cigarette.

The two wiped the tears off their faces as they were interrupted by stationmaster Mohan Das.

"There is plenty of food. Why don't you two eat, and I will retire for the day. Both of you can stay here tonight, and if you need something, please ask Moji.

"Moji, please make sure these gentlemen are comfortable."

Hari and Daler stayed at the station, catching up on days in Peshawar until sleep got the best of them. The next morning, Maya opened the door of her father's office and set the tea on the table.

"Good morning, gentlemen. Tea is here," Mohan Das announced as he sipped the tea from a clay cup. "The train to Rampur will be here in about one hour."

Hari and Daler both freshened up and exchanged addresses.

Soon, the train to Rampur was there. Daler folded his hands to thank Mohan Das. Hari realized Daler and the stationmaster knew each other very well. As a stationmaster, Mohan Das was known in the area and was a kind man, so people respected him a lot.

Before boarding the train, Hari asked to buy the ticket.

"You don't need to buy the ticket. You can board any compartment. They know you are my guest."

"No, I must."

"Excellent, Moji. Get the sahib a ticket to Rampur."

As Hari walked to the ticket window, Mohan looked at Daler. "Look, Daler, I like this young man. God willing, I think he will be a great match for my daughter, Maya."

"Mohan, he is from a great family. You would be blessed to have him in your family."

"Can I count on you to make it happen?" Mohan Das looked at Daler in anticipation.

"It would be a blessing to be part of it. For this to happen from my hand would be small payback for all the good his family has done for me and many others." Daler teared up, and Mohan Das patted his back.

# Endnotes

This book is inspired by the stories that my father told me about his family in Peshawar before their haveli was attacked in Qissa Khwani Bazaar. My father was the only one who survived, as the servants took him to Kabul River for his safety every day as partition violence raged. Many of the prominent characters in this book are real, although their names have been changed. There are fictional characters added or two real characters combined to create one fictional character. A lot of events have been adopted from India's partition history in the story, and references to history and historical figures are added. Overall, the book tells the history, but there is a lot of fiction used in writing this book.

# Acknowledgments

Thanks to my lovely wife Priyanka for her support. Thanks to everyone who continuously asked me about the progress of this book. Their interest in this book has kept me motivated to complete it.

Copy/Line editing: Kaz Moran
Proofreading: Samantha Gove

Sikh man image on book cover used with permission from Nihang Teja Singh
Afghan horse rider image used with permission from Ali Afghani

# Characters

**Listed in no particular order**

Kalyan Dil (Baba Kalyan) and his two sons Jawar Dil and Jurnail Dil (Baba Jurnail) and daughter Sukhi

Jawar's three sons - Jai, Mehar, and Bhole; Jai's wife Lakshmi and their son, Hari

Mehar's bride Kirat; Bhole's wife Mary

Amrit - Kalyan's sister and mother of Balwant (Baba Balwant), Sarup, and Sucha

Sukhi's and her sons Satwant and Zorawar; Satwant's son Jigar and daughter Raji

Lakhbir (son of Hajoor) – Balwant's grandson assigned to his care and protection

Partap Maggu, his daughter Lakshmi and two sons, Kedar and Anand

Kedar's friends and business partners, Mangat Bakshi, and twins Tej and Ved Sahani

Diwan Prem Chand Uppal – Rich merchant in Peshawar

Bakshi's wife Svitri and their servant Inder

Jung – Jawar's friend, Kirat's father

Dostan Khan –a Pashtun tribal leader and childhood friend of Jawar and Jurnail; his son Ullas Khan

Joga – head of Dil clan's militia and his son Daler (Dil clan's estate manager and security)

Masood Khan and Haji Khan - tribal leaders hostile to Dil clan

Ajmal Khan and Ismail Khan - Masood Khan's henchmen

Azmat - Ali's father, a Dil clansman loyal to Jawar

Arfan - Azmat's father-in-law, a hardline Muslim cleric

Messa Khan, a Sufi saint and dervish; His son Abdul

Dil clan servants: Rustam (cook), Zahir (helper), Lal Singh (driver), Bazam Lohana (worker), Amira(maid)

Hamdard – kahwah vendor and Dil clan's loyal informer

Chaman Talwar – Dil family attorney; his son Kishan

Girdhari – Vaidya, an ayurvedic doctor

Daya Shankar - Dil family priests in Holy city of Haridwar

Jivan Singh -Hari's co-worker at the foundry

Paul McDermott – Manager at the car dealership

Kedar's wife Jamuna, Jamuna's father Sant Das, and brother Mani Das

Mohan Das stationmaster and his daughter Maya

Captain Bhag Singh – Gorkha military officer in Indian Army

# Real Historical Characters

**Gandhi** (Mohandas Karamchand Gandhi)– Proponent of non-violence against British Colonial rule in India

**Bacha Khan** – real name Abdul Ghaffar Khan – Pashtun Leader for India's independence struggle against British, Founder of Khudai Khidmatgar/Red Shirt movement

**Dr. Khan Sahib** - Dr. Abdul Jabbar Khan – Pashtun leader of the Indian independence movement

**Jinnah** (Muhammad Ali Jinnah) – Founder of Pakistan, primarily responsible for the partition of India

**Nehru** (Jawaharlal Nehru) - First Prime Minister of India and leader of Indian National Congress

**Olaf Caroe** – British Governor of Northwest Frontier Province (now Khyber Pakhtunkhwa, Pakistan)

**Khanna** - Mehr Chand Khanna, Indian Politician in Peshawar

**Syed Ahmed** Brelvi - Indian Muslim revivalist, regarded as the initiator of Jihad movement

**Maharaja Ranjit Singh** - Maharaja of the Sikh Empire

**Guru Nanak Dev** – First Guru of Sikhs, considered as Founder of Sikhism

**Lodhi** – Lodhi Dynasty in India

# Glossary and Terms

### Salutations and Titles

Acharya - a Hindu or Buddhist spiritual teacher or leader

Baba – wise old man

Bhai – brother

Bhabhi – brother or close friend's wife

Chacha – father's brother, male cousin, or close male friend

Diwan – the title of respect for someone trusted with governance or someone from an elite family

Darvish – in Islam can refer broadly to members of a Sufi fraternity

Ji – in India, a suffix placed after a person's name or title as a mark of respect

Janab – sir

Lala – a male salutation of respect for men, rich merchants; big brother

Madrasa -school, usually Islamic school

Mahatma -great soul

Mawlawi – Islamic religious title was given to Muslim religious scholars.

Mullah- a Muslim learned in Islamic theology and sacred law

Pandit – Hindu religious scholar

Sahib – title or honorific of respect

Sardar – chief (also used for a Sikh man)

Vaidya – a Sanskrit word meaning "doctor" or "traditional physician" versed in Ayurveda medicine

## Nouns

Baraat – a groom's wedding procession in India and Pakistan

Beedi – a thin cigarette or mini-cigar filled with tobacco flakes and commonly wrapped in a tendu leaf

Bhakta – worshiper

Dharma - in Hinduism, a cosmic law underlying right behavior and social order

Dera – camp, settlement, or monastery

Dhaba – roadside restaurant in the Indian subcontinent

Firangis – white men, British, (derogatory)

Gotra - Hindu lineage

Halwais – Indian confectionery and sweets maker

Haveli – mansion

Islamist – someone who uses Islam as a political weapon to grab power, usually with violence

Jutti – footwear common in Northern India

Janeu – the sacred strand of threads worn by orthodox male Hindus

Kahwah – traditional green tea consumed in Afghanistan, Pakistan, India, and some other countries

Khatri-Kshatriya – Hindu/Sikh warrior caste

Mubarak – greetings, congratulations

Nikah – Islamic marriage

Pakol – a soft round-topped men's hat

Perahan Tunban – male clothing worn by Pashtun men (and other ethnicities) in Afghanistan and Western Pakistan

Rakhi – a festival to formalize and celebrate the bond of protection, obligation, and care between brother and sister

Sadar – cantonment; garrison

Sabzi – vegetable dish in India

Tiffin – packed meal (India)

# Ethnic Groups

Afridi – a Pashtun subtribe

Baloch – an Iranian people who live mainly in Baluchistan (Iran, Pakistan, Afghanistan)

Gorkha or Gurkhas- are soldiers native to South Asia of Nepalese nationality

Huns - ancient nomadic Central Asian tribes who (White Huns), via Khyber Pass, entered the Indian Subcontinent at the end of the fifth or early sixth century

Kalash – Indo-Aryan indigenous people in Chitral, Pakistan

Marathas – Marathi-speaking warrior group from the western Deccan Plateau (India)

Nikpikhel – a subclan of Yousafzai Pashtun in Swat

Pashtun – a dominant tribe in many parts of Pakistan (Khyber Pakhtunkhwa) and Afghanistan

Popalzai – a Pashtun tribe of Afghanistan

Sindhi – an Indo-Aryan ethnic group in Pakistan and India from the state of Sindh (who historically lived alongside the river Sindhu or Indus)

White Huns – a subtribe of Huns

# Religions

**Hinduism** - people of India that follow a common set of beliefs such as rebirth, reincarnation, and the basic set of fundamental duties (Santana Dharma). In Hinduism, all thoughts and ideas about God's existence and nature that are supported by reasoning are acceptable. The origin of the term, Hindu, is mostly geographical and implies people who live east of the Sindhu River (Indus River), and many times is used as a term for identifying a common culture. People who identify with Hinduism fall into many religions and sects.

Arya Samaj – Hindu reform movement that promotes the supremacy of Vedic texts

Sanātan Dharma – an alternate name for Hinduism; describes duties according to a person's spiritual identity (atma) and personal duty as individual

Hindu God/Goddess names mentioned in this book:

Shiva – Hindu God, also called Adiyogi, or first yogi and considered as the founder of Yoga

Shakti – Hindu Goddess, Shiva's wife, considered energy behind the creation in cosmos

Brahman –the ultimate reality behind all that exists, including soul, considered as the source of all consciousness

Maya -(illusion), it represents everything in the cosmos in the material world that can be measured, but since it constantly changes, it is unreal.

Lord Krishna –Hindu God, Considered as Perfect or Complete Incarnation of God in Hinduism. Believed to be born 3228 BCE

**Sikhism** – people of a sect or offshoot religion of Hinduism that includes some hardline stances on the nature of God from Islam, such as idol worship being considered blasphemous; although, Sikhs do pray and bow in front of their religious book because it represents knowledge about the nature of God.

Sikh Sects mentioned in the book:

Nirankari – a form of Sikhism

Namdhari – an offshoot sect of Sikhism

**Buddhism** – Buddhism is an Indian religion founded on the teachings of Gautama Buddha

**Jainism** – a nontheistic religion founded in India in the sixth century BC by the Mahavira. Jains don't believe in the existence of a god, but they believe humans can attain perfection and become close manifestations of the concept of God.

**Islam** – Abrahamic religion teaching that Muhammad is the last messenger of God

Islamic Sects/Movements mentioned in the book:

Wahabi – any adherent of the orthodox/puritan Islamic reform movement of Sunni Islam

Deobandi – and Islamic revivalist movement within Sunni Islam that formed during the late 19th century around the Darul Uloom Islamic seminary in the town of Deoband, India

Religious Books mentioned:

Bhagavad Gita - one of the holy scriptures for Hinduism

Guru Granth Sahib - the central holy religious scripture of Sikhism

Japji Sahib - the Sikh thesis that appears at the beginning of the Guru Granth Sahib

Made in the USA
Monee, IL
22 February 2022